HEARTWARMING

In My Dreams

—

Muriel Jensen

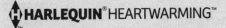

Recycling programs
for this product may
not exist in your area.

ISBN-13: 978-0-373-36708-5

In My Dreams

Copyright © 2015 by Muriel Jensen

Printed in U.S.A.

www.Harlequin.com

Muriel Jensen lives with her husband, Ron, in a simple old Victorian looking down on the Columbia River in Astoria, Oregon. They share the space with a loudmouthed husky mix and two eccentric tabbies. They have three children, eight grandchildren and four great-grandchildren.

Their neighborhood is charmed, populated with the kindest and most fun-to-be-around people. Who would have guessed that the eight-year-old who lived across the street and came to watch television and eat cookies after school when he'd misplaced his key would grow up to inspire a book and its hero?

No one is safe from the writer's reach.

Select Books by Muriel Jensen

HARLEQUIN HEARTWARMING
Always Florence
Love Me Forever

HARLEQUIN SUPERROMANCE
Trust a Hero
Bridge to Yesterday
In Good Time
Candy Kisses
Husband in a Hurry
The Fraudulent Fiancée
The Little Matchmaker
First Born Son
Second to None
The Third Wise Man
All Summer Long (Home, Hearth and Hayley)
Man with a Mission
Man with a Message
Man with a Miracle
Man in a Million
The Man She Married

HARLEQUIN AMERICAN ROMANCE
Four Reasons for Fatherhood
Fatherhood Forever
Father Formula
Father Found
Daddy to Be Determined
Jackpot Baby
That Summer in Maine
His Baby
His Wife

Visit the Author Profile page at Harlequin.com for more titles

To Sgt. Sean M. Johnson
Apache Troop 3rd Squadron, 89th Cavalry Regiment
4th Brigade, 10th Mountain Division

This handsome young man, who has lived across the street from us since he was a child, has grown up to be a credit to his parents and his own sense of honor. When I told him I wanted to dedicate this book to him for all his help with the first chapter, and the psyche of my hero, he said, "Dedicate it to all those who've served and sacrificed their lives, and for all who still put their lives on the line."

He is now Officer Sean Johnson with the Cannon Beach, Oregon, Police Department, and has a beautiful wife, Allison, and brand-new son, Odin Curtis-Wayne Johnson, born July 17.

CHAPTER ONE

THE AIR INSIDE the Humvee was thick with dust and heat. Under his camo jacket, Jack's skin prickled with the threat of danger as he scanned the road ahead. The escort of Special Forces to a chicken farm in Southeastern Iraq where the farmer was dealing in rockets and missiles had been uneventful, but it was insurgent strategy to let them pass, plant IEDs when they were out of sight, then wait for the patrol to return and watch the jihad happen.

Sweat broke out along his spine. He had leave in a week and a half. He was just imagining trouble. He was going to be fine. The day was quiet. He was a cavalry scout, the best of the best, the baddest of the bad, able to take on the world—or so the scouts told each other. Ego could keep you alive.

"You feel that?" Bolton asked. He was a teacher from New Jersey and claimed to be "in tune with the universe." He sat beside Jack.

"Yeah," Jack said. It wasn't anything audible, just hung in the air like a weight. "What is it?"

"I don't know. But something."

Everything inside Jack sharpened—his senses, his instincts and his primal sense of survival. This close to the end of his tour, fear no longer had meaning. He couldn't function with it. Simple, steady common sense and remembering his training became the focus of every moment on the road.

The flash of light burst all around him like some personal supernova. Later, the other joes would talk about the deafening explosion, but he never heard it. There was only the light and the diffusion of everything beyond its circle.

When Jack came to, Bolton was slumped in his seat and the whole right side of the vehicle, which included the computer and a rifle, was gone. Above Jack's head, Curry, the gunner, was praying urgently. "Help me. Please, God, help me."

Jack forced himself to assess. He ran his hands up and down his arms, felt his thighs, his knees. He was okay. He pushed at Bolton's shoulder. "You okay? Bolton?"

Bolton didn't answer. There wasn't a sound from the three other vehicles in the convoy. Jack's heart beat fast enough to choke him.

He checked Bolton for injuries and found a lot of blood on his right side. But he had a pulse.

"Help me," Curry continued to pray. "Please help me."

Jack leaped out on his side and climbed into the turret. Curry's face was white and his blood was everywhere. The explosion had blown away most of his right forearm, still held on by something stringy—a tendon, maybe. Swallowing the need to hurl, Jack pulled a tourniquet from pieces of the first-aid kit in his pocket. He tied it just above Curry's elbow.

That's when he saw the figure approaching from the west and drew his sidearm. It was a column of white walking out of the dry desert grass on the side of the road.

The caftan billowed in a whisper of breeze as the figure took a step forward. Jack aimed his weapon, widened his stance and shouted, "Stop!" The figure kept coming. Jack shouted again and held up his hand in the universal signal to halt. Still, the figure kept coming as though simply on a stroll. Jack fired above his head, but the figure didn't stop.

Jack aimed for the chest, his finger on the trigger, but confusion made him hold back.

Why wasn't the attacker returning fire? He could see both his hands, scanned his body for a weapon and saw none—unless a bomb was strapped to his chest. Jack's heartbeat accelerated and sweat ran into his eyes as the guy closed the distance between them.

Then he realized it was not a man. The walk was fluid and graceful. A woman. She could be as lethal as any man. He took aim again and then the pistol went slack in his hands as the woman raised her head to reveal a beautiful, wholesome face. The last time he'd seen that face, he'd been eight years old and the world as he knew it had ended.

"Mom?" He heard his astonished whisper.

The face's soft beauty suggested the complete opposite of the drug-hungry woman who'd had three children she'd ignored while going through man after man in her attempt to stay high. Blue eyes met his and honey-blond hair ruffled as she pulled off the hijab.

"I'm going, Jack," she said in the slightly slurred voice he remembered. She came to a stop near the vehicle. "You'll be fine."

Now two little girls who hadn't been there a moment ago held her hands. One of them was dark featured and about four. The other was just a toddler with blond hair. Both pulled away from their mother and reached for him, crying his name. "Jack! Jackie!"

He felt a burning in his gut, as though she'd shot him.

He was Section 8. He'd been afraid this would happen. The guys who survived emotionally in this bubble of hell managed to somehow exist outside it. After living through an ugly childhood, he'd thought he was strong enough to get through anything, but apparently he wasn't. After all he'd seen and done and survived, he was now hallucinating. His mother had been in jail for over twenty years, and he hadn't seen his sisters in about as long.

His mother called his name, but it couldn't be her; it was his brain playing tricks. He screamed for the image to go away or he'd shoot again. Now the girls were gone and his mother climbed the turret and took hold of his forearms.

"No!" he shouted and used every ounce of strength he had left to push her away. She screamed as she fell backward.

"JACK!" SARAH SHOUTED into his face, pushing at his chest with both hands. It was like trying to move a refrigerator. She wanted to think he wouldn't harm her, but he was caught in one of his nightmares and in this one, she seemed to be a threat. Since he was a well-honed fighting machine, she had to wake him. "Jack! Stop! It's me!"

Whatever was going on in his mind had twisted his handsome face into a mask of pain.

"Jack!" she said again. "Wake up!"

His eyes opened and he blinked, confusion, disorientation in his face. She took advantage of the moment to push harder against him and roll him over so that she knelt astride him and pinned him to the mattress. *"Wake up!"*

"Geez!" A strong male arm suddenly circled her waist and pulled her off Jack. "What happened?" Ben demanded, setting her on her feet and holding Jack down with his other hand.

Ben, a Beggar's Bay, Oregon, police officer, was Jack's brother and her boyfriend. She smiled feebly and indicated Jack, who was now clearly awake and trying to sit up but for the hand to his chest. "He was crying out. I was starting breakfast and came in to see if he was okay."

Jack pushed Ben's hand away and swung his legs over the side of the bed. He wore boxer shorts and a T-shirt, revealing bulging arm and thigh muscles. He smiled apologetically. "I was dreaming that she was going to make me eat oatmeal again today," he said, his brown-eyed, bloodshot glance teasing. "I want bacon and eggs."

"Funny man." Sarah took a steadying breath and turned to give Ben a quick kiss. He looked stressed out. "Hi. My hero." She put her hands on her hips and frowned good-naturedly at Jack. "You know, I'd like you better if you didn't try to kill me when I come over to make your breakfast."

She'd promised Jack and Ben's parents that while they were at their winter place in Arizona, she'd prepare meals and keep an eye on Jack. She worked for Coast Care, a home health-care provider.

Neither brother had kitchen skills and the Palmers had been concerned about Jack's nightmares. He'd been cleared of mental health issues upon discharge two weeks ago. He insisted he would be fine as soon as he put the past six years away and reclaimed his civilian life.

To ease his parents' minds, Ben had assured them that he and Sarah would look out for his brother. To that end, he'd temporarily vacated his condo and moved into their childhood home. Sarah had been coming daily as promised. This was the second time Jack had mistaken her for an Iraqi insurgent.

"I'm fine," Jack insisted. "Sarah doesn't have to come anymore. I can make our breakfast."

"Toaster waffles are not breakfast," Sarah stated.

"Says who? They're whole grain."

She sighed. "You should start the day with fruit, protein and whole grain that aren't processed into pastry." She made a beckoning gesture. "Come on. I brought vegetarian sausage, cheese and veggies for an omelet, and grainy bread for toast."

Jack shook his bed-head at Ben, wearing a weary grin. "She's such a tyrant. I don't know what you see in her, apart from beauty and brains."

"She's already paid off her student loans, so if I marry her, she can start on mine. I've got a sunny future sewed up."

Sarah shook her head and looked from one brother to the other, then gave Ben a quick hug, loving the easy relationship between them. She'd met Ben when he'd stopped her doing fifty through town on her way to work five months ago. She'd been late and he'd been charming, even though he'd still given her a ticket! He had a degree in Business Administration, but loved police work. And she loved him because he cared about his family and his community.

"Come on, Jack," she encouraged. "If you're starting work today like you said, you need nutrition. I know you can't recover overnight from all you've seen and been through, but a healthy breakfast would be a good start." She glanced at her watch. "I've got an hour before Vinny."

"Vinny?"

"Vinny Caruso, my first client of the day. He's eighty-four, about five foot six and maybe a hundred and forty pounds. He was an insurance salesman and a musician on the side. He's about as skilled in the kitchen as you two. But he lives across town, so let's get moving."

"All right, all right. I'm right behind you."

Sarah was now very familiar with the Palmers' large, comfortable kitchen. Twenty years ago, Gary Palmer, Ben and Jack's father, had renovated the inside of the spacious Victorian home on the edge of town to suit his family's purposes. The more recently updated kitchen looked out onto a wide lawn that sloped to the bay on the central Oregon coast. Four fat blue hydrangea bushes now turning green and purple in the September weather crowded a simple wooden gate at the edge of the slope. The gate served no purpose, but Gary had put it there, thinking it provided a pretty sight from the kitchen window.

The room was painted an herbal green and the cupboards and details were rustic with hinges and pulls Gary had salvaged from an old bakery. Sarah loved working in this room; it made her feel connected to past generations. As someone disconnected from her former life, she appreciated that.

Ben placed bread in the toaster while Sarah dropped the sausage into the frying pan. She pulled a bowl of fruit out of the refrigerator and spooned some into three bowls. She topped them with strawberry yogurt, then turned the sausage.

"You all right?" Ben asked, pushing the toaster lever down and moving closer to study her. He frowned at a bruise on her upper arm.

"I'm fine."

"I warned you not to try to wake him."

"Ben, he was screaming. I can't hear someone cry out and not investigate. And, if you recall, when you came to my rescue, I had the upper hand."

"Upper hand," he repeated skeptically. "I

hate to disillusion you, but the self-defense class you took at the college wouldn't hold up against military combat training. Had he been a little deeper into that dream, you'd have been in three pieces."

She rolled her eyes. "Next time he screams, I'll ask what's wrong from the doorway."

She turned the sausage patties again and pointed to the toaster where browned bread had popped up. "I put a jar of strawberry jam in the fridge."

"Do you have a night job tonight?" he asked, retrieving the jam.

"No. Just Vinny and Margaret. No Jasper today. He's gone to Portland with a friend. But I do have a meeting with my boss after lunch." They'd all been her daytime regulars for the past few months. Vinny loved her cooking, Margaret was a lady of the old school and loved Sarah because she was willing to iron her sheets, and Jasper Fletcher, a blind man in his late fifties, counted on Sarah to listen as he told her about what he'd learned from books on tape. Her goal was to make their diets nutritious, as well as to keep them active and social. "I'm done in the middle of the afternoon."

"Good. I'm off to Eugene in the morning

for a weekend cop conference. Want to have dinner tonight?"

"Sure. I'll fix something for Jack."

"He's planning a *Blue Bloods* marathon."

"Wouldn't you rather stay with him? You'd probably love a *Blue Bloods* marathon. We can have dinner another time."

He leaned over to kiss her gently. "We haven't had an evening alone together in two weeks. Prime rib special at the Farmhouse tonight."

"Okay, I'm in."

"Seven o'clock."

"It's a date."

"It is," he said, a different note in his voice. "We have things to talk about. I'll pick you up."

"No, I'll stop by to deliver something for Jack's dinner. What do we have to talk about?"

He narrowed his gaze on her, as though looking for something in her eyes he wasn't finding. "A lot," he finally replied.

His tone put her on alert. So far, theirs had been just an easy, romantic friendship. Today, though, he looked very serious. She hoped he wasn't thinking what she suspected he was thinking. He'd make a wonderful husband and father, but while she'd like to have the one, she didn't intend to ever have the other.

JACK WALKED INTO the kitchen, doing his best to look well-adjusted despite his earlier freakout. That was just a small indicator of his serious problem. Behaving in a normal way in the kitchen he'd grown up in since age eight, in the small-town life that had been all about fishing and building and girls, when just two weeks ago he'd carried an M4 carbine and jumped out of helicopters, was harder than it sounded. Bullets had whistled by his ear, people around him had died or suffered unspeakable injuries; he'd exchanged gunfire and felt a time or two as though he might die. And somehow he had to dial down the adrenaline that pulsed into his blood and figure out how to live again in this kitchen, in this life.

"A step at a time, Jack," his shrink at Fort Polk used to say. "A step at a time."

Sure. Easily said. But even if he managed to cope with old memories, what did he do about new ones? Like waking up with his brother's girl straddling him? He could still feel her knees pressed against his hips, smell the floral-vanilla fragrance of her clinging to his T-shirt.

He shook off the sensory image and took the plate of buttered toast from Ben, put it in the middle of the table, then went to get utensils. He smiled reassuringly at his brother and Sarah as he passed them. He took the opportunity to keep thinking.

Why in God's name had he seen his *mother's* face in his dream? Images of his little sisters had haunted him for years, ever since they'd all been separated when their mother had gone to jail for manslaughter after murdering her boyfriend. He'd had nightmares since then of himself running away through a dark, blurry night, the girls screaming and footsteps right behind him, gaining on him. But he'd always been very much alone. What was his mother doing in his dreams? And in Iraq? He scowled fiercely.

"Jack?"

He looked up at the sound of his name and saw Sarah holding up an egg. "You okay?" she asked.

"Sure."

"Good. Two or three eggs in your omelet?"

He smiled. "Two, please."

Ben put the jam down in front of him. "You're starting to scare me, bro. You sure you're okay?"

Jack kept smiling. "Thanks, I'm good. You know how real dreams can be. I'm just having trouble putting it out of my head."

"Afghanistan?"

"No, Iraq. For whatever reason, it was the Humvee explosion in the middle of my first tour that keeps coming back to me."

"You can talk about any of that, you know. I'd be glad to listen. I know I wasn't there, but I kind of understand war."

"Thanks." Jack knew cops saw ugly things all the time. But terrible memories of war entangled with ugly childhood memories made for an awful hybrid.

It would be hard to explain to Ben what was going on in his head. He and Ben had been friends as children, then brothers when the Department of Human Services had allowed Ben's parents, Gary and Helen Palmer, to adopt Jack. At the same time, his younger half sisters had been sent to live with their respective fathers.

"I'm going to be fine," Jack insisted. "I just have to get my head together."

Ben looked him in the eye, clearly trying to read what Jack wasn't saying. "You know it's more than that. No one can survive such things without venting it to somebody."

He'd been doing that to his shrink at the fort, and although being home again was gradually pulling him away from the past six years, the sharply revived memories of his childhood and the big-time return of his dreams were driving him toward the only solution he could think of to get his life on track again.

"Actually," he said, "I have an idea about how to help myself."

Ben put down his fork. "What's that?"

Jack met his waiting gaze and said, as though it was going to be easy, "I'm going to find my sisters."

CHAPTER TWO

BEN SHOOK HIS head and stabbed his fork into a bite of sausage. "Jack, it's been too long. You have no idea where they are, and they have different names."

"Yeah. But technology puts the world at my fingertips. I'm going to find them."

Sarah saw the zealous light in Jack's eyes and the defining caution in Ben's. They were two very different men with one very strong connection. They weren't brothers by birth but by the courage that brought them together as boys and now defined them as men—the soldier and the cop.

"I hate to see you get hurt, Jack. And you're kind of...vulnerable right now, don't you think? You've had about all the pain you can deal with."

Jack shrugged as though he had no control over his need to reconnect with his sisters. "I have to do this."

"Why can't it wait until you're...adjusted?"

"Because 'it' has waited so long already. And this is as adjusted as I'm going to get until I find them. I promised our mother that I'd work on the carriage house out back. That'll help me regain my carpentry skills, hopefully, so I can get Palmer Restorations going again, and in my spare time, I'm going to start looking for Corie. Or Cassie. Whoever I get a lead on first."

Sarah knew that Helen Palmer had long dreamed of fixing up the old carriage house, now used as a storage shed, to rent it out to writers. For the past ten years Helen had been a freelance editor for a Portland publishing house. Over the years she'd hosted several writers in this home while they'd discussed revisions. She'd often talked about how good it would be for a writer to spend time in a comfortable spot in this country setting with more privacy than the guest bedroom could provide.

"What are you going to do with all the stuff in there now?" Ben asked.

"Rent a Dumpster, throw away the junk, save the good stuff and store it in your room." Jack spoke with a straight face and spread jam on his toast while Ben looked heavenward.

Since Ben had moved back into his old

room, he'd been less than tidy. It had become a family joke.

"I mean, really," Jack went on with a grin at Sarah. "You could hide an elephant in there. You'll barely notice lumber and storage boxes."

"You're hilarious."

"I'll clear a corner of the basement," Jack said seriously. "You can look over the iffy stuff with me. We'll save a pile for Mom to check out before I throw it away."

"Yeah, well, much as I'd love to do that, I'll be busy busting perps and saving lives. I'm afraid you're on your own."

"Does it really come to that in Beggar's Bay? I mean, isn't it more directing parking at the fairgrounds and taking runaway dogs to the animal shelter?"

"Just the other day," Sarah said gravely, "Ben jumped into the bay to catch a drunk driver evading arrest, remember?"

Jack wrinkled his nose. "Hard to forget. He smelled like a salmon for two days."

"But, still. Heroic."

Ben made a sound of distress and turned to Sarah, pretending hurt feelings at her dubious defense. "Hey. For better or for worse, in sickness and in health, remember?"

"That's for married people, Ben." She gave him a wide-eyed look of innocence, phony but very sweet. It gave Jack a mild case of arrhythmia for a minute. "People just dating get to harass and annoy."

Ben stopped her, laughing, and leaned toward her for a kiss. Jack had seen enough. As if his life, his recovery from the ugliness of war and his bizarre nightmares weren't complicated enough already, he had to be attracted to Sarah Reed, his brother's girlfriend.

He pushed away from the table. He could deal with it. Attraction, after all, was such a small thing as far as love was concerned, and attraction was all he was going to allow himself to feel. He hoped.

Fortunately, neither Sarah nor Ben had noticed.

The table was littered with empty plates. "All right," Jack said, standing and pointing to Ben. "You go save lives." He smiled at Sarah. "And you get to work before Vinny and your other clients expire without you. I'll clean up."

There was no false reluctance to leave him with the task. They were both gone in an instant. He cleared the table, loaded the dishwasher, then grabbed a jacket and went outside to check out the contents of the carriage house.

SARAH DROVE THROUGH the three-block commercial area. She passed the Episcopal Church and continued up the hill, past the nearly finished retirement village and the elementary school across the road, toward the over-55 development where Vinny lived.

As she drove, Sarah breathed as though she were in a Lamaze class. Since Jack had come home, she and Ben had talked a lot about family, but very little about children, except that he'd asked her once if she liked them. She'd said that she did, just hadn't mentioned that she didn't want any of her own. But now that she felt certain marriage was on his mind, she had to tell him that and explain why.

Her first job after acquiring her Bachelor of Science in Nursing had been as a pediatric nurse in Seattle. Her dream had been to go on to a Master of Science and work toward becoming a Pediatric Nurse Practitioner.

For several years she'd loved the work. Eventually, however, it became evident that while nothing could compete with the emotional highs of success in children's care, nothing was as dark and ugly as failure.

At first she'd been philosophical about doing the most that could be done for sick children. Then a five-year-old patient, Jerica Warren, had been admitted with the flu. Despite an underlying asthma issue, she hadn't been vaccinated against the flu because it was early in the season. Sarah had told Jerica's worried parents how hard the doctors worked at Puget Sound Children's Hospital. How they'd used every medical advancement known to man and saved nine out of ten children. "She has to live, Sarah," Jerica's father had said. "Because if she doesn't, we won't survive, either."

Jerica had been brave and trusting, held Sarah's hand while the doctor put a line into her small arm to fill her with antibiotics. But not only had she had Influenza B, but also MRSA, a superbug infection. Sarah had sat with the family as Jerica's organs began to shut down. She remembered every moment of those awful days.

Jerica died on a sunny day in early October, and the look on her parents' faces had been like eternal winter. That had been two years ago. Sarah had stayed on the job another month but had been unable to shake the sense of loss and a new lack of faith in a medical system that should be able to save all children. The good work done at the children's hospital couldn't make up for Jerica's loss.

Sarah quit, spent a month with her parents,

helping around the house and in the garden, and simply absorbing the comfort of being home. Her sister, Kate, who was married and had beautiful four-year-old twin boys, visited regularly. Sarah had enjoyed them until they coughed or sniffled, whereupon she'd found herself listening for wheezing sounds and checking skin color while unreasonable fears mounted inside her.

"You're just burned out, sweetheart," her father had said when she explained her feelings. "You'll recover. Or maybe you should find some other kind of nursing that isn't so hard on you."

Conducting a job search online, Sarah had discovered Coast Care in Beggar's Bay and had worked for the owner, John Baldrich, for the past year. Most of her clients were seniors. They were sometimes cranky, but for the most part, they appreciated her visits.

Sarah guided her sturdy white Jeep through the maze of homes that made up the community and pulled into Vinny's driveway. His house was a small two-bedroom with bright colors and a lot of style. Vinny's wife, who'd died the year before, had had an eye for design.

Vinny met Sarah at the door as he always

did, leaning heavily on his cane as he ushered her inside. He wore a bright red flannel shirt with gray sweatpants and had combed his thin gray hair. Horn-rimmed glasses sat on a formidable nose over a bright smile of original teeth.

"How are ya, gorgeous?" he asked.

She gave him a quick hug. Good. One of his cheerful days. "Great, handsome. How are you today?"

"Hungry! What are we having?"

"Vegetarian sausage and cheese omelet, and I brought you a few fat-free brownies for later, but don't eat them all at once. Like you did the lemon bars, remember? Walgreens ran out of Tums because of you."

He followed her into a small but well-equipped kitchen. Photos of his wife and children covered the refrigerator. "I had no regrets," he said. "Those were the best lemon bars I've ever binged on. Want to get married?"

She turned the heat on under a frying pan and smiled at him over her shoulder. "Not today, Vinny. I have a meeting later with John Baldrich about you guys buying the Cooper Building to use as a seniors' center." She added sausage to the pan.

"What kind of meeting? I thought all we had to do was form a nonprofit corporation and the city would let us have it. We did that."

"Unfortunately, it's not that simple. There's another buyer involved."

He frowned. "Who?"

"Not sure. But I like to think city council will give priority to the seniors."

"What does city council have to do with it?"

"They make the decision on whom to sell it to, because the city took possession of the building when the owner defaulted on three years' worth of taxes."

"What's the decision based on?"

She turned the sausage and then added the omelet mixture she'd brought in a plastic container. "I think it all depends on how the city's code is written. John's checking it out."

Vinny nodded. "He's a good guy. I can't imagine he makes a fortune. His rate for having you come every day during the week for an hour is ridiculously reasonable." He grinned at her. "And you always do more than you need to. I hope he pays you more than I pay him."

She made him toast, poured his orange juice and served his breakfast at a small table in a sunny window. While she cleaned the kitchen, she listened to stories she'd already heard about his great-grandchildren and his daughter's promotion.

After breakfast she drove him to the seniors' center in a building that the owner had decided to boot the seniors from to refurbish for a tenant who could pay higher rent. She helped him out of her car and walked him to the door. He leaned on his cane and squeezed her hand with his free one. "The omelet was delicious. Thanks, Sarah."

"Have a great day, Vinny."

"You too, gorgeous."

His friends came to greet him and she left him in their care, probably to play pool and solve the world's political problems. She drove on to Margaret's.

AN ELEGANT WOMAN in her early eighties, Margaret Brogan lived in a little apartment in a downtown complex. She used a walker because of a fall that had left her with a painful limp. She dressed in soft, pretty colors, and her carefully tended helmet of white hair looked precisely the same every day. She always wore jewelry and lipstick and smelled of some spicy floral scent.

She always prepared her own breakfast of fruit, granola and yogurt, but loved to have morning coffee with Sarah. Suffering from mild depression, she refused medication, wanting instead to work through the issue herself. Her doctor thought the regular visits of someone who cared might help.

Margaret's apartment was spotless. It had a blond coffee table with matching end tables, and a comfortable burnt-orange sofa and chairs. The tall, filigreed birdcage that stood by the window had plants in it, tendrils of ivy spiraling out. Three dining stools were lined up in front of a white Formica-topped bar that separated the living room from the white-and-yellow kitchenette. The rooms looked dated but stately, like Margaret herself.

"What did you bring today?" Margaret asked as she led the way to the kitchen.

"Blueberry muffins from the Bountiful Bakery. You got coffee going?"

"Yes. You have a date tonight?"

Margaret was very interested in Sarah's social life. She, herself, had had a very active one as a young woman. It had resulted in a long marriage, three children scattered across the country and a lonely old age.

"I do, as a matter of fact. Ben and I are going to the Farmhouse." Sarah put the muffins on plates and retrieved low-fat margarine from the refrigerator. She helped Margaret sit at the table.

"How's Jack doing now that he's back? My daughter lived a few houses down from Jack and his biological mother, Charlene Manning, when Jack was a boy. I used to babysit my grandson Marty at my daughter's while she worked. Marty's a lawyer now, you know..." She trailed off, then came back to the subject of Jack. "He and Marty often played together. Jack wasn't wounded, was he?"

Sarah remembered the nightmare that had landed her on top of a very agitated Jack. "No, no serious injuries. I haven't known him very long. I met Ben *after* Jack was deployed to Afghanistan and met Jack for the first time a couple of weeks ago."

Margaret cut her muffin in two. "It's unfair that a boy should have to go through even more than he did as a child." Margaret seemed to be looking at an image in her mind and shook her head at what she saw there. "Charlene was a terrible mother, but she was as beautiful as a movie star. She used to sing, you know, but after Jack's father died, men came and went from that house as though she sold sporting goods."

Sarah arched an eyebrow at the appropriate

simile. "A few of them were not very good to those children. I often heard angry shouting. I called the police several times, but they never took action. I don't know what she told them, but those children stayed with her till the day she shot and killed that last boyfriend."

Ben had told her a little about Jack's childhood and the murder that had resulted in him becoming one of the Palmers. But she didn't know very much about Jack's mother. "You wonder how that can be allowed to happen."

"That family was all over the front page of the newspaper. It doesn't seem right that a child should witness a murder at eight years old and then have to go to war and see men get killed when he's an adult."

"It's a rotten world sometimes."

"It is. More for some people than for others."

Ben had told her Jack had been blown up in a Humvee on two separate occasions, involved in several firefights and nicked in the earlobe by a bullet while he'd been loading a mortar shell on his last deployment. She couldn't imagine how life altering it must be to come so close to death.

"I gave them things to eat on more than one occasion," Margaret said. "If it hadn't been for that boy, those little girls would have gone hungry. He took care of them all the time. And then that murder happened." She shook her head despairingly.

No wonder Jack had nightmares, Sarah thought.

"Well, shall I tell him you said hello?" Sarah asked, poking at her half of the muffin. Her appetite was waning. "Would he remember you?"

Margaret nodded and smiled. "I think he would. Tell him I'm the lady with the peanut butter cookies."

"I will. How come *I've* never had your peanut butter cookies?"

Margaret reached out to pinch her cheek. "Because you're not a hungry little waif with a world of sadness in your eyes."

JOHN BALDRICH, WHO'D been an ER nurse before he'd started Coast Care five years before, welcomed Sarah into his small downtown office at the back of Johnson Medical Supply. He was tall and professional looking with gray hair and glasses. His office, too, with its dark paneling and wall of medical books, looked scholarly and tweedy.

After exchanging pleasantries and asking

about her clients, he smiled, his manner becoming paternal.

"Sarah, I know how you feel about your experience in caring for children, but it's almost criminal that you've signed on here as a home-care worker rather than as a licensed nurse. You cook and make beds and do laundry, rather than assess your clients' conditions, give medications and make more important contributions to their health. You're like an orchid disguised as a daisy."

He grew orchids at home and won competitions all around the state for his perfect specimens. She appreciated the sincerity of his compliment. "Thank you, John. But I really like what I'm doing now." She wanted nothing to do with a more important role in patient care. She liked this one.

He nodded, though the expression in his eyes seemed troubled. "Margaret calls me once a month to tell me how much she likes you. That you're caring and conscientious and go the extra mile."

"Good. I'm glad she's happy."

He shuffled papers on his desk and shifted position in his chair, clearly preparing to change the subject. "About the Cooper Building," he said.

"Yes."

"All the agencies that serve seniors are getting together to put on a fund-raiser to help them buy the building. Each group is sending a representative to form a committee. Will you be ours? I'll clear you for whatever time you need to make meetings and do whatever you have to do. And I'll pay you for that time because I know you're living partly on savings."

"Goodness, John…"

"I'd like this to work for the seniors," he went on. "It would be nice if they had a place of their own where they couldn't be ejected on a landlord's whim. I'm not sure of the status of plumbing and wiring, but that can always be fixed once they have the building."

"That's expensive stuff."

"It is, but I know a guy…" He grinned. "So, will you do it? Represent Coast Care?"

"I guess. Usually, I'm not much of a meetings person. I like to do what I want to do without a lot of haggling."

"It's not haggling, it's negotiating, compromising. And anyway, a lot of the prep work is already done. Also, somebody knows a thirty-ish member of the Cooper family who originally owned the building. Bobby Jay Cooper's not exactly a country-western star, but he does the state fair circuit and has a few CDs that have sold very well. He's willing to come to Beggar's Bay to perform for us. Plus, we'll have a talent show and he's agreed to be the judge."

"A talent show," she repeated doubtfully.

"Your client Margaret Brogan taught music in the school system for years. She should be able to recommend some participants for you. As well as participate herself."

"Why do we need that if we have a country-western singer?"

"Just to get more people involved. People love to come out and see their neighbors embarrass themselves."

She had to smile at that. "Sure. I'll do it. As long as *I* don't have to sing."

"Great." He handed her a slip of paper. "First meeting is next Tuesday. Library meeting room."

JACK MADE FOUR piles in the backyard to organize the redistribution of the contents of the four rooms in the carriage house. It had a main room with a small fireplace, a small bedroom, a tiny kitchen and a tinier bathroom. He had a pile for lumber his father had saved from various projects—Gary Palmer owned a construction business—and one for empty boxes that could be useful sometime but were in the way right now; he could break those down and tape them together when the need arose. Plastic tubs of Christmas decorations were handier to have in the carriage house than in the basement, where they had to be hauled up and down steep steps, but he or Ben could do that when the time came, and there were a few boxes of childhood toys and games his mother still brought out when friends with children came to visit.

He filled a trash barrel with pieces of wood that had warped. A branch from an old cedar tree had gone through a window at the back during the last windstorm and had apparently not been noticed. The box that had been stored under it was wet.

He pulled the shards of glass out of the window and placed them in an empty box. Then he used the bottom of another box to cover the hole until he could replace the window.

He hauled the barrel and the box of glass outside and surveyed the now almost-empty carriage house. He felt himself drift backward into the memory of hiding out in here when he and Ben were seven, before his mother had killed Brauer and his life, such as it was, had fallen apart. Ben had broken a kitchen window with an awesome but slightly misdirected two-base hit and Jack had been staying out of Roscoe's way. Roscoe Brauer had been the fourth man in his mother's life that he recalled, and the worst.

When he was three, his father had died somewhere over the desert when the light plane he was transporting illegal drugs in experienced engine failure and crashed.

After that, his mother had taken up with Miguel Ochoa, who'd kept her supplied with cocaine. Elizabeth Corazon—they'd called her Corie—Ochoa was born when Jack was four. She'd been pretty homely, but had grown a little prettier and been a complete pain in the neck. She'd broken every toy Jack owned.

Miguel, who'd been a relatively nice guy despite his occupation, left a year later after many prolonged arguments with Jack's mother. That had begun her serious descent into despondency and mindless addiction to methamphetamines.

Cassidy, or Cassie, had been born the following year, the result of his mother's brief and tragic relationship with a counselor who'd tried to help her and fallen victim instead to her charm and beauty when she was sober. It was brief because she'd lasted less than three months in the rehab program, and tragic because Donald Chapman had left.

His mother had played a game with the Department of Human Services people. She had been sober when they'd visited and able to express sincerely her desire to keep her children, a declaration they'd believed because it had played into their mission of keeping families together. But when they'd left, it was back to life as usual.

A drug dealer named Roscoe Brauer was her next conquest. Or, rather, she'd been his. Roscoe had been big and menacing. Jack had avoided him whenever possible and kept Corie and Cassidy away from him.

Though Brauer had been a nasty piece of work, he'd been a good provider and, unlike the times their mother was without a man, there had been food to eat, oil for the furnace and clothes for school.

Until she'd killed him and the girls had been sent to their fathers. Because Jack had been fatherless and, then, motherless—Charlene had signed away all rights to him—he'd been adopted by the Palmers.

Impatient with himself for thinking about the past instead of going forward—such as spending time looking for his sisters—Jack closed the door behind him and went back to the house.

But it wasn't easy getting his head out of the past. He didn't understand why he'd successfully suppressed his childhood most of his life and now, finally, when he was free of the army and able to do what he wanted, all he could think about—and have nightmares about—was his childhood.

He put a mug under the Keurig and went to the refrigerator for the take-out ribs he'd bought for dinner, since Ben and Sarah were going to be out. The self-indulgent rehashing of his past stopped now.

A LIGHT RAP on the back door was followed by Sarah poking her head around it. A waft of fragrant September air swept in as though she'd brought it.

Jack took a moment to appreciate how pretty she was. Her light brown hair, usually tied up in a knot or caught back in a ponytail when she was on her way to see her clients, was flying free. It highlighted the beautiful shape of her face, her smooth, eggshell-delicate skin and her blue-gray eyes. She smiled, her lips a moist rose color. He experienced that arrhythmia again.

"Ben home yet?" She stepped into the kitchen, her pink dress dropping to a vee just above her breasts, hugging her waist and moving gracefully around her knees. A covered casserole sat on the flat of her hand.

"No. What's that?" he asked.

"Broccoli, chicken and potatoes in a light cheese sauce."

He smiled with difficulty. Even cheese sauce couldn't save broccoli. "Thanks, but I'm having ribs tonight."

"Jack..."

"Sarah, the army has set me free, and while I appreciate your efforts to make me healthy, I started back to work today—well, I cleared out the carriage house—and think I deserve to spoil myself."

She shifted her weight and studied him consideringly. He tried not to notice how the fabric of her dress moved with her, clinging here, swirling there. "What are you having with it?"

"Potato salad."

"From the market?"

"Yes."

"You know that's as much mayonnaise as potato."

"I do." He smiled widely. "And I don't care."

"There's some leftover three-bean salad in the refrigerator. Would you consider having that instead?"

"No. And I'm probably going to add a brownie. You have to deal with it, Sarah."

She shook her head with disapproval in the face of his unapologetic smile. "If your cardiovascular system is still functioning tomorrow," she said, "I'd appreciate your help with something. If you don't mind that it's Saturday."

"Sure." He went to the kitchen table and pulled a chair out for her, then sat across the table. "What do you need?"

She sank smoothly into the chair. "The seniors in Beggar's Bay have to move their center. They've formed a nonprofit and would like to buy a building the city is offering for sale. Would you look at it with me and see what you think?"

He thought a minute. "I'd be happy to, but you should have the building inspected. You'll want experts to check for mold, pests, whether or not the heating system is sound, the plumbing and electricity are..."

"I think our lawyer's already arranged for that, but I'd just feel better if someone I know would look at it and talk to me about it in words I understand."

"Why are *you* responsible?"

"I'm not, really. I'm just nosy. Thorough. If I'm going to help raise money for the seniors to buy it, I'd like to make sure it isn't going to collapse around them or make them sick."

"Sure. What time do you want to go?"

"Sometime in the afternoon…"

"Okay, I'll pick you up."

"I have a meeting with my insurance agent and I'm not sure how long it'll take. Can I come for you?"

"Are you a good driver?" he teased.

"At least as good as you. I've never had a vehicle blow up around me."

"Good. Probably not a lot of IEDs on Main Street."

She looked immediately apologetic. "Sorry. That's nothing to joke about."

Watching her expression, he thought of how she was usually cheerful and kind, though he noticed quick changes of mood sometimes, the sudden dimming of a smile. He'd like to know what was behind that. "It's all right," he said gently.

Suddenly he wanted to know more about

her. "Working with seniors can be rewarding, I think. Is that why you got into nursing?"

She was silent for a few moments, then, apparently deciding she could trust him with the truth, said, "No. When I graduated I went straight into pediatrics."

"Wow. That's the complete opposite."

She laughed. "My first day at Puget Sound Children's Hospital, I walked down the corridor and paper airplanes, balls, various missiles were flying about. The children were sick, but not quiet. That gave me a laugh and encouraged me."

Jack watched as that dimming took place.

"But…caring for children is sometimes worse than there are words for, you know?"

She looked into his eyes. He looked back, knowing exactly what she meant. Different battlefields, but death was death. "I do know."

The moment stretched. Abruptly the back door burst open and Ben stood there in a dark jacket and slacks, a grin on his face. It was a look Jack remembered from their childhood. Ben had it all and he knew it.

He looked from his girlfriend to his brother, an eyebrow raised in question. "What's going on? You two are looking grim."

"I just asked Jack if he'd come with me to

look at the Cooper Building. The seniors want to buy it for a new seniors' center."

"I thought Ken Forman had it sewed up."

"Is that the lawyer who also wants to rent the building?"

"Yeah."

"Not yet. We're still in the running. And the town's getting together to raise money so the seniors have more money to offer. City council is split on whether to add to the tax rolls or do something for the common good."

Ben raised a skeptical eyebrow. "A better offer than Forman, a divorce lawyer, can make?"

"Maybe. This is a generous town."

He let her have that, but clearly didn't believe it. "Okay. But let's shelve all that for now and go have some dinner." He looked at Jack. "You got everything you need?"

"Ribs and potato salad."

Ben made a sound of approval. "Heaven on a plate."

That earned him a scolding glance from Sarah. He turned back to Jack with a theatrically swift change of expression. "What's wrong with you? Don't you know that could clog your arteries and…"

Sarah pitched in. "Stop his heart."

"Yeah. Stop your heart." Ben looked firm. "I'm sure Sarah brought you something gross and grassy that would be much healthier…"

She smacked Ben's arm with her purse, fighting a laugh as she headed for the door.

"How's it going with the carriage house?" Ben asked, backing toward the door.

"Pretty well. Took everything I couldn't throw away into the basement."

"Okay." Ben waved at Jack as he turned and left. "Enjoy the ribs."

CHAPTER THREE

JACK WENT TO the front window to watch his brother and Sarah drive away. Even in the third grade, Ben had been a secure and confident kid. Jack had acted like one, but Ben had really been one. His parents were nice, normal people, and they'd loved him. Jack, on the other hand, had had a mother who was always in a twilight world, somewhere he couldn't reach, and he'd been scared all the time because there was usually no one around to tell him what to do.

Sometimes a friend of his mother's would take his sisters for a few days and he'd spend the time at Ben's without even being missed. He'd dreamed of having the life Ben had.

One day he did, but getting what he'd wanted had taken a terrible toll on everyone else. Ben's parents had taken him and his sisters in that night and he'd heard Ben campaigning to keep them. They hadn't been able to, of course, because the girls still had fathers who wanted them, but Ben had been eloquent.

"It's been just me all this time," Ben had said vehemently. "Well, I could really use a brother. So, you know, I learn to share and stuff. So I don't get spoiled. 'Cause I could use help with taking out the garbage and the errands."

Jack had heard Gary reply, given with a trace of humor. "All right, then. We'll make Jack your brother."

There'd been a moment's silence. Then he'd heard Ben's voice, high with thrilled disbelief. "Really?"

"Really. But you have to be quiet about it until the girls are gone."

Until the girls are gone. Jack had felt elated at the prospect of living with the Palmers, but the elation had drained from him at the knowledge that his sisters would have to go to their fathers.

He found it odd as an adult that children would be sent to live with a parent who'd abandoned them, but knew the Department of Human Services' optimum solution with disrupted families was to put them back together. And both Miguel and Donald had wanted their daughters. In all fairness to them, his mother had had the DHS caseworker convinced she would do better—as she probably believed herself—so they'd probably believed a prolonged custody battle wouldn't have been in anyone's best interest. Which was why the girls had stayed with their mother.

Since his mother had been put in prison, however, that had all changed. Ben and Jack, living under the same roof, had loved each other, barely tolerated each other sometimes, wanted to beat each other to a pulp often and actually tried a few times, had each the other's back against the Duffy boys, bullies in middle school, and as they'd matured and begun to appreciate the value of a brother who is chosen, supported each other in every way they could.

Jack went back into the kitchen. As he carried his dinner to the table and turned on the news, he remembered that for all he'd lost in his childhood, he'd gained so much.

BEN PARKED HIS classic red Mustang on a knoll overlooking the bay. A few lights picked out boats bobbing on the water; otherwise the night was dark and cold. Sarah hadn't eaten very much, a little worried about what Ben had to say. He'd been the perfect companion all evening, bright and funny, all his attention focused on her. Now he was subdued.

He turned in his seat to smile at her and then reached across the gearshift to kiss her. His eyes were shadowed in the dark car and he pulled back to look into hers. He took her hand. "So, what are you doing for the next sixty years?" he asked. "Want to spend them with me?"

She'd always thought that proposing to someone took a lot of courage. You could presume you knew the answer, but it was impossible to be absolutely certain. It was brave to put your heart out there like that.

She'd worried about this moment all day and still hadn't found a painless way to explain to Ben what she felt. She opened her mouth to try, but he pulled a small box out of his breast pocket. He opened it to reveal a round-cut diamond ring that sparkled brilliantly, even in the darkness. "My dream is to marry you and do my best to make all *your* dreams come true."

She expelled a breath that sounded as anguished as she felt. She couldn't imagine a more perfect proposal.

Ben was a good cop, commended on more than one occasion for defusing domestic disputes or calming an angry mob. He straightened, apparently reading her well, his expression a combination of hurt and confusion. "Why did that sigh sound distressed rather than happy?"

She was silent a long moment, struggling to find the right words to explain. Finally deciding there weren't any, she just spoke directly.

"Ben, we've never talked about children."

He waited a beat. "True. You're not going to tell me you want a dozen, are you?" he joked, still looking worried.

"No," she replied. "I'm telling you I don't want *any*."

He stared at her, his confusion deepening. "You said you liked children," he reminded her gently. "And I've witnessed it. When you helped with the department's Christmas party, you seemed to enjoy watching and helping the kids."

"I did." She inhaled to steady herself. "I love kids. And I love them most when they belong to somebody else." She was about to go on to explain when he turned on the car's ceiling light.

"You're saying..." He paused, as though not quite believing what he was about to say. "That...you don't want your own? Ever?"

"Yes," she replied, looking directly into his

eyes so there'd be no misunderstanding her conviction.

He looked away, shook his head, then turned back to her. "Okay. You're very serious. I see that. But…why?"

"Remember that I told you I used to be a pediatric nurse?"

"Yes."

She reeled out the whole long story about Jerica. "The average person," she said, her voice growing raspy, "has no idea how vulnerable children are to what appear to be the most innocuous things, or things that one child can survive, hardly noticing it, while it takes another child's life. I dealt with it for years and accepted that working with children was just going to beat me up every day, but the successes made it worth it. Until Jerica died and then…well, it feels like nothing's worth it."

He listened quietly, clearly affected by her story. "I'm so sorry, Sarah," he said, holding both her hands.

"I led her parents to believe that if anyone could save Jerri, we could. But we couldn't. Anyway, in the end, I could no longer deal with the death of children day after day. I know someone has to, but it doesn't have to be me."

"I understand that. I wouldn't want to work with dying children every day. It's hard enough to see them at risk from abuse or neglect." He put a gentle hand to the back of her head. "But, Sarah, *all* you saw was sick children. Most children's lives are never threatened by serious disease or injury. I don't know what the odds are, but I don't imagine they're that high. We could have perfectly healthy children who grow up to have perfectly healthy children of their own."

"Or we could have one who has problems." She caught his wrist and pulled his hand down to hold it in her own. "I *do* know the odds. Between fifteen and eighteen percent of children live with chronic disease. I can't accept the ring, Ben. I'm too messed up about children."

Ben squeezed her hand and looked out the windshield. "You're not messed up. You've just been…hurt, wounded."

She tugged at his hand so that he'd turn back to her. She asked into his eyes, "Can you live without having kids?"

He considered, and then shook his head regretfully. "I don't think so. But I don't like the thought of living without you, either."

"I'm sorry, Ben."

"Look, let's not do anything hasty. Let's just

give it a little time. That's what dating is for, isn't it? To learn about each other and discover what you can deal with and what you can't?"

That was a tolerant attitude, even enlightened, but she had to make her position clear. "I wouldn't hurt you for anything, Ben. But I'm not having children. Ever."

He didn't seem to want to believe her. "There might be some magical solution out there we're just not thinking of."

He brought her hand to his lips and kissed the finger that he'd hoped would wear his ring. "I'll take you home. I'm leaving early in the morning for the conference."

"I picked up two night shifts over the weekend," she said, "because I've arranged for lighter duty next week so I can work on the fund-raiser. But I'm still going to make dinner for you guys Monday."

He looked sunken. She hated that. "Okay," he said.

Ben kissed her good-night in front of the fourplex where she rented an apartment. His manner was warm and affectionate, as it always was, but she caught an undercurrent of sadness he did his best to hide.

She gave him an extra hug.

As he held her to him, he said, "It's okay.

I know you can't help how you feel. See you Monday." Pushing her gently away, he headed back to his car.

She'd left the drum-shaded lamp lit on her desk on the far side of her small living room. She checked for messages on her phone and heard her mother's cheerful voice.

"Sarah!" she said excitedly. "I know you don't need a formal invitation for Thanksgiving, but I thought I'd extend one anyway. It seems so long since we've seen you. It'll just be us and Kate and Randy and the kids. Hope all's well. Love from both of us." Her mother said goodbye and her father chimed in, shouting, "Love ya, Sarah!" in the background.

She put the light on in her kitchen, filled the kettle and gave the new stove her landlord had provided an affectionate pat. Then she stopped and looked around her at the tiny pink-and-white room. She'd thought pink an unusual color for a kitchen, but she'd grown to like it. In the dark of the Oregon winter, it was warm and cheerful. A lace valance decorated the top of the window over the sink, and pink woven place mats were ready for guests—or, one guest—at the two-person round table in the corner.

Was this all she would ever have? she wondered. It wasn't that she wanted *things*, but she longed for room to have friends over, a large dining table that could accommodate ten, a hall tree for hanging hats and coats, room to line up boots and umbrellas. She felt a stab of pain when she realized what she wanted was...a family.

She just didn't have the courage to have one. She'd seen what families of sick children went through and she couldn't do it. She didn't *want* to do it.

She folded her arms and turned to look out at her nine-by-twelve living room decorated in pale blue with burgundy accents. The place was perfectly adequate for her needs. Maybe there was no point in wanting a bigger apartment if she was never going to have a husband and children. She couldn't imagine there were a lot of men out there willing to give up fatherhood for a woman. Despite Ben's insistence that they not do anything hasty, she feared for the future of their relationship.

The kettle boiled. She turned off the burner and made a cup of Yorkshire Gold tea. Above her stove was a plaque that read, "A woman is like a tea bag. You never know how strong she is until she's in hot water."

So here she was. In hot water. Her relationship with Ben probably suspended, her hard-earned skills as a pediatric nurse abandoned in favor of cooking and housekeeping duties because she wanted to be safe.

Was anyone ever safe from the vagaries of life? she wondered. She didn't know, but if she could be the first, she'd like to try.

JACK HAD SET up his computer in the kitchen because the light was better than in his bedroom. He'd put Corie's and Cassie's names in Facebook to see if finding them could possibly be that simple. He'd had to start somewhere. And, of course, it had not been that simple; he'd got nothing. He'd put in their fathers' names. Nothing. He refused to be discouraged. He'd try other social media and follow the first lead. If the girls were in touch with each other, finding one could bring him both.

The kitchen door opened and Ben walked in. Jack glanced at the clock, noting the early hour, then back at Ben's grim expression. He concluded that something had gone wrong with his evening. The confident lift of his shoulders he'd left with was now a slouch. Ben poured himself a cup of coffee and turned to Jack. "Want one?"

Jack held up the mug he was already working on. "Everything okay?"

Coming to sit at a right angle to him, Ben pulled off his jacket and yanked at his tie. "No. You working on something important?"

"Some preliminary research looking for Corie and Cassidy. But I'm finished for now. What happened?"

Ben put down his mug and said, "This'll probably seem like nothing to you because you've been dealing with life and death."

"*You* deal with life and death every day," Jack said with a grin, trying to lighten the mood. "Well, fairground parking and animal relocation, but still." He sobered when Ben didn't smile. "If it's important to you, I'm happy to listen. Something with Sarah?"

Ben turned in his chair to pull a ring box out of his coat pocket and place it in the middle of the table.

"Oh, man." Jack looked into Ben's face and figured it out. "You proposed and she said no."

After staring moodily into his coffee, Ben finally looked up. "She said, 'I don't want to have children.'"

Whoa. "Really. Why not?"

"She was a pediatric nurse before she went to work for Coast Care. Watching children die was hard…understandably. But then she lost a child she'd grown attached to, and that did it for her."

"Grief's a bugger." Sarah had explained some of that to him just today, though she hadn't told him the loss had led her to make such a decision. Poor Ben. "Takes a while to get your brain back in working order."

Ben nodded. His voice seemed to come from far away. "I understand. Who wouldn't? But that means I have to either live without children or live without Sarah."

Jack said, "You know, it's entirely possible she could change her mind a couple of years down the road."

"I don't know. And what if she doesn't?"

"I guess if you can't live with that possibility, then make sure you think it through before you go any further."

Ben shrugged. "I'm thinking…you know… maybe it'll somehow resolve itself." He ran a hand over his face and groaned. "Yeah. Like that'll happen."

"Having kids is a tough choice for some people. If you think disease is hard on children, you should see what war does to them."

Jack understood Sarah, he just didn't agree with her. He wanted children—an SUV full.

Yeah, kids were very vulnerable to all of life's evils, but he'd survived a childhood at least as toxic as a horrible disease.

He'd decided in Afghanistan that the best way to save the warring world was to populate it with peaceful people who were loving and tolerant. They would become that way by being loved and tolerated themselves. He imagined all the things he'd longed for as a child… Someone to smile at him, not just once in a great while but every day. Someone to put a loving hand on him, to offer him security and comfort and love him just because he existed. He'd decided to give all that to his own children so they wouldn't be haunted by bad memories and old fears. So that, one day, *they* could change the world.

All he had to do was find a woman who agreed with him.

He understood Sarah, but she was wrong.

SARAH PULLED UP in front of the Cooper Building on Saturday afternoon. The string of sunny days continued, and shoppers were wandering around downtown, determined to enjoy the weather before it turned to the usual Oregon coastal wind and rain of mid-fall and winter.

Jack stepped out of the passenger side and looked up at the two-story Italianate structure built of brick and stone. Arched windows on the second floor softened the line and empty window boxes on the first floor begged for a gardener's touch.

He stood for a long time. Sarah looked up at his pleated brow. "You don't like it?"

"No, I do." He came out of his thoughts to catch her arm and lead her toward the door. "It's just that I know this place."

She redirected him toward the rear door. "I don't have a key," she said. "But the cleaning crew usually leaves it open. If you've lived here all your life, I'm not surprised you know it. It started out as a bank at the turn of the twentieth century, but it's had all kinds of incarnations since then."

"When I was a kid," he said, opening the door for her, "it was a nightclub called Cubby's. My mother sang here."

Sarah stopped just inside, the large main room to their right dim and quiet. "You were allowed in?" she asked in surprise.

"Only in the back." He turned left instead of right into a smaller, windowless room, twelve by twelve, according to the building specs she'd printed out for herself. He shone the flashlight he'd brought around the room. A built-in bookcase stood against the opposite wall. "In those days," he said, walking in, "I used to play in this room while my mother worked. Somebody from the kitchen would bring us something to eat. I remember liking the crème brûlée."

Sarah smiled in the dark, happy he had some good memories of that time. "Pretty sophisticated palate for a little kid."

"No. It's just really good custard." He walked up to the bookcase and put a hand on it. "This was a storeroom then, but the guy who owned the place used to keep games and books in here for us."

"Us?"

"Yeah. Corie was just a toddler, but she came when Donald wasn't home to watch her, and there was another kid. Can't remember his name right now. His mother played guitar. He had red hair and freckles and his front teeth were missing. I used to feel sorry for him, but he was always cheerful. He liked to play with a red Tonka dump truck Mrs. Brogan—I think she's one of your clients—had given me. She'd filled it with cookies—I ate all of them—but he filled it with gum balls. There was a machine by the back door and for twenty-five cents in pennies, he could almost fill it."

Sarah laughed at that picture. "Good times, huh?"

"Yeah." He turned off the flashlight. "I'd forgotten there'd been any."

Together, they walked through the main room. Tall windows let in the bright afternoon. Two Ionic columns flanked an arch at the back of the room that had once separated teller windows from the vault when it had been a bank, the sales floor from the cash registers when it was a clothing store and the dining area from the kitchen when it was a nightclub. The restaurant that had most recently occupied the building had put in a large kitchen at the back, on the right.

Jack looked up at the stains on the ceiling.

Sarah looked up with him. "The city assures us the roof was fixed when the restaurant was here," she said. "They also rewired, but there's still a problem in the room where you played. They're not sure what happened, but the power was fried in there and still doesn't work. Plumbing's a little old, but functional."

Jack glanced around at the walls that had once been a soft gold but were now dull with age. "No cracks," he said. "That's good." He turned his gaze down to the pockmarked fir floor. "This flooring will be beautiful once it's sanded and restained."

"That's what I thought." She was happy with his observations so far. "Come see the kitchen."

The walls were white and the floor and backsplash were black-and-white tiles. "It's institutional looking," she said, "but the appliances are big because of the restaurant, and the specs say they work." The window looked out onto the green wall of the fabric store next door.

"Is the water on?"

"Yes."

Jack went to the double sink and turned on the hot faucet. The pressure was strong and steam rose almost immediately.

"That's good," he said. "If anything, you might want to turn the water heater down a notch. There's an elevator, as I recall."

"Yes. At the back, just beyond the kitchen."

The slightly musty-smelling car was small and a little rickety, but there was a new inspection sticker near the controls. Sarah and Jack stood side by side while the car rose.

JACK PUT HIS hands in his pockets. Awareness of her closed in on him, applying more pressure on his body than the rising elevator. It was difficult to see her pretty profile and the soft roundness of her and know she didn't want children. She seemed so perfect a vessel! But he *did* want kids and he wasn't a perfect prospect for fatherhood at all. He guessed everyone put limits on themselves that greatly underestimated what they were capable of.

Still, in her case it seemed a shame. And Ben had gone off to work that morning looking as though someone had hammered him into his clothes. Jack was determined not to mention her refusal of Ben's proposal unless she brought it up.

The elevator doors parted on a big room, empty except for two men wearing ventilators, who were putting a pile of trash into black plastic bags.

"What was up here?" Jack asked.

"Living quarters for the people who owned the restaurant. They moved out in the middle of the night a couple of years ago to escape their creditors. Their furniture's been given to Goodwill."

Suddenly she smiled brightly. "Can't you see this with three or four sofas, lots of comfortable chairs, craft tables to work on, a couple of televisions and earphones, and a small library in one corner?"

"The real one is right across the street."

"True, but it might not have *Crochet Monthly* magazine and all the history books Vinny loves."

It always surprised him how well she knew her clients. And how much she cared.

"I'd say if the inspection your attorney is arranging comes out well—" Jack turned slowly in a circle, looking the room over again "—this seems ideal for the seniors' center."

Her smile widened further. "Great! That's what I thought. Maybe you'll want to bid on the work if we get to move in. We'll have to repair, do the floors, put in new light fixtures, all kinds of stuff."

He nodded. He needed work.

In the elevator on the way down, she seemed to lose some of her sparkle. "How was Ben this morning?" she asked.

"Brokenhearted," he replied truthfully.

Arms folded, she leaned against the wall of the car. "He told you about it?"

"Some. About children."

"You think that's awful?"

"Of course not. Misguided, maybe. But everybody has to do what works for them. It's just hard to deal with when the same things *don't* work for the person you love."

She smiled faintly as the doors parted. "Thank you for understanding," she said.

Their footsteps rang on the floor as they walked to the back door.

CHAPTER FOUR

ON MONDAY, SARAH hosted her favorite clients in the community room in the building where Jasper, her blind client, lived. She'd done a circuit of town to pick up Vinny and Margaret and they now all sat together in a large room with a wall of windows that looked out onto the ocean. A mountain ash on the back lawn had lost its bright red berries and was just beginning to turn from green to gold. There was a discernible bite in the air that said October.

She carried a plate of oatmeal-raisin bars she'd brought along from the small kitchen area to the coffee table. "I apologize for sounding like a page of an Agatha Christie novel, but I've gathered you all here to tell you about the talent show fund-raiser for the Cooper Building, hopefully the new home of your seniors' center."

Jasper, whose head was perpetually tilted in an attitude of listening, frowned in the direction of her voice.

"Talent show?" he repeated ominously. "You mean like singing and dancing?"

"Yes. Or acrobatics and juggling." She waited for a smile from anyone. None came. "Dramatic readings," she went on in a teasing tone. "Wild animal taming. Darts."

"I'm good at darts," Jasper said. He was average height and white-haired, though only in his late fifties. Then he grinned. "But one of you will have to stand in front of the bull's-eye, talking so I can throw at the sound of your voice."

Sarah laughed, but neither Vinny nor Margaret even cracked a smile. She had this problem with them every time they got together as a group. They liked her visits as long as she didn't ask them to do anything outside of their comfort zones or at a time that interfered with their favorite television shows. They were happy in their apartments, at the seniors' center and at the supermarket, but trips out of town were out, as was anything that disturbed their routines.

"Sure," she said to Jasper. "If you give me a minute to duck first. Vinny, you played in a band on weekends before your wife died, didn't you? Margaret sang with a traveling choir in her twenties and taught music in the school here in Beggar's Bay. Maybe the two of you could pair up to do a song together."

The look the two exchanged should have been accompanied by the heavy, threatening music that announced the arrival of Darth Vader.

"No," Vinny said simply.

Sarah didn't mind putting him on the spot. "Why not?"

"Because he knows I wouldn't want to do it, either," Margaret replied for him. "Vinny's kind of…"

Sarah understood her hesitation. Vinny was difficult to describe.

"Jazzy," she finally said. And it was no secret that they didn't particularly like each other. Vinny was often outrageous, and Margaret tended to be stiff and formal. "My approach to music is more serious."

"Guys." Sarah let them see her disappointment. "I need your help. We need all of us— seniors and all of us who work with you—to support this project so that you'll have this great place to meet. Have you been in the Cooper Building? It's wonderful."

"I was in it," Vinny said, "when it was still a bank. It would be nice to have a place that was ours, a place we couldn't be kicked out of with little warning."

"Right. So what if you each did something individually?"

"I might be able to get some of my old band together." Vinny picked up one of her oatmeal-raisin bars and smiled in anticipation before taking a big bite. "My drummer is still in town," he said after a moment, "and Boseman, my guitarist, lives in Newport. I'll bet I could get him to come down. Mmm. Delicious."

"Excellent." Delighted to have a positive word spoken, Sarah steered the conversation back to the general plan. "The fliers I gave you explain that all the proceeds go to your nonprofit's bid on the building."

Margaret looked skeptical. "Could that make us enough money? That lawyer who wants it, too, has to have more money than we do."

"Someone on the school board knows a country-western performer whose family once owned the building." Sarah ramped up her enthusiasm, hoping it was contagious. "That should draw a lot of people. And he'll judge the talent show. My boss seems to think people will be happy to support something that al-

lows their friends to stand up in public and...
be brave enough to perform. Of course, you
two are so good you don't have to be brave.
You're professionals." She touched Jasper's
arm so he'd know she was talking to him.
"What do you want to do? I'm not sure I'd
be comfortable with the dart thing, after all."

Jasper rolled unseeing blue eyes at the ceiling. "Well, let's see. I could juggle knives, leap
through a ring of fire, saw a lady in half..."

"I volunteer Sarah." Vinny passed her the
plate of treats. "Have one."

"Cute, Vinny," Sarah said. "I'll be working
just as hard as you are, but behind the scenes.
We're here to work as a team."

"Okay." Vinny picked up another bar and
wrapped it in a napkin. "Thank you for the
treats. I'll get in touch with my guys and see
what we can do. When do I have to let you
know?"

"As soon as possible. Everyone involved
will rehearse together twice—once the week
before and once for the dress rehearsal the
Friday night before our performance. That'll
be the Saturday before Thanksgiving in
the high-school auditorium. Where are you
going, Vinny? Don't you want me to drive
you home?"

"No, thanks." Vinny checked his watch, pulled on a dark blue cotton jacket, put the napkin-wrapped bar in a pocket and grinned at her. "Jasper's driving me home."

"Ha, ha."

"Actually, I have a friend on the third floor and I arranged to spend a little time with him, then my son's picking me up for dinner." He punched Jasper in the arm, code for wanting to shake hands. "Want to come, Jazz? It's Nick Crawford. You know him from the seniors' bus that takes us shopping."

Jasper shook his head. "Thanks, but I'll stay to hear the entire plan."

Sarah looked from Vinny's eager-to-leave face to Margaret's obvious reluctance, but refused to let them stop her plans. Getting them to participate in this would be good for them.

"I'm not finished, Vinny. But if you have other things to do, I can catch you up later."

"Okay." Vinny headed for the door. "Thank you, Sarah," he said stiffly. "Good day, Margaret. Bye, Jasper." And he disappeared into the hallway.

"Okay, Jasper." Sarah cleared her throat, wondering for a moment what made her think dealing with senior citizens would be easier than dealing with children. "No knives, no ring of fire, no saws. I know you were kidding, but I'd like you to get serious for a minute." Jasper had been sighted for thirty years until an industrial accident caused a toxic adhesive to be thrown into his face. Of the three men standing with him at the time, he was the only one to survive. Now, at fifty-eight, he was determined to do everything he'd done in his youth. His courage alarmed Sarah and everyone else around him, and he seemed to delight in that.

"What about doing a recitation?" Sarah asked. Jasper had a deep, resonant voice. "You have such a good memory."

He seemed surprised, then asked, "Will I have a teleprompter?"

"Jasper. Didn't I just ask you to be serious?"

"You did," he replied, smiling. "But did you expect that I would? I guess I could recite something."

"Great. What do you think, Margaret?"

She seemed surprised to be consulted. "I think he'd do well. He always does well."

"Thank you," Jasper said. "So are *you* going to sing, Margaret?"

Sarah read the retreat in her face. She wanted to refuse. "I'm counting on you, Margaret," Sarah said. "You and Vinny are both adults. You don't have to perform together, but you can coexist in the interest of ownership of a new building for the seniors' center."

"I don't know, Sarah."

"I do. I'd like you to sing 'Among My Souvenirs' just like you sang it for me for my birthday in June."

Margaret made a face at her. "No one wants to hear that but you. It's sentimental and there's no electric guitar."

"It was beautiful. I'm signing you up for that."

"Sarah…"

"I think you'd have a good chance at winning. We'll talk about it while I drive you home."

THE AFTERNOON WAS a Northwest fall postcard as Sarah followed the coast road across town. Sunlight embroidered the ocean and seagulls called loudly as they circled and dove in search of lunch.

"I apologize," Margaret said, "for being less than enthusiastic. But Vinny annoys me."

"He knows that and likes to push your buttons."

Margaret puffed up a little. "I wouldn't date

him when we were kids because he was just the way he is now."

Sarah turned up Margaret's street and parked in front of her apartment building, interested to finally know what the problem was between them. "Really," she said. "He's a nice man at heart, Margaret. Do you think you can work with us if you'll have to see Vinny regularly?"

"I'm not sure."

Sarah stepped out of the car and walked around to help Margaret out. "That's a pretty old grudge to hold on to. Maybe it's time you two talked it out. You probably hurt his pride. He's kind of a peacock, you know."

"Yes," the old woman agreed. "All feathers and no bird. We simply avoid each other. Now, if you're going to be throwing us together..."

"You don't have to help if you don't want to."

"Maybe Vincent shouldn't be helping."

Sarah saw her chance. "But he's getting his old band together, and you seem reluctant to..."

"Fine, I'll do it. But I'll perform alone."

"Got it. So were there any stars in your music class that would make good competition for the show?"

Margaret suddenly brightened as they reached her back door. "Actually, Jack and Ben Palmer. Jack inherited a little of his mother's singing talent, and Ben's just a good showman with decent pitch."

"Really."

"Really. They and the De Angelis boys used to sing for the neighborhood when they needed spending money. One time…" Her smiled widened as she thought back. "They'd outgrown their bikes and wanted new ones. So they built a stage and set up chairs in my backyard. They charged admission and sang songs from those boy bands. They were great."

"So they got their bikes?"

Margaret's smile dimmed. "Ben and Mario and Rico did. Jack bought shoes for his sisters and a couple of new bike tires for himself."

"Geez."

"Yes. Thank you for the treats, Sarah." Margaret held up the leftovers Sarah had packed for her in a plastic bag. "It was a nice afternoon, despite Vinny. Before you sign me up for the song, let me work on it and see if I can still do it."

Sarah hugged her. "Thanks, Margaret. See you Monday."

Sarah drove home, thinking that Jack must

have been a remarkable boy. Maybe that was why he'd matured into such an interesting man. Margaret was right. One person shouldn't have to deal with so much.

She stopped at the grocery store for ingredients for the dinner she wanted to make—chicken couscous—as well as a few things for breakfast at the Palmers'. If only she could transplant their kitchen into her apartment! But at least she did have a new stove—only two burners had worked on the old one.

Finally home, Sarah decided to cook the couscous dish here. As she cut up the chicken and preheated the oven, she made a mental note to call her mother back about the Thanksgiving invitation.

Working in the cramped little room, Sarah imagined what it would be like to have yards of counter space, enough cupboards that she didn't have to store canned goods in the bottom shelf of the small linen closet in her bedroom, and room to put a KitchenAid, a Keurig coffeemaker and a dishwasher. How she'd love a dishwasher!

Reminding herself not to waste energy on what she couldn't have, at least at the moment, she focused her attention on slicing lemons, then browning the chicken pieces in a large frying pan.

When they seemed done, she glanced out the kitchen window and noticed the play of sunlight through the gnarled oak tree in the backyard. She pushed the window open. The air was cool, but its fragrance could have been imported from an island that grew spices and exotic flowers. She took a deep breath and let the aroma fill her being.

She blamed the sudden acrid smell in the kitchen to preheating an oven that was brand-new. She'd had it only a few days, not even long enough for an errant spill. All thought stopped when a line of flame flared out of the wall just above the stove. She stared at it, unable to believe what her eyes were seeing. The flame was just an inch tall for about a second, like the flame from a candle, then it ate its way up the wall while she watched, openmouthed, until it was halfway up, then angled left, toward the window, obviously following a line of electrical wiring. The curtains ignited, terrifying her.

Spurred into action, she ran to the narrow utility closet for the fire extinguisher. She scanned the instructions and then, with shaky hands, aimed the nozzle at the flames.

Her filmy curtains were already gone and the flames were dancing along the row of tea towels and pot holders hung on a rack there.

She gasped in alarm as the foamy stuff seemed to be drawn out the window, rather than to extinguishing the flames. Even worse, the line of flame was still running along the wall, perforating the living-room wallpaper as it went. It passed behind a glass-covered photo of her parents' wedding, the heat of it bursting the glass from behind and knocking it off the wall.

Mouth agape, she stared, then aimed the extinguisher at it. The tank fizzled.

She fought panic as heat and smoke quickly made the room uninhabitable. She snatched her purse off the table and ran out the door.

She dialed 9-1-1 on her cell and gave a shaky but clear account to the dispatcher, who told her to get her neighbors and go across the street, that the fire department was coming. "There's no one in the building but me right now," she said, breathless.

"All right. Wait across the street."

David Lester, who lived next door to her, was in his second year at Coast Community College and seldom came home until late, but she pounded on his door anyway. No answer.

The Moffits, the young couple who lived next to the empty apartment upstairs, were on vacation.

Sarah hurried across the street. A crowd had begun to gather as dark smoke billowed out of her windows and flame was visible in the upper floor.

She was losing everything, she thought with an odd disconnection that probably had something to do with shock. It didn't look as though there would be anything left. Her clothes. Her computer. Jerica's bear! Sarah had bought it for her and the child had loved it. Her parents had given it to Sarah when Jerica died.

The whine of a siren announced the arrival of a police car. Ben and his partner, Grady Nelson, leaped out. Sarah ran across the street toward them, a dark SUV screeching to a halt as she crossed its path. She waved a distracted apology and continued to run.

Ben had already disappeared into the fourplex. As a fire truck screamed its arrival, she raced into the building. She heard Ben shouting her name from inside her apartment. She followed the sound.

"I'm here!" she screamed, trying to find the tiny hallway to her bedroom so she could retrieve Jerica's bear from its spot on the bed.

She reached a hand out in the blinding smoke, sure she was at the hallway, when another strong hand caught it.

"Sarah!" Ben shouted. "What are you doing? Get out!"

"Okay, but I have to—"

"Get out, Sarah! *Now!*"

"No, I have to get the bear!"

"What? No!"

She yanked away from him. "Please, Ben..."

He pushed her bodily ahead of him and out the front door. He pointed across the street when she tried to push around him to get back inside. His face was smudged with smoke and his eyes hard with determination. This wasn't the sweet man she'd been dating. This was the cop doing his job.

She tried to explain.

"No!" he interrupted, pushing her toward the sidewalk. "You can't go back inside. Whatever's in there isn't anymore. Is there anyone upstairs?"

"No."

"Pets?"

"Not allowed."

He led her across the street, shouted, "Stay here!" then raced back to join Grady as he emerged from the building.

She stood across the street with her neighbors in silent disbelief. All around them, onlookers were talking about old buildings, smoke alarms, homeowner's insurance, but she wasn't following any of it. As they watched, the side window blew out and flames caught the grass that led to the concrete pad where residents of the apartment parked their cars. Her Jeep, the closest to the building, caught fire.

"No!" she cried, taking several steps toward it, but an onlooker stopped her.

"Not smart, ma'am," the man said. "Look. That fireman's going to get it."

A fireman working that side of the building aimed his hose at the car. By the time he was able to extinguish the fire, the tires were gone. The car listed sadly, like a big, broken toy.

She was homeless. And she was probably afoot for a while, too. A weird calm overtook her as she realized that now she had no possessions. She began to pace, watching Ben and Grady run back down the front steps. Grady was on the radio attached to his collar, probably reporting in to Dispatch, and Ben was on his cell phone.

Sarah imagined tomorrow's *Beggar's Bay Bugle* headline: "Bay Apartments Burn to the

Ground. Residents Unhurt But Lose Everything."

What was she going to do? She'd think of something, but at the moment, her brain didn't seem to be operating.

"Sarah."

Sarah turned at the sound of her name and was surprised to see Jack standing there in the paint-smeared jeans and sweatshirt he wore to work in the carriage house. On his head was a pale denim baseball cap with the insignia of the Cavalry Scouts—crossed swords in gold—and the words *US Cavalry*. His eyes, under the bill of the cap, were dark with worry.

Emotion swelled in her and threatened to rise in her throat in a sob. She inhaled a breath and forced it down.

"Hi," she said, her voice shaky and a little thin. "What are you doing here?"

"Ben called me." He placed his hands gently on her arms as he looked into her eyes. "Are you okay?"

Before she could answer, he shook his head. "Forget that. Stupid question. Of course, you're not okay." He turned his head in the direction of the fire and swore under his breath.

Then he refocused on her. "What I meant to ask was, are you hurt?"

She had to take another breath to keep the sob at bay. "I'm not hurt. Just sort of…" What? Shocked? Scared? Alone?

The sob erupted anyway. She tried to swallow it and that somehow made it louder.

"Yeah," he said and wrapped an arm around her. "Come on. You're going to stay with us. Ben said he has to ask you some questions about the fire, but he can do that later."

How could she move into the same house as the man whose proposal she'd just thwarted? "What? No. I can't just…"

"Sure you can." Ignoring her attempt to argue, Jack pointed to his battered SUV parked at the curb down the street. "Why don't you go sit in the car? I want to let Ben know that I've got you. I'll be right back."

She did as he suggested. As she sat in the front passenger seat, she caught a glimpse of Ben and Jack in conversation. Jack pointed toward his SUV and Ben looked in that direction. She waved.

Behind Ben she saw the blackened shell that had been her side of the fourplex: a smoky ruin in the middle of a grove of oaks dressed for fall. The outside of the apartment above hers was charred, all the windows were blown out and there was a hole in the roof.

That's a picture of my life, she thought. Windows blown out. A hole in the roof.

She put her fingertips to her throbbing forehead, refocusing her thoughts. Other people were involved here besides her. It was hard to assess the damage to the two apartments on the other side, but they looked far less affected. She hoped that was true for the sakes of David and the Moffits.

It was clear that her life was about to change direction. She belted herself into the passenger seat and pulled down the makeup mirror.

She was horrified to see that she looked a little like a briquette with a nose and ears. The heat had done something to her hair and it stuck out in all directions. She groaned and dug in her jeans for one of the hair ties that lived in every pocket she owned. She caught her hair in a bunch and tied it up, catching the tail in the band, too. It was far from glamorous, but so what?

She braced herself as Jack loped back to his SUV. She was feeling disoriented and a little scared. She'd been off balance in her life before—angry, heartbroken, hurt—but she didn't remember ever being truly frightened. This was new—and unsettling.

She thought philosophically that she should probably get used to *new*. All the *old* stuff in her life had just gone up in flames.

CHAPTER FIVE

JACK CLIMBED IN behind the wheel and surveyed his passenger. She looked as though she'd been dragged through the proverbial knothole. Her face was smudged with smoke and she'd done something weird with her hair. She took a bumpy little breath while he watched her.

At last he said, "Okay, Sarah. Hang in there for a few minutes and we'll get you home."

She looked back at the burned building. "It isn't there anymore," she said.

"Home can be anywhere you hang your hat." He started the vehicle and smiled encouragingly. That was a concept most people didn't understand, unless you'd moved around a lot as a child, made camp with a hundred other guys in the most godforsaken places and had to find a way to stay sane. He was a master at it.

She wasn't buying it. She rolled her eyes upward to indicate the top of her head. "You'll notice I'm not wearing a hat."

"Ah." He pulled off his ball cap and put it on her head. "Problem solved."

She gasped a laugh and had to make some adjustments, pulling the bottom of her pony-tail out of the band and putting it through the sizing hole. She looked into the mirror and groaned. "I look a fright."

Even with her cheeks blackened and her usually gorgeous hair tied like a bunch of green onions, she was still the prettiest thing he'd ever seen.

"A hot shower will fix that."

"I have nothing to wear after the shower."

"I've got a shirt and a pair of pajama pants someone gave me that you can use to get you through today." Jack shook his head and ex-plained: "I sleep in my Skivvies, so the pajama pants are still in the original packaging. Then you can make a list of what you need and I can take you shopping if you want— Oh, there might be something in Mom's closet you can borrow. She's shorter than you are, but about the same proportions."

"I can't take her things," she objected.

"Okay, we'll call her and ask."

Jack drove home in silence. Sarah sat with

her head against the rest, her eyes closed. He took that to mean she didn't want to talk, was probably overwhelmed. He understood completely.

Jack led Sarah upstairs to his parents' bedroom at the back of the house. It was a nice room in blue and pale yellow with a quilt that matched the curtains. There were pictures all over the walls of him and Ben when they were kids. She stood in the doorway and looked around, then turned to him, her expression disconsolate. "Jack, it's beautiful, but I can't just move into their room."

"They're away until Christmas. You know that. They won't mind."

She stood stubbornly in the hallway and wouldn't cross the threshold into the bedroom.

He dialed his mother and explained briefly what had happened. He had to hold the phone away from his ear when she expressed her horror.

"Ben told me to put her in your room," he went on to his mother, "but she's afraid you'll object."

"Put her on," Helen ordered. She was a vibrant woman with a lot to share. That included giving orders to those she loved.

"I'll put you on speaker," Jack said.

A very one-sided argument ensued, with Sarah unable to get much in, just the occasional "But—" and "I—" while his mother kept talking.

"You will take over our room and that's the end of it. And if you need clothes, you're welcome to whatever's in my closet. I have just warm-weather clothes with me, so there are sweats, sweaters, jackets. My jeans would probably be too short on you."

"Mrs. Palmer…"

"Helen," his mother corrected. "This is perfect. I mean, of course it isn't perfect because you've lost all your things, but 'things' are just that. No one was hurt. That's a good outcome to anything. When we come home, I have a Realtor friend who can help you find something to rent. But, for now, you'll be there to help Ben and keep an eye on Jack."

He rolled his eyes at that and Sarah smiled. "Also," his mother went on, "in my Christmas-gifts-I'll-never-use drawer, second one down on the right, under the black lace teddy—honestly, I don't know what Gary was thinking—is an evening purse with my mad money in it. Help yourself to it if you need to buy some things."

"But I—"

"We'll settle up when we get home. Now, anything else?"

Assured that there wasn't, love promised all around, Jack turned off his phone and looked at Sarah. "You go in and do whatever you need to do to get comfortable, and I'll find those things I was telling you about." He pointed to the television on the wall above the Colonial dresser. "I believe the remote's in the bedside table on Dad's side." He pointed and then put a hand to the wardrobe-closet doors on one wall. "The clothes Mom talked about are in here." He pushed open another door in the corner. "Bathroom. And feel free to take a nap, if you need one. We have some of the salad you made the other day for dinner and I'll call for a pizza. Nobody has to worry about cooking."

He thought she looked a little deflated suddenly, as though the reality of having lost all her possessions had just struck her .

He wanted to help, but he knew platitudes weren't going to do it. He called on his military experience.

"You've heard the expression 'Embrace the suck'?" he asked as he moved toward the door.

Sarah dropped her purse on the bed and sat beside it. "Nancy Pelosi, Minority Speaker, said that when her party had to compromise on something or other. Don't remember what."

"Actually," he said, "she borrowed it from the American soldier. Sometimes, when things are so bad and there's no escape, there's a certain comfort in metaphorically wrapping your arms around the misery and making it a part of you. Eventually, your strengths will make inroads and it'll change into something you can deal with."

She met his eyes. "Did that happen to you in Iraq?"

"Somewhat," he admitted. "It started ugly and remained ugly, but I figured if I didn't resist having to be there, the ugly wouldn't overwhelm me."

"Did it work for you?" she asked with a certain interested courtesy, as though the question was part of a clinical study. "I mean, is it still a good thing if the ugly invades your dreams?"

Good point. He was never as together as he pretended to be. But she looked so invested in his answer that he was as honest as he could be, given his lack of understanding about what was going on with him.

"Frankly, I'm not sure." He folded his arms and rested a shoulder against the doorjamb.

"My nightmares are a mixture of my childhood and the worst of my military experiences."

She turned more fully toward him, hiking a knee up on the bed, a pleat forming between her eyebrows. The intensity of her attention was at odds with her blackened cheeks and nose. He would have smiled if he hadn't been trying to explain the darkest places in his soul. And if she hadn't looked so serious in her eagerness to understand.

"In my nightmare, there's an incident," he continued, "where the Humvee I'm driving hits an IED and a few of my buddies are badly hurt. I see myself in the turret on top, tending to one of the guys whose arm was blown off and then I see a woman walking toward me down the lane. She's wearing a white caftan and hijab. My gun is drawn because women sometimes strap bombs to their bodies and try to take out as many of us as they can. As she comes closer, I realize…she's my mother."

He paused, wondering how to explain to her what his mother had been like. He said simply, "She was pretty awful at the mom job. I loved her because she was my mom, but my sisters and I were usually her last priority."

"I'm sorry."

He was, too, but he was over it. "The last words she said to me were, 'Get away from me, Jack.' Then, when she went to prison, she wanted no contact with any of us and refused all mail. Helen wrote her to tell her I was healthy and happy and doing well in school. It was returned declined."

"Maybe she didn't want to interfere with your adjustment to your new family."

"Maybe. When I was ten, DHS told us she'd died of an overdose in prison, possibly bad drugs. She must've got them from a guard, and I can only guess she'd made the same deal with him that she made with every other man she lived with."

It was clear to see in her horrified eyes that such a mother was an alien concept to her. He told her more about his nightmare, how his mother climbs onto the turret, struggles with him when he tries to push her away. "That was the morning I shoved you. I'm sorry. In that place between sleep and wakefulness, you were her."

"Maybe," Sarah said after a moment, "the awful things in your life have come together because of the way you take them on." Apparently warming to her thought, she stood, that bent knee bracing her on the bed, her gaze distracted as she thought it through. "You know...the embracing-the-suck thing. The way you took care of your sisters and bought new bike tires rather than a new bike. You take things head-on, you don't try to side-step them and you don't waste time on self-pity. So the bad stuff stays in your face, trying to survive." She refocused her gaze on him and then laughed at herself. "Clearly, I know nothing about psychoanalysis, just that everything bad in us wants to hold on. Badness has a pulse, a soul. It lives. At least, that's been true in my life."

She'd said so much else he wanted to talk about, but he had to ask, "How do you know about the bike tires?"

She smiled easily. "Margaret Brogan says her daughter was your neighbor. She gave you peanut butter cookies when you were little."

His confusion cleared and he remembered the very formal woman who had always dressed and spoken like royalty but behaved like the grandmother he never had.

He smiled at the memory. "Yeah. Ben and I used to hang around with her grandson. She was always feeding my sisters and me."

"She also said that you inherited your mother's singing voice. That I should ask you and Ben and the De Angelis brothers to sing in the talent show. The four of you could reprise your role as neighborhood stars." She grinned broadly.

Much as he enjoyed seeing that, he had no intention of singing in front of an auditorium filled with people, however noble the cause.

"I don't think that's going to happen," he told her. That seemed to douse her momentary cheer.

"Jack, you've been through the building with me. You know how much it would mean to the seniors." She wrapped her arms around herself as though warding off a chill. "You don't want all those sweet old people to be without a place to get together, do you? This way they can own their own place and never have to move again."

"Please." He stood firm. "That's shameless emotional blackmail."

"It is. Bobby Jay Cooper is coming to sing, so we should get a good turnout. I'm trying to get strong participation for the talent competition because he's going to judge it for us. The police department is helping. Firemen are taking part. The director of parks and recreation is juggling. Don't you think you should, too?"

"Juggle?"

She frowned at his deliberate misunderstanding. "Participate."

"No. It's easy for the police department. They're armed." He shifted his weight, wanting to return to what she'd said earlier. "Back to your analysis of my nightmares. You said the bad things that have happened to me stay in my face to survive."

"It's just a guess, but it sounds reasonable."

"Is that what happened to you with the young patient you lost? The grief stays in your face and makes it hard for you to be the nurse you trained to be?"

She looked affronted for a moment, then seemed to reconsider. "Hard to hear, but true. It stays there to remind me how much it hurts. So I don't try it again." She stood a little straighter, as though realizing what she'd just said, mulling it over. "So, what's in my face is fear," she added finally, looking up to share the discovery.

That was remarkable self-confrontation, he thought, for a day when the ground had fallen out from under her feet. She was silent for another minute, as though still confused. "But *you're* fearless," she said at last. "That can't be what's causing your nightmares. Ben told me you were decorated several times."

He shrugged that off. "Physical fear is relatively easy to deal with. In a combat situation, we're all dependent on one another. We don't want to fail each other, so we do what's going to help us all survive." He hesitated to consider what was churning in his mind, what had eluded understanding since he'd come home.

"Emotional fear is different. When I was a kid, I used to sit alone in the dark and wonder what I had done to make my mother not want to be with me, why she always had to be high on something and beyond my reach. Then in school, I'd watch all the other kids who had nice clothes and packed lunches and wonder how they were able to get their moms to take care of them like that. It had to be something wrong with me."

Sarah shook her head at him as though to deny that.

"In high school, I used to wonder if I'd ever have a girlfriend. My mother had quite a reputation, so what girl in her right mind and from a good family would want to be with a low-class guy like me?

"Then in the Army, we talked each other up, stroked each other's egos and told ourselves we were so tough nothing could defeat us. But in the back of my mind, I was always afraid that I wouldn't measure up because of where I came from. So I tried harder, took more chances, did reckless things to try to prove myself."

There was a certain satisfaction in admitting all that and pouring it out to someone who listened attentively and seemed to care. He heaved a sigh. "Anyway—" he straightened away from the door "—you take a shower, have a nap, relax, whatever you want to do, and I'll leave those things on the table in the hallway right by your door. Pizza, whenever you come down. I suppose you want nutritious things on it, only vegetables or chicken and—God forbid—spinach."

He was surprised when she exclaimed, "Heavens, no! Pepperoni, sausage, olives, hot peppers, but get whatever you want and I can pick off anything I don't like. But I do like thin crust. I suppose you're a deep-dish kind of guy?"

He was. "Usually. But I'll make an exception tonight. See you later." He started to close the door behind him.

"Jack?" she called.

He turned. "Yeah?"

She stepped closer, smudged and earnest. "You put your life on the line for your friends, for your country. That's amazing generosity. I'd say you've overcome your childhood."

He wanted to believe that, but he had proof to the contrary. "Then why is my mother in my nightmares? See you later."

He closed the door before she could say anything else.

CHAPTER SIX

SHOWERED AND WRAPPED in a towel, Sarah searched the bathroom shelves and drawers until she located a blow-dryer. It even had a comb attachment. She dried her hair, then caught it back in the scrunchy she'd found in her jeans' pocket. She put on the robe that hung on the back of the bathroom door.

After emerging from the bathroom, she went to the bedroom door and peered out into the hall. There was a small stack of things on the hall table as Jack had promised. She brought the stack inside and sat on the bed to examine it.

There was a pair of thick, oatmeal-colored socks with a green stripe around the top, a pair of black-watch plaid pajama pants still in their plastic packaging and a simple gray sweatshirt that smelled of laundry soap and softener.

Sarah put her underwear back on, pulled on the sweatshirt, cuffing back the sleeves a couple of times, then climbed into the pajama pants. They were a foot too long, but she fastened the tie at the waist as tightly as she could, rolled it up and then cuffed the legs to just above her ankles. She did a turn in front of the cheval glass in the corner and had to laugh. She would definitely not be invited to Fashion Week, but she was warm and comfortable.

She closed the curtains against the darkness outside, then emptied the contents of her purse onto the middle of the bedspread to calculate how much money she had and how long it would last.

There were forty-two dollars in her wallet, and most of this month's paycheck was still in the bank. There was just under a thousand dollars' credit available on her card. She could easily pay room and board here for a couple of weeks, anyway, until she could find another apartment with appliances. She could probably find furniture at Goodwill or in any secondhand store. But she didn't have to think about that right now. Her main concern at the moment was to make sure she did her part for the Palmer household.

She called her mother to tell her what had happened.

"Oh, my God! Will. Will!" Her mother

shouted for Sarah's father. "Pick up the extension. It's Sarah. Are you all right, sweetheart? You weren't hurt?"

"No, I'm fine." She explained that she'd lost everything, though, and was staying with friends temporarily. She made sure they had her cell phone number and gave them the Palmers' land line number. "I'll be here for a couple of weeks at least. Please don't worry."

"Are these 'friends' Ben and his family?" her father asked. She'd told them about Ben.

"Yes."

"I thought his family was in Arizona for the winter." That was her mother, who never missed a thing, or the opportunity to call you on it.

"They are. Ben's brother, Jack, is home from Afghanistan and their mom hired me to cook for them and, you know, keep an eye on things. So, she invited me to move in."

"From Arizona?"

"We spoke on the phone, Mom."

"What things are you keeping an eye on?"

"Janice," her father said quietly, and as though repeating something he'd said before, added, "she's a grown woman with good sense and we know she can take care of herself."

"Thank you, Dad."

"If she could take care of herself," her mother said in the same tone, "she wouldn't have moved away to escape her life."

Sarah and her father groaned in unison.

"I'm not trying to escape," Sarah denied patiently. "I just took another bend in the road. It's still my life. I'm still a nurse..." Technically, that was true. She kept up her license; she just preferred not to use it.

"We bought your mother a used Volkswagen Beetle," her father said, obviously trying to change the subject. "I'll email you some photos."

"That'd be gr—" she began, then remembered that her computer had been lost in the fire. "No computer, Dad. That's gone, too. But I'll see if Ben or Jack will let me access my email through theirs."

"You mean, you've lost *everything*?" her mother asked.

"Yes. Well, I got out with my purse and the clothes on my back. My Jeep caught on fire, too, so I don't think it's—"

"Why don't you come home? You can stay until you make a new plan."

"Thanks, Mom, but I'm working my old plan. I like Beggar's Bay. Everything's going to come together."

"Read me your routing and bank account numbers," her father said, rustling papers. "I'm going to send you some money. And actual photos of the car."

"No. I have—"

"Sarah."

She knew that tone and read him the numbers.

"It's just a loan," he said, "so don't get huffy. I can charge you exorbitant interest if that'd make you feel better."

"That's not necessary." She laughed lightly.

"You can bring Ben for Thanksgiving," her mother said.

"Sure," she lied. Things were too complicated at this moment to explain about Ben.

"If his parents are still in Arizona, you can bring the brother, too. What's his name again?"

"Jack."

"Jack. Did he come home in good health?"

"He's a perfect specimen," she replied before realizing how that might sound to them. She added before they could comment, "No injuries, a few medals. He's getting ready to reopen the family's restoration and remodeling business."

Her mother was silent. "Oh yeah?" her father said, sounding interested.

"Are you two doing okay?" Sarah asked before either of them could take that any further.

"We are," her mother replied. "Your father is already planning his light display for Christmas. Saints preserve me. Maybe it'll be up when you come for Thanksgiving."

"Okay. I'll look forward to that. Well, I just wanted to check in, let you know I'm fine and that you can reach me on my cell or on the Palmers' number for the next couple of weeks. I love you."

She turned off her phone with their goodbyes ringing in her ears. It humbled her to know that, even though they were several hundred miles away, there were people for whom she was still priority one.

The phone rang again while still in her hand. It was her landlord.

"Sarah!" he said, sounding relieved to hear her voice. "Are you okay? The police told me there wasn't time for you to save anything."

"Hi, Mr. Potter. Well, I got my purse. All my important records are in a safe-deposit box. I lost all my clothes and furniture, car, too. But the insurance company will pay me as soon as the fire department determines what caused the problem."

"Do you have someplace to stay?"

"Yes. I'm with friends."

"I'm so sorry," he said sincerely. "The whole building's looking like a loss. We'll have to bulldoze it and start over. I'll stay in touch. You call me if there's anything I can do."

"I will."

She turned off her phone and sat quietly for a moment, thinking how surreal it was that just earlier this afternoon she was trying to gently bully her seniors into supporting the fund-raiser, as though she had nothing else to worry about. Ha. The best-laid plans…

The sound of an automobile engine in the driveway got her on her feet. She looked out the window to see a pizza delivery car. Pocketing her phone, she started toward the door, then noticed the cap Jack had put on her head in the SUV. She'd tossed it on the bed when she'd gone into the bathroom to shower.

She noticed a hook on the middle of the window frame between the pair of windows. She guessed it was leftover from a rod that had probably supported the bottom half of café curtains before the long panels had been installed. She placed the hat on the hook.

Home is anywhere you hang your hat, Jack had said.

She ran downstairs and found that Jack had taken the bowl of leftover salad and two plates to the table, but had apparently been distracted by the laptop on his place mat from setting the table completely. She found tongs in the utensil drawer and dished out salad as he paid the pizza deliverer and carried the aromatic box to the table.

Sarah put a ten-dollar bill on Jack's keyboard and then went to find something to drink. He noticed the bill and began to protest. She looked around the refrigerator door at him. "I'm going to do my share," she said firmly, then ducked back to reach for the bottle of cola.

He went to get dinner plates and glasses, then met her at the table with them. "Tonight you're a guest," he said.

"Nope. I've officially moved in for a while and the only way this is going to work is if you let me pay my way."

"And not argue with you, right?" He grinned as he pulled out her chair. "Am I allowed to do the gentlemanly things or does that not let you feel like an equal-share roommate?"

She smiled and took the seat. "No, that's

very thoughtful. Thank you. But from now on, pretend I'm the sister you and Ben never had."

He made a face as he closed his laptop and moved it aside, then sat opposite her. She regretted her remark instantly. "I'm sorry," she said quickly. "You do have sisters. I didn't mean—"

He shook his head. "No, no. I made a face because…" He hesitated, then met her gaze and said frankly, "I'd have difficulty thinking of you as a sister."

She opened her mouth to ask why, then changed her mind. There was something in his eyes and something in *her* surprisingly willing to accept it. Her nerve endings fluttered. Uh-oh.

"You mentioned that you've officially moved in," he said, getting up again to get the Parmesan cheese shaker and pepper flakes. "What makes it official?"

"I hung my—your hat on a hook." She forced a light tone, trying not to think about how substantial he looked in a dark blue thermal shirt and clean jeans and the work boots he preferred. Her fears seemed to have dissolved and that didn't make sense. She'd lost everything and just a couple of hours ago she'd been afraid.

Of course, this new nubbin of confidence might not be because of him. Her father was sending her money, and despite her nagging, her mother always made her feel as though she meant the world to her.

He pretended shock. "You don't mean you're taking something I told you to heart?"

"No." She smiled again. "I mean I found a handy hook, and I put your hat on it. I'll give it back tomorrow."

"That would un-officialize the whole thing. You hung it up. It's your hat."

"Un-officialize?"

He shrugged. "The word's a stretch, but it says what I mean. Incidentally, Ben called. They're down a man tonight and he's splitting a shift with someone. We should save him some pizza."

So she was alone with Jack. That was fine. They were adults, and though he'd said he couldn't think of her as a sister, that didn't mean he thought of her as anything else, even though her pulse tripped a little at the thought. But maybe it just meant that he had sisters he loved and no one else could take either one's place.

"Okay," she teased, "but Ben's part comes out of your half."

"Oh, no. We'll just put a third aside for Ben. Something tells me you'd have been a bratty little sister."

"I was. No excuses. I do have a great sister, Kate, two years older than I am, who would tell you that I broke a few of her dolls because I needed patients in my hospital when I was seven." She grinned across the table at him as she pulled a piece of pizza onto her plate. "I thought I was going into orthopedics in those days. I didn't know what orthopedics was, but I saw a cowboy in a movie put a splint on a friend's broken leg and I was sold. Oh. I also let her take the blame when I broke the turkey platter on Thanksgiving—she used to bring that up every holiday—and I ratted on her when she told our parents she was going to a friend's to study and she was really meeting Damien Fortin. I was a rotten little sister."

He was enjoying her confession. "What happened to the turkey platter?"

"We were emptying the dishwasher while Mom and Dad were having a much-deserved rest after Christmas dinner with my aunt and uncle in front of the television. Kate snapped me with a towel. I was holding the platter and smacked her on the backside with it. I had no idea she was stronger than the platter. She had the two pieces in her hands when my mother walked in, so I said she broke it."

Jack looked shocked. "Sarah, I hadn't imagined this side of you. To let your sister be punished for your—"

"She wasn't really punished, she was just scolded. And she started it, anyway, by snapping me with the towel. But about Damien..."

"Well, that I get. I mean the guy's name was Damien—the evil one from *The Omen* movies."

"He was also the speeding one. His younger brother was in my class and had just had to contribute his allowance to help pay Damien's speeding ticket so his father wouldn't find out. I really didn't want Kate to end up in a crash."

"Did she see it that way?"

"Of course not. She didn't speak to me for a week. About *your* sisters," she asked. "Find anything yet?"

JACK LIBERALLY SPRINKLED pepper flakes on his pizza. He was trying not to get too down about his search. He'd known it would be difficult when he started, but it would be so encouraging to get one little glimmer of either girl. Girl. They were women now, possibly with families of their own. Considering how their childhood had been, it occurred to him for the first time that they might not have the same interest in finding him as he had in finding them. They'd adored him as little girls, but they might have found worthwhile connections by now and be happy to just forget the past.

"Nothing yet," he admitted. "I've tried every social media I can think of—Facebook, Myspace, LinkedIn and a few others I'd never heard of till I started searching. I've used the phone books with the last place I knew them to be and just can't make a connection. Tons of Ochoas and Chapmans, but no right combination of middle initials and connected family. Of course, it's been so long, I can't claim to know their families. There were no names I recognized."

"Do you remember their fathers' first names?"

"I do. I tried that. Corie's father was Miguel Ochoa, so I tried it and found an obituary for someone by that name in Odessa, Texas, who died fifteen years ago."

"Could that be him?"

"Possibly. He was living in Mexico when she was sent back to him, but people run back and forth across the border all the time—legally and illegally. Corie's name wasn't among the family left behind, though."

"I'm sorry. Miguel is a pretty common given name in Mexico. And there must be lots of Ochoas. What if Miguel was a middle name?"

He smiled wryly. "Yeah, but if he was Juan or José or Pablo Miguel Ochoa, it isn't going to help me anyway. I also searched Michael and Mike Ochoa, but found nothing."

"What about Cassidy's father?"

"Donald Chapman. Don't know his middle initial, so I tried to go by age, but the only one I could find that might be appropriate was in Paris, France. That seems unlikely, but who knows? I'll just keep working on Corie because I'm deeply into it at the moment. They're out there somewhere. I just have to keep trying."

After dinner, she took over the cleanup. "I left about twenty dollars' worth of chicken couscous ingredients on my stove top and kitchen counter," she complained as she loaded the dishwasher. "When the fire started, I just grabbed my purse and ran. I wish now I'd thought to grab some of the food, but I didn't think of it. Or the bear."

"The bear?"

"Jerica's bear. It was on my bed, but everything was catching fire so quickly, I didn't think and just ran. When I remembered and tried to get back in, Ben pushed me out again."

"I should hope so. I'm sure the bear is important to you, but…you're important to Ben. He wanted you to be safe."

She acknowledged that with a nod and then turned away from him to look through cupboards. He wasn't sure why he'd reminded her that Ben cared.

Something about knowing she'd be here every day made her more appealing than ever, and filled him with a fatalistic acceptance of the fact that her presence meant big trouble. Ben cared for her and wanted to work out their relationship issue. Though whether or not to have children was a big issue, and Ben was on the wrong side of it. Then again, so was he.

And he'd thought the Middle East was complicated.

FOR AN HOUR Jack searched websites while Sarah padded quietly around the kitchen in his socks. Her slender frame swam in his sweatshirt, her small hands working among familiar kitchen things with a grace his eyes kept going back to. He sighed and forced himself to focus on his task. He was vaguely aware of her mixing something in a bowl and then pouring it into a pan that went in the oven.

Ben came home to take her into the living room and question her about the fire. He was gone in twenty minutes.

Sarah eventually came to look over his shoulder, drying her hands on a towel. "Are you finding anything?"

"No." He closed his laptop and pushed it slightly away from him. Her nearness seemed to make the air crackle. "I'm done for tonight." Pulling himself together, he made an effort to appear removed from this intimate moment in the kitchen. "Did you call your insurance company?" he asked.

Her eyes registered surprise at the sudden change in him. "I did. They're investigating. They'll be in touch."

"Did you call your landlord?"

"*He* called *me*." She smiled at his questions, apparently deciding the new mood was not a problem for her. "He was apologetic and also investigating. Margaret said you were a great big brother, always looking out for the girls. See, this familial relationship between us could work."

Yeah. Right. "I'm going to clean up in the

carriage house. I left a mess when Ben called me to come and get you."

She looked slightly off balance again. "I apologize for the disruption to your life."

He shook his head. "Please. It's not a disruption. Well, not an unpleasant one, anyway."

"Thank you. I'm baking blond brownies." She made a production of hanging the tea towel in her hand on the oven handle. "I know, I know. Not the kind of food I generally eat. But you and Ben do, so... Want me to call you when they're ready?"

Did he? No. "Yes. Please."

In the carriage house he worked like a wild man, filled with a new energy he hadn't experienced since he'd been home. He swept up sawdust, threw odds and ends of molding in a bucket, scrubbed down the shower stall and decided it didn't have to be replaced, though new doors would be a good idea.

The main room and the bedroom were in good structural shape and he'd replaced a broken window. He looked around and tried to imagine someone living here. It was small, but the fireplace would make it comfortable, and the stylish details his father had added—elegant molding, woodsy light fixture overhead, a window seat in the bedroom—lent it the same turn-of-the-twentieth-century air the main house had. His mother had picked out paint before she and his father had left for Arizona.

Sarah called from the open back door, then wandered in. She looked around the main room, apparently noticing the nice lines visible even with construction clutter all around.

"Wow," she said, stepping carefully around a tarp-covered vanity that was going in the bathroom. She stopped in front of the stone fireplace he'd cleaned with trisodium phosphate. "This is going to be so elegant," she said, squatting to study the old filigreed fire screen he'd buffed up.

"There should be flowers in there in the summer," she said. "Those blue hydrangea from the bushes by the back gate. Then you can put them on the mantel when it's time to build a fire." She straightened, her cheeks pink, her eyes bright. She avoided his eyes.

"Did you know," she went on, wandering around the room, "that you can put hydrangea in water and just let the water evaporate and they'll dry beautifully?"

"I didn't know that." He wasn't sure he cared, but she seemed to, and as long as she was wandering and talking and avoiding him, he could continue to watch her move around in his clothes and pretend that their situation was less complicated than it was.

She peered into the bathroom and then headed for the bedroom. It was small and empty, wood debris from the molding he'd replaced in one corner still piled there. "I used to painstakingly hang the flowers upside down, one by one, from a clothesline I'd strung in the bathroom over the tub…" She kept talking as she looked. "And then a nurse friend told me I didn't have to go to all that trouble. That they'll dry beautifully all by… them…selves."

He'd been watching her from the doorway and she turned to come out. It would have been simpler if he'd just moved, but no part of his life had been simple—ever—and he held his ground. She was forced to look at him. Her blue-gray eyes were soft and a little wary in her roses-and-cream face, a few wisps of light brown hair at her forehead and temples. If he ignored the sweatshirt and sleep pants, she looked like a woman from a Pre-Raphaelite painting. He couldn't stop staring.

"She said…she saw it…on Martha Stewart's show."

"Who?"

"My nurse friend."

"Yeah. What?"

"The flowers."

"Yeah."

He wanted to kiss her more than he wanted anything, but he wasn't sure that she felt the same. The warrior in him wanted to kiss her anyway, but he was trying to put that guy away and live in peace. Peace with Ben. Peace with himself.

He leaned toward her because the moment stretched, her eyes widening a little, her pink lips parting. The tension seemed to heighten his senses and draw his mouth toward hers.

Then it snapped back painfully as a voice shouted from the doorway. "Jack? You still working?"

He straightened away from Sarah at the sound of Ben's voice. Sarah walked out of the bedroom and stopped in front of Jack to greet Ben.

"Ben!" She spoke with surprise, as though she'd never seen him before. Jack guessed there was a little residual tension in her, too. "Hi. I thought you were working tonight."

In uniform, Ben always looked like a poster for the perfect cop. His eyes went from Sarah's face to Jack's with that incisive gaze that never missed anything. Jack was sure he saw their mutual attraction, if not in Sarah's eyes, then in his.

Ben arched an eyebrow. The glance that fell on Jack held an element of angry surprise. Or maybe he was just imagining it.

"I am working," Ben said. "But I asked the fire department to be on the lookout for this and they found it. I'm sorry it's in bad shape." He pulled a scorched, foot-long blond teddy bear out from behind his back. One side of it was black, the ear missing, and the rest of it was soaked, one button eye in place.

Sarah took it from him and caught it to her. All she must have felt at the time the little girl died passed through her eyes and she let out a strangled sob. Then she reached up an arm to wrap it around Ben's neck. "Thank you," she said. "I'm so happy to have it."

"Sure. You're welcome." Jack caught Ben's glance over Sarah's shoulder. His expression was difficult to read. It might have been triumph, but it was possible Jack was just feeling paranoid. "I've got to get back to work," Ben said.

"Your pizza's in foil in the refrigerator," Jack heard Sarah tell Ben as she followed him toward the house. "You should take it with you."

Jack stayed behind, unwilling to get in the way. The hug, he thought, was just gratitude for the mangy bear that was so important to her. She'd thought Ben hadn't understood her need for it, but he had. When he'd made her leave the burning building, he'd just been doing his job as a cop to keep her safe. Or had it been his job as the man who still loved her?

Great, Jack thought. *Now I'm jealous of my brother. Well, that should be grist for an interesting nightmare tonight.*

AND IT WAS, although Ben didn't figure in it. Jack stood atop the turret, trying to stop Curry's bleeding, when the woman in white appeared again. From behind the dream, he tried to tell himself that she was his mother, that he should fire in her direction and hope she runs away. But his dream self couldn't hear him. He drew his weapon but watched her come as he had before, demanding that she stop. But she didn't.

His little sisters weren't there this time. Just her. And she kept coming. Then she was on the turret with him and when he struggled with her this time, she tried to take his gun.

He put a foot to her stomach and kicked her ruthlessly off the Humvee. She sailed off with a scream, as though free-falling off a cliff.

He awoke with the shrill sound of it in his ears, his breath coming in rapid gasps, beads of sweat on his face. Then there was absolute silence. No sounds of running feet, no door flying open. No Sarah pinned to the mattress.

Pity. On several counts.

CHAPTER SEVEN

"I CALLED MY DRUMMER," Vinnie announced while Sarah applied a medicated skin cream to an angry dry patch on the sole of his foot. "And found my old guitarist. We've decided to do a Sinatra medley."

"Everyone loves Sinatra." She worked the residue of cream into her fingers and capped the container. "That should make you very popular with the romantics in the audience."

"Margaret's doing 'Among My Souvenirs,'" he confided, his tone suggesting a complete lack of interest. Odd, she thought, since he'd brought it up.

"How do you know that? I thought the two of you don't speak."

"Her friend June Wheeler is friends with Jasper. He told me."

"Hmm. She's good. Probably be stiff competition for you."

"Nah. We're better. The girls used to swoon over us in the old days." He laughed. "I can't imagine forty years have made that much difference. So I'm two inches shorter and my hair's white instead of black. So's hers and it's sprayed so hard you could wear it into battle."

Sarah stifled a laugh. It was true. Though a wonderful woman, Margaret could use a little loosening up.

"Be nice. She's a lady, and you can be a little much sometimes."

He rolled his eyes. "She thinks she's better than everybody else."

She put his white cotton sock back on and handed him his shoe. "No, she doesn't. She's just reserved."

"Stuffy, you mean."

As much as she wanted to see her favorite clients become friends again, Sarah had to agree that was true. She washed her hands at the counter and started Vinny's breakfast.

"What's on the menu?" he asked, tugging on the Velcro strap on his shoe.

"Omelet with green onions and turkey sausage." She smirked at him over her shoulder. "Can you eat that, or would you see eating turkey as cannibalism?"

He opened his mouth to reply, then, realizing he was being teased, made a face at her.

"Is harassing your clients part of your job description?"

"Come on, this has to be fun for me, too. Grated cheddar or Swiss?"

"Swiss. This conversation is full of holes, anyway."

MARGARET DIDN'T WANT to talk about Vinny.

"I just asked," Sarah said, slicing the raspberry-cream-cheese coffee cake she'd brought, "because you're doing that Sinatra number for the show, and I know Vinny and his band will be doing a Sinatra medley. Would you rather be scheduled before him to make a big impression or after him so that your performance will linger in the judge's mind?"

Margaret studied her suspiciously, her helmet of hair catching Sarah's attention. "It isn't like you to show preference to one client over another. You're doing this to try to make me sing *with* him, aren't you? It won't work, Sarah. We hate each other. Why are you looking at my hair?" She put a hand up to it, patting it, checking for disorder.

Sarah shrugged, carrying coffee to the bar. "I just think it would be very elegant to have an entry that was a throwback to the forties. You know. The big band era with heart-tugging music from a handsome band with a beautiful chanteuse at the microphone. We'd have to put a little movement into your hair, so that it gleams under the lights."

The elderly woman looked embarrassed. "Please. Beautiful? Gleaming hair? I'm way past all that."

Sarah sat opposite her and leaned forward conspiratorially. "Is a woman ever past all that? Is a man ever past noticing that she's still got it?"

Margaret frowned. "I haven't got it. I never *had* it."

"Margaret, you do."

AT JASPER'S PLACE, Sarah did a load of laundry and folded sheets before making lunch. Jasper played a reading of Walt Whitman he'd gotten at the library. "Did you know he had a romantic side?" he asked, stopping the disc. "We love him for his patriotic works and his Americana, but he wrote love poems, too."

"No, I didn't know that. Does that mean you have a romantic side, too, Jasper?"

"No, it means I happened upon his by accident. I had the love of my life as a young man and now I'm just…a student of the world, I guess."

Sarah dropped the sheet into a plastic basket. "What happened to her?"

"She left," he said without offering further explanation. Sarah smiled at the thought that he didn't know *her* very well if he thought she'd settle for that answer.

"When?" she asked. "After your accident?"

"Yes. She was wild and free and I loved that about her. So when I could feel the change in her, I told her she could go."

"If she went—" Sarah carried the basket to his bedroom, then came back "—she wasn't the love of your life. If she was, she'd still be here."

He hunched a shoulder. "I guess there are times when someone can be the love of your life, but you're not the love of theirs. I couldn't see the things she saw, we couldn't talk about them in that way, remember them, let them be part of a shared experience. I was out of the equation. And that diminished life for her." He smiled a little self-consciously, admitting, "Then, of course, there was the confinement of having my hand on her arm all the time so she could guide me, the limiting of our world a little bit."

She carried a stack of dish towels into the kitchen. "I've never noticed that your world was smaller than other people's. I've seen you all over the place. I think you're very brave, an adventurer, even."

"Real adventurers are often alone. It isn't everyone who wants to share that kind of life. Anyway, I was thinking of reciting 'I Hear America Singing' for the show. Do you think that would appeal to anyone today?"

"I do." She put coffee at his left hand and a plate of coffee cake in his lap. "In a couple of weeks we'll have our first rehearsal and see what kind of reaction we get from the other participants."

"I wonder if Vinny found his old drummer."

"He did. They're doing a Sinatra medley. I'm trying to talk Margaret into joining them for a number. I think it would be wonderful."

He frowned in Sarah's direction, a forkful of coffee cake halfway to his mouth. "Then it would turn into a murder-mystery dinner, rather than a talent show."

She admitted as much with a sigh. "True. But I'm going to keep working on them. They used to be friends once."

"Things change, Sarah. You can't fix everything for us. You can fix meals and wonderful treats, but you can't fix our lives."

The notion made her stubborn. A lot *he* knew.

JACK STOOD SEVERAL rungs from the top of an ancient, rickety ladder, changing the lightbulb in what was now Sarah's room. It smelled of her already, he noted, that subtle blend of flower notes and vanilla. He removed the inverted bowl fixture and placed it on the bucket shelf, then unscrewed the spent bulb.

"What are you doing?" Ben asked.

Screwing the bulb in with one hand, Jack glanced down at his brother, who was still in uniform. "I'm changing a bicycle tire. Must have picked up a nail." At Ben's groan of impatience, he asked, "Well, what does it look like I'm doing? One bulb was burned out, so I thought I'd change them both. Sarah said we should think of her as a sister and not do everything for her, but I wouldn't ask a sister to get up on this shaky ladder."

"Dad says that was the first thing he bought when he started the business." Ben's voice was less defensive now. Jack felt his own defenses relax.

"Yeah. I'm not wild about using it, but it

was on the back porch. Handier than getting mine out of the carriage house."

"Is she settling in okay? I haven't seen much of her."

"Seems to be." Jack removed the second bulb and handed it down to Ben. "This still has a little life in it. We can put it in the basement. The one over the dryer is starting to flicker."

"Right."

The air was heavy with Ben's unasked question.

"We were talking about hydrangea," Jack said into the silence. He screwed in the second bulb. "Blue ones."

"What?"

"When you walked into the carriage house with Sarah's bear, and got all bent out of shape when you saw us together. She was telling me there should be dried hydrangea in the fireplace in the summer." He picked up the glass fixture.

"Yeah, well. I'm not as stupid as I look, Jack." Ben sounded testy.

"That's a relief. We'd have to hide you from the asylum if you were."

Ben ignored his smart remark and said, "It

doesn't matter what you were talking about, I know what *you* were thinking about."

Jack held the fixture in place with one hand and screwed in the pin with the other. "Now you're a stupid mind reader. Those two qualities aren't usually found together."

"You like her."

"She's a likable woman."

"Damn. I'm going to shake this thing until you fall off it, Jack. I'm trying to discuss a problem here."

Jack climbed calmly down. He knew Ben hated cool reason when he was passionate about something. And he was clearly still passionate about Sarah. "*Why* is there a problem here?" Jack asked. "*You* invited her to live with us. *You* asked me to pick her up at the time of the fire and bring her home. *Your* department's understaffing keeps you away at unpredictable hours, so there will be times when the two of us are alone together. You can't blame me for that, Ben. I know you'd like to, but you started all this."

"Just admit that you're attracted to her." There was little subtlety in Ben.

Jack could be subtle but not reticent. "I'm attracted to her."

Ben glared back at him. "I don't *want* it to

be over between Sarah and me. And if you aren't in the middle being...*you*..." The simple word had a distinctly condemning connotation. "She might just wake up one day and decide she does want children. And me."

Jack wanted to be offended, but he wasn't sure if that remark warranted it or not. "Being *me*? Who do you want me to be?"

Ben tossed the bulb down on the soft bedcover and walked out of the room, calling over his shoulder, "You know what I mean."

He didn't. And he thought their conversation was beginning to sound like something from a counseling-session workbook. Jack followed him into the kitchen where he was pawing through the refrigerator.

"I *don't* know what you mean."

"I thought *I* was the stupid one."

"That still holds true. Tell me what we're talking about."

Ben slammed the fridge door closed and leaned on it. "We're talking about Sarah, who doesn't want children, but would probably change her mind for *you*." Again, that angry emphasis of the pronoun.

Desperate to make sense of all this, Jack struggled to remain calm. "If she was going to change her mind, why wouldn't she do it for you? I'm the one with the bad mother and the father who was stupid enough to fly while high on drugs."

Ben growled. "What your parents did were personal choices. They had nothing to do with you. Somehow, their faulty genetics produced *you*—the golden child who came out of a hideous situation and got everything right."

Jack was getting angry. "You think I'm somehow charmed, is that it? Or does this have to do with *our* parents and not just mine? You never liked that I wanted to work with Dad when you didn't, that I have the same interest and skill set he has. He's *your* natural father, not mine. Do you hate that our parents love me, too, even though I'm grafted onto this family?"

Ben untied his creaky leather belt with gun, flashlight and handcuffs, and placed it on the back of a chair.

"Afraid you'll be tempted to shoot me?" Jack taunted, going to pour two cups of coffee.

Snorting scornfully, Ben retrieved a bottle of brandy and carried it to the table. "I could take you down with one hand. Don't need a bullet."

Carrying the mugs to the table, Jack snorted

back. "Yeah, right. Remember the old Chevy incident?"

They'd fought over driving an old Camaro their father had held onto for them to use through high school. They'd had to share it, and one particular summer evening when they'd gone to a beach party with a pair of sisters, they'd fought over who would drive home. Ben had had two beers more than Jack and Jack had fought for the keys. Jack had won, but only because Ben had been somewhat worse for wear.

"I thought we decided not to bring that up since I have no real memory of what happened," Ben said. "You could be lying to me for all I know."

"So, what's your problem then?"

Ben poured a tot of brandy into each mug. He pulled one toward him and leaned back in his chair. He looked grim, clearly reluctant to say what was on his mind.

"Are you still on duty?" Jack asked. "Should you be drinking?

"No. Have to take my uniform to the cleaners, so I just wore it home." He tore open the top buttons of his shirt.

"Just spit it out," Jack advised. "Don't try to sugarcoat it. You hate me, after all?" He took a sip of the laced coffee to fortify himself in case the answer was yes.

"What I didn't like as a kid," Ben replied, his voice a decibel lower than it had been, "was that Mom and Dad did seem happier after you came." He sighed heavily, drank his own fortifying sip of coffee, then looked Jack in the eye and admitted, "I know it's a small-minded thought, but I can't help it. It's there. You sort of filled things out. Made it better."

Jack looked into his brother's eyes and couldn't remember a time when Ben had expressed any resentment of him. They'd fought, competed, been jealous of each other, but all that had been classic sibling stuff. "*You* lobbied for them to adopt me," he reminded Ben.

"I know. You were important to me then, and you're important to me now. I just hate that you're sometimes—often—better than I am."

"What?" Jack stared at him in disbelief. "You're a cop who's been commended over and over. You have a million friends in a town of only 4,000 people. You're on the fast track for promotion and women love you. I don't see—"

"Sarah doesn't," Ben interrupted.

"That's bull. She doesn't want children. You

don't know that she doesn't want *you*." What was he doing?

"If she truly loved me," Ben asked morosely, "wouldn't she consider thinking about having children...for me?"

"Well, yeah, but the reverse is true, too, isn't it? If you truly loved her, wouldn't you consider living without children...for her?"

"God."

"Yeah."

Ben nodded broodingly into his coffee and then looked up at Jack as though he had more to say.

"Go ahead," Jack encouraged. "I can take it."

Ben sighed and took a long pull on the cup. "I saw a look in her eyes when she was with you in the carriage house that she's never given me."

Jack gave himself a minute to absorb that, trying not to react. Was that true? "You were jealous and imagining things."

"You know me, Jack. I don't imagine anything. I deal only in reality—passionately, but honestly. You're going to make this fall apart for me."

Jack thought he should probably do the noble thing and back away, but the past six years of his life had been about stepping up, pushing through. It was who he'd become. "Ben," he said levelly, "if you're dealing only in reality, think about it. If you and Sarah disagree on the issue of children, there's already a lot against you."

Ben's expression was indecipherable, except that it was absolutely black. "Are you hoping to pick up the pieces?"

I wish, Jack thought. Aloud he said, "Maybe. But I want kids, too. The only difference between you and me is that I've lived most of my life wishing I could change things. Facing reality is good, but figuring out how to reshape it has kept me sane—with my birth mother, in the Middle East and…right now."

Running a hand over his face, Ben said bleakly, "So we're in love with the same woman. Seriously."

"Looks like it."

Ben stood abruptly. "You get no quarter because you're my brother."

Jack took that threat as a good sign. He still called him his brother. Jack nodded. "Neither do you."

"All right." Ben took his mug to the counter. "She's late tonight," he said as though they hadn't just discussed a life-altering love for the same woman.

"She's at a Coast Care meeting."

"I'm going to meet Mario and Rico at the Water Dog. Want to come? There's a baby shower or something and the ladies are out."

"No, thanks. I'm still trying to find some sign of my sisters."

Ben wandered back to the table, the subject of Sarah shelved for the moment. Jack had pulled his laptop toward him and Ben leaned over him to look. "What have you tried?"

Jack listed all his efforts, then told him about finding Miguel Ochoa's obituary. "I thought that might be her father, but she isn't listed among the family."

"You know, there's a website called Tomb-Stones.com where family and friends can leave a message on the deceased's page. If that was her father and she was alienated from the family or something else separated them, she might use that as a way to, you know, let the universe know she still cares. We use it in investigations all the time. And the site logs not only the message, but where it came from. You might try it."

When Ben left, Jack went to that website. He put in Miguel Ochoa's name and the date of his death, and came up with his page. There was a photo of his tombstone and one message: "Your daughter forever, Isabel." Jack remembered that Isabel had been mentioned in the obituary. No messages from Corie. Or Elizabeth. Well. He'd been crazy to think it would be that simple.

With a groan of exasperation, he turned off the computer and went to the carriage house where he prepared to paint the bedroom. If he exhausted himself before he went to bed, maybe he wouldn't dream.

SARAH PULLED HELEN PALMER's RAV4 into the driveway and parked beside Jack's SUV. Thank God for the extra car that was left behind when the senior Palmers went south for the winter, and for Helen's fall and winter wardrobe from which Sarah had borrowed jeans that were too short, but passed when worn with the boots she'd been wearing when she escaped the fire, and a nubby red sweater that was wonderfully cozy. Sarah was happy to see Ben must have met friends for dinner or drinks, as he often did.

Her living with him and Jack now made everyday things so much more awkward than they'd been before. She saw it in Jack, too. She was attracted to him, but she put that down to all the trauma of the past week, the status of her relationship with Ben changing and the strangeness of having lost all familiar possessions. But Jack seemed uncomfortable, too. There was a tension between them like an electrified fence.

She guessed things were a little iffy between Ben and Jack, also. Both of them were courteous to her, but a little less so with each other. The last thing in the world she wanted was to cause a problem between the two of them.

She saw a light on in the carriage house and was surprised that Jack was still working. Maybe that was good. She was too tired tonight to deal with whatever little drama they had going on.

She carried her purse and cooler bag into the house and set them down on the kitchen table. The house was absolutely quiet. She made a cup of tea, put the things from her food bag into the dishwasher and then went upstairs, thinking that going to bed early sounded wonderful. She was bone-weary.

Her room was cool and dark. She hit the light switch with her elbow and was surprised when every corner of the room lit up. She dropped her bag on the bed and looked at the light fixture. Two bulbs were visible through the glass. Jack must have changed them. Ben had been gone all day.

Jack Palmer, she thought. *Bringer of light.*

CHAPTER EIGHT

SAME THING AGAIN. Jack was watching the action from outside himself. His mother was walking down the dusty Iraqi lane, but his dream self didn't know it was her. He tried to tell him, but he wasn't listening. He was standing on the turret, this time steeling himself to hold the M4 steady.

She climbed onto the turret—always a surprise because it was hard for a man to swing up there, but she did it easily. He told himself to shoot, but he still wasn't listening. He saw his own horrified look as she grabbed his hands and fought with him for possession of the weapon.

He tried to kick her away, but as they struggled, fingers on one hand locked, the gun between them in the other, she looked into his eyes. Hers were deep blue, like Cassidy's eyes, and for the moment there was no drugged glaze, no lack of recognition. They were a mother's eyes, a sober mother's eyes. She told him silently that she knew what she had done to him, to the girls.

And in that moment of his distraction, of their rare emotional connection, he loosened his grip on her and she got the gun away. He knew she was going to kill him. She'd been a danger to him since he was a baby. She'd dropped him, forgotten to feed him, let him do pretty much what he'd wanted without fear for his safety.

Now she was going to finish the job.

He watched his shoulders square, felt his spine stiffen with resolve. He'd spent his entire life surviving her against impossible odds. She wasn't going to get him now. At least not today.

He tried to grab for the gun, but she danced out of his reach. "No, Jack," she said in an eerily quiet voice. "No."

The distant him, watching the struggling him, knew it was over. But he had to try. He flung himself at her and they flew off the Humvee together, struggling for the gun.

SARAH WHACKED AT Jack with the wooden spoon he was trying so hard to get away from her. He was dreaming again, and while she'd promised Ben she'd keep her distance, she was too much the nurse to watch that painful struggle and not try to do something about it.

She'd better take a strength-building class, she told herself as Jack grabbed for her and went sailing off the bed, taking her to the carpet with him. Her body trapped under the steel of his, she was unable to move, except to whack him with the wooden spoon she still held.

"Wake up, Jack!" she shouted in his ear right next to her lips. "It's Sarah. This isn't Iraq and I'm not your mother! Jack!"

She felt him come awake. The tension in his body held for one moment while he propped himself up on his elbows, probably assessing where he was, guessing what had happened. His body straddling hers, he looked into her eyes, his angry and hard, then softening as he understood the situation. She was aware of every inch of him in contact with every inch of her. A small shudder rippled along her nerves.

"God," he muttered, then pushed himself off her and sprang to his feet. He was wearing only boxer shorts and a T-shirt.

He was gorgeous, she thought.

"Give me that." He took the wooden spoon from her and tossed it on the bed, then offered both his hands. He had a few red welts on his cheek and forehead, she noticed.

She took his hands and let him pull her to her feet.

"Again," he said, squeezing her fingers, "I'm sorry. You've got to stop coming in here when I'm having nightmares."

That would be right, of course, if she wasn't conditioned to care for someone in distress—and inclined to care about this someone in particular.

"I can't just listen to you crying out and not do something about it."

The apology in his eyes was now replaced by humor. "Well, if the something you're going to do is hit me in the face with a wooden spoon…"

It was a relief to laugh. "You kept trying to take it away from me. And when you tackled me to the carpet, it was my only defense."

"Yeah. Sorry." His voice was just above a whisper. "In my dream, it was a gun."

Suddenly overwhelmed with empathy for what he must be going through—memories of a terrible mother, sisters now lost to him, pictures in his mind of war and suffering, she instinctively wrapped her arms around his neck. "It'll get better, Jack. The bad memories will fade and you'll find your sisters. Another year down the road, this will be behind you and you'll have so much to look forward to."

They shared a moment of stillness, then her own body recognized the instant her embrace stopped being about comfort and became something else.

He had relaxed while she held him, but every muscle with which she had contact was now a steel coil. The gentle arms that had enfolded her now held her with purpose.

"Sarah," he whispered.

He pushed her slightly away, looking down into her face. She looked up, snared by his gaze. His mouth came down, hers reached up. The kiss was a gentle communication—for about a second—then it seemed to take his eager initiative and her tentative participation and give them sudden power. His fingers caught in her hair, hers clutched at his shoulders and they kissed away all the shadows that made a relationship between them seem impossible.

They kissed until she had to pull away and gasp for air.

He wore a look of complete surprise. She wasn't sure what to make of that.

He said, as though confused, "Ah…"

Deeply affected by the kiss, Sarah looked into his face and worried that it hadn't had the same impact on him. So she punched him playfully in the gut. "Relax, Jack. It was just a kiss. Now, if I can have my wooden spoon back, I can go."

He gave her the spoon and then caught her wrist as she headed for the door. He looked out of sorts. She felt worse.

"That was *not* just a kiss," he said.

Her pretense collapsed. "You look like you don't want it to be more." Though he *had* said he couldn't think of her as a sister. "So—" she sighed wearily, suddenly exhausted by the scare of his shouting, the tussle off the bed, the pressure of his weight and muscle on top of her "—we won't let it be anything more."

He dropped her wrist, but the turmoil in his eyes kept her rooted to the spot.

"It's not that I don't want it to be important," he said. "I just wonder if you understand the problem."

"Problem?" she asked. She felt encouraged to know that it had been more than just a kiss to him, but if that something more was a problem for him, she was glad she held the wooden spoon. "What was problematic about that kiss? It was…" She struggled to find the right word and finally settled for "Wow."

Wow. Yes, that said it. He couldn't stop staring into her soft blue-gray eyes.

Didn't she get it? "The kiss wasn't problematic. The fact that my brother wants you, too, is."

She swallowed and studied her fingers. "But he wants children."

He shifted his weight and folded his arms. "So do I. Not that we're anywhere near that place, but there it is."

"Yeah," she whispered and walked away, a terrible sadness in her eyes.

She heard him follow her.

Annoyed with him because he couldn't just make things easy for her, she stopped abruptly in front of the kitchen table and put a hand out to prevent him from bumping into her. "If you recall, I'm the one who said it was just a kiss. Forget it, Jack. It was all the result of a dream."

He stood at her back. "Was it?"

"Yes." She turned to look him full in the face, needing to hurt him. "You have such awful stuff to deal with. I felt sorry for you, so I kissed you."

He looked shaken for a moment, then something ignited in his eyes and he shook his head. "Nice try. That was *not* a pity kiss. We have to deal with this."

What neither had noticed was that Ben had just come home and was standing inside the kitchen door, his uniform hat in one hand, a bag from McDonald's in the other. Sarah spotted him over Jack's shoulder and felt embarrassed and a little upset that it must now be clear to him what she and Jack were fighting about.

"Good morning, Ben," she said. She met his gaze, refusing to look guilty. She wasn't. She'd turned down his proposal. She hadn't done anything wrong. He wanted children. He should just move on and find someone else to love.

Her interest in Jack wasn't wrong, at least in regard to fidelity. Sanity was another matter.

Jack turned toward him, his expression giving nothing away. "Hey, Ben."

His brother smiled blandly. "Still talking about hydrangeas in the fireplace? Blue ones? A variety called kiss, maybe? I heard a lot of talk about kisses."

Sarah ignored him and dug coffee cartridges out of a drawer, while Jack went to get utensils.

"No, huh? Okay. Well, I brought breakfast home, and a good thing, since the two of you have obviously been too busy to cook anything for the man who left early this morning. I had to take the last two hours of the shift of a guy who got the flu or something, and I've been risking life and limb ever since without sustenance." He indicated the ingredients for pancakes spread out on the counter but clearly ignored, then frowned at Sarah. "Aren't you late for Vinny?"

"No," she replied with a glower. "The seniors' bus took everyone to breakfast, then grocery shopping."

"Ah." He put the sack in the middle of the table and dug out all the contents. "Three Sausage McMuffins, six hash browns because Jack and I like to double up on them, and three yogurts with fruit." He turned to Sarah with a theatrically questioning eyebrow. "Do you think you could trouble yourself to make coffee?"

"Depends," she replied. "How much of your smug smartness do we have to listen to before we can eat?"

"That was it," he replied. "Please make the coffee and come and eat. Or would you like me to leave so you two can continue your argument?"

"Shut up, Ben," Jack and Sarah said simultaneously.

"Right."

JACK STOOD IN the middle of the carriage house's bedroom. Sarah had taken off after breakfast for a fund-raising committee meeting, and he was assessing his skills as a painter. He'd done well. The pale green color his mother had chosen was relaxing, the white woodwork a crisp, sharp contrast. Glenn Stapleton, an old friend who installed hardwood floors, was coming the following day. His mother had left new curtains to hang and a coverlet for the bed.

He could install the new, wrought-iron curtain rods, but he might need Sarah's help with the curtains. That could be iffy. She'd left without speaking to him. Ben had given him a look that spoke volumes—lethally.

He needed counseling. He'd been attracted to Sarah from the first time he'd seen her, and that attraction was now turning into outright lust.

No, it was worse than that. It was love. When he'd had her in his arms after his nightmare and felt her, soft and pliant under his hands, he'd understood just how much he wanted her. Then the kiss had proved that she shared his feelings. He'd had a clear opportunity to tell her how he felt and he'd brought up obstacles instead. Though the fact that his brother loved her, too, *was* a serious obstacle. What was *wrong* with him?

He was a damaged human being, that was it. He loved his brother's girlfriend, though he'd die before he hurt Ben. He loved a family he hadn't seen in over twenty years, and he wondered if the family who'd adopted him and given him everything his life had lacked for eight years would understand. It was as though his life was stalled. The war finally over for him, yet there was no apparent peace in his future.

He went back to the kitchen in the main house to pour himself a coffee, desperate for caffeine. He heard a car, then the front door opening. Sarah must be back.

She walked down the hallway toward the main part of the house without noticing him. He cleared his throat noisily.

Footsteps came back and her head peered

around the kitchen doorway. She was pink cheeked and she'd tied her hair back. He liked it best when she wore it down, but pulled back had the effect of making her eyes seem enormous, and they were interesting now with their turbulence and flash.

She had a sheaf of papers in her hand and she thrust one at him. "I've just been to the printers. This is the flyer for the talent show I was telling you about. Ben and the De Angelis brothers have agreed to participate, but they say their group doesn't work without you." She paused for a breath and gave him a look intended to intimidate. "You have to help us."

"I told you I don't—"

She silenced him with saying, "Jack. You have a good voice. You run your own business and therefore set your own hours. You'll have lots of time for rehearsals and to psych yourself up to appear in front of an audience."

He caught the strap of the little purse that was draped across her body and pulled her to him. It was one thing for her to be upset with him, but another to let her think she could push him around. She could, but he was pretty sure it wasn't good for him to let her think she could. He looped his arms loosely around her.

"I might be charmed into helping," he

said, noticing that she wasn't struggling to get away, "but telling me I have to help isn't going to do it."

"If you don't agree," she said in a reasonable tone that belied the deepening pink in her cheeks, "Ben and the De Angelis brothers won't do it."

"Ah. So it isn't as much that I *have* to do it as you *need* me to do it."

She considered that. "Yes," she said finally.

"Then, maybe..." He tipped his head back as though thinking through a solution. "Oh, something like 'Jack, I need you' might spur me to be helpful."

Her lips quirked wryly. "Honestly, Palmer. You can be such a pill. And pills used to be my line of work, so I know whereof I speak." He watched her fight against a smile.

"Hmm. That didn't sound like 'Jack, I need you.'"

"Is that going to guarantee me anything?"

She met his gaze and doubtless realized that he considered the scope of those few words went beyond the context of the talent show. Her eyes softened and he felt their pull as he tugged her closer. "In the right tone of voice, those words could get you anything you want."

When she didn't immediately reply, he said,

as though reconsidering, "Or one could consider my offer to renovate the Cooper Building at cost enough of a contribution that I wouldn't—"

This time *she* kissed *him*. He had to get past the shock he felt to realize she held his face in her hands, met his lips with fervor and impressive skill, then wrapped her arms around him and held him as though he was the only steady handhold in a storm-rocked world. Then she sighed, dropped her hands and stepped back.

"Jack," she said, her manner sharpening a little, though the kiss lingered in her eyes, "I need you. Are you in or not?"

That didn't sound as though he got the words out of the context of the talent show, but it was progress of a sort.

"The Wild Men really weren't very good," he said. "I mean, I can carry a tune, but I'm no Bruno Mars."

"The Wild Men?"

"Our group."

"Oh. I don't care."

"What if the audience boos and hisses?"

"I imagine your ego can deal with that. If they start throwing things, we'll have a lot of cops participating, so we'll have built-in crowd control."

He exhaled noisily. "Then I guess I'm in."

"Thank you." She started to walk away.

"Do you want to seal the deal with another kiss?" he called after her.

She turned and walked back to him. His pulse quickened and he reached a hand out for her. "No," she said, keeping herself beyond his reach. "But maybe you could put that offer to work at cost in writing."

"YOU TOLD HER the Wild Men needed me?" Jack confronted Ben in the driveway. He'd gone out to the truck to get another tarp and Ben was on his way to work a swing shift. His schedule was now completely crazy. The number of officers who weren't down with the flu was continually diminishing.

Ben opened his door. "Yeah. If I have to do this, so do you. And why don't you *want* to do it for her? Don't insult my intelligence by denying that anything's going on between you, because you're both wearing it like hazmat suits."

"I'm doing it, okay? It's just that the Wild Men weren't really very good."

"We'll rehearse."

"I doubt seriously that will help."

"Community talent shows are about effort and good humor, not real talent. Which, I admit, is a good thing in our case. A willingness to laugh at ourselves will work in our favor. But the Cooper guy is bound to be a big draw." Ben climbed into his truck. "I've got to go."

Jack tapped on his window. "One more thing," he said when Ben opened it.

"Yeah?"

"Are you still in love with her?"

Ben looked him in the eye. "Of course. Are you going to nobly step out of my way so I can keep seeing her and convince her that she'd love to have my children, after all?"

"No."

Ben grinned with what appeared to be satisfaction. "She seemed to be pretty mad at you this morning."

Jack had to let him have that one. "That seems to be the way this relationship rolls. She's mad at me a lot."

"I don't ever remember her being mad at me."

"Maybe that means something. Deep feelings aren't always easy to manage peacefully."

His smile dying, Ben stuck a hand out the window and pushed Jack out of the way for his own safety, then sped backward with a squeal of tires and raced away. Jack felt both guilty and triumphant. But that was his life's story. He'd always felt responsible for everything and everyone, treasured his small victories, then felt guilty about being happy. The fact that his happiness would come at the expense of Ben's was hard to accept. But he couldn't help exulting over Sarah's kiss.

Then he had a new thought. There was a solution to this tension among the three of them that didn't involve giving up Sarah. Granted, it was only temporary, but it might alleviate some problems. And it would prevent him from throwing Sarah around while he was dreaming.

JACK WAS CARRYING BEDCLOTHES, a pillow and a suitcase out the kitchen door when Sarah came home from work. It had been a long day. She felt a stab of alarm at what appeared to be a moving-out process. "What's going on?" she asked.

"I thought it would be better if I moved into the carriage house for a while," he said casually, apparently trying not to make a big thing of it. But she knew it kind of was; all three of them were at odds with one another far too often. "This way, if I'm shouting in my sleep, you won't hear me and be tempted to help me and I won't throw you off the turret."

"The turret?" she asked. She followed him down the walk and into the carriage house, holding up the dragging end of a blanket. They turned into the bedroom.

He dropped everything onto the mattress and nodded. "My mother always climbs up onto the Humvee's turret to confront me. That's when I throw her off. And you."

She hated this. "I'm sorry my being here is causing problems between you and Ben. I should be the one to find someplace else to live."

"No, this will work out fine. I'm going to take a few things from the kitchen in the house for the kitchen here."

"You have to come to the house for breakfast every day. I promised your mom I'd cook for you."

"What she doesn't know won't hurt her."

She punched him with a look. "We're not lying to your mother."

"It's not lying, precisely."

"When you have to add 'precisely,' it's lying. We can't run away from the problem." She was upset and confused and couldn't imagine how she'd gotten into this, or how she could ever resolve it. And what did it matter, anyway? She didn't want children and Ben and Jack did. So, nothing could happen for her with either man. Fate, however, didn't seem to know that.

He turned on her hotly. "I'd love to just let myself fall in love with you, but Ben doesn't want it to be over between you. I keep telling myself that I've never in my life sat back and let Ben take something from me just because I owe him for getting me into his family. But this time…"

"What's different about this time?"

He met her gaze, his own sad and perplexed. "This time, it's you. And you're right between my brother and me. Not your fault, just the way it is. All that's kept me sane through the nightmares was the thought of finding a woman to love and raise children with." He made a rueful gesture in her direction. "I found the woman, but she doesn't *want* children, and my brother loves her. Damn."

On the brink of tears, her mouth trembling dangerously, she turned abruptly and headed back to the house. As much as he wanted to, he couldn't just let her go. With a growl, he headed for the house, too.

He found her in the kitchen. "Sarah."

He had a ringing sense of déjà vu when she turned to him angrily and declared, "I'm not the issue, here. The two of you can't decide which way to split this relationship the three of us have going. I think it's because you don't know what to do about each other. You love the Palmers, but you have to find Corie and Cassidy because they're your family, too, and Ben wants to support you, but he's afraid that if you find them, it'll somehow intrude upon the *Palmer* family. I'm just a sort of symbol of the discord." As she spun out her theory, she understood it for the first time. Or so she thought.

He shook his head slowly, hands on his hips. "I am not confusing you with whatever issues I have with Ben, except that he loves you. You're a complete problem all by yourself. I love you—" there, he'd said it "—but you're afraid to bring more risk into your life by having kids."

His confession of love sent a thrill through her, but then she brought her focus back to the more important issue. "I've seen children suffer and die."

"I have, too. Not in a hospital, but in war. Whatever pain comes with that is just a fact of life. Nobody gets to escape that."

That wasn't true. She'd been telling herself for more than a year that she was on the right track. She *could* escape. "I know what I'm doing."

"Really?"

"Really."

"Then how did you end up with two men in love with you?"

The question left her speechless.

He took a deep breath and conceded, "Okay, stupid question. Obviously not your fault that you're so..."

Her breath was suspended as she waited for him to come up with the word.

"Everything," he finally said.

She must have looked puzzled, because he seemed to feel obliged to explain. "Yes. Inadequate word. But whenever I think about what would make me happy in a woman... well, you have it all."

Rattled to her core by that simple, humbling explanation, she felt compelled to resist it. "Shouldn't you be thinking about what *you* would do to make a woman happy?"

"Same answer applies," he said, spreading his arms helplessly. "Everything."

His simple, generous answer slapped the fight right out of her.

"Gotta go," he said. "Lots to do."

He left, probably headed for his self-imposed exile in the carriage house.

Good. She wouldn't have known what to do or say if he'd stayed.

CHAPTER NINE

JACK WORKED THE following two weeks as though the President and First Lady were arriving to take up residence in the carriage house. He left the installation of the new pedestal sink and the water-conserving john to the plumber, who brought the towel racks and toilet tissue holder his mother had ordered earlier. He did everything he could to avoid the main house and the two vases of hydrangea there, one in the middle of the kitchen table and the other on the fireplace mantel, obviously drying, as Sarah had explained.

He painted the walls the Caribbean blue his mother had chosen, and scoured catalogs looking for the "interesting" mirror she wanted. He found one while sitting on a stool pulled up to the kitchen counter in the carriage house, eating Chinese takeout and paging through the last catalog he had. He spotted a simple mirror trimmed in what looked like sliced glass bricks. He photographed the catalog item and sent it to his mother's phone. And while he was at it, he photographed the newly installed john and sink and sent those, too.

He came back from his morning run the next day to find Ben standing in front of the carriage house door, a covered plate of what looked like a breakfast casserole balanced on the palm of his hand. He did not look happy, but then, he seldom did lately.

"Morning," Jack said, rotating his shoulders as he pushed the door open. Apparently his usual cooldown was going to be interrupted. "What are you doing standing out here?" He gestured Ben inside, then followed him.

Ben went into the kitchen and put the plate on the counter. "Since you're living here, it would be like walking into your house. I wouldn't do that. Actually, Sarah saw you heading home and sent me over with this. She's says all you've done is order takeout. Apparently she's keeping tabs on you."

In dark shorts and a gray bike shirt, Jack held both arms out to his sides. "Do I look food deprived to you?" He felt invigorated by the run, and all the heavy work to finish the carriage house was good for his body's general condition. Apart from emotional confusion, he felt great.

Ben looked him over, his expression grudgingly approving. "No, you don't. You make even a police academy graduate look flabby. But you know how she is about her promise to Mom, so please eat it or I'll have to listen to more of how you and I are making her job impossible."

"Sorry."

"I hope so. Because now that you're not there as a buffer, I get all the angst over why the three of us can't get along, and all the news about her seniors and the talent show." To illustrate, he leaned a hip against the counter and asked, "Did you know that Vinny and Margaret still aren't speaking, and the first rehearsal with everyone is in two weeks?" Ben reached behind him to the utensil drawer, removed a fork and handed it to Jack. "And someone's doing a Whitman reading and she's worried about it. I'm not sure why that's a problem."

Jack took the fork. "Probably because it's Jasper and he's blind. I'm sure it's a recitation rather than a reading."

"Oh. Didn't know that." It seemed to offend him that Jack knew those details and he didn't.

"I'm sorry you have to deal with Sarah's distress. It's better that I'm out of the way.

Maybe you two can work it out if that's what you want."

Ben pinned him with a look. "I thought *you* wanted to work it out with her."

He didn't know what he wanted anymore. He was going mildly crazy back here, but he hadn't had a nightmare since he'd been sleeping in the carriage house. Or since he hadn't been around Sarah.

"I don't know what I want," he admitted, pulling the plastic off the plate of food. Wonderful aromas of sausage and cheese arose, along with that of roasted potatoes and scrambled eggs. "But since you do, you should have the chance." He forked a bite of sausage with potato and groaned. It was delicious.

Ben turned to go. "Wild Men practice tonight in the church basement. Seven sharp. Be there, or I'll come get you."

SARAH COULDN'T STOP staring at the action on the stage. She sat beside Margie De Angelis in one of the folding chairs scattered around the basement of St. Peter's by the Sea Catholic Church. Margie, who was married to Mario and very pregnant, did bookkeeping for the Coast Care office and was helping Sarah coordinate the talent-show lineup. Sarah knew her fairly well because in the few months Sarah had dated Ben, they'd all gone out together a couple of times.

Trina, a pudgy-cheeked toddler with dark hair and eyes, played with colorful plastic toys on a blanket at her feet. Margie and Mario expected their second baby in December.

"Aren't they gorgeous?" Margie whispered, her brown eyes alight with affection and excitement as she watched the four men on the small stage. Her gaze was fastened on Mario, and Sarah couldn't take her eyes off Jack. She told herself it was because she hadn't seen much of him lately, and the tight jeans, casual jacket and mussy-hair look of the boy bands of the nineties had nothing to do with his appeal.

Jack, Ben and the De Angelis brothers had all been a little inhibited when they'd begun rehearsing, but responding to the cheers and good-natured harassment from friends and family, they were giving the performance of "Bye, Bye, Bye," NSYNC's famous hit, their over-the-top all.

Mario and Rico, both on guitar, flanked Ben and Jack. Jack had an impressive tenor voice as lead singer, while Ben supported with surprisingly good harmony. Maybe they weren't destined for a Grammy, but they might be the act to beat at the talent show.

Jack's voice hit a sour note and his companions began to smack him with rolled-up sheet music until everyone dissolved into laughter.

As they resumed their places to run through the number one more time, Margie stood and stepped over her daughter. "Sarah, I have to run to the restroom. Would you keep an eye on Trina? I promise I won't be long."

Before Sarah could say, "No. I never told you, but it hurts to even look at babies. I don't want to. Please don't make me," Margie was gone.

Sarah expected the inevitable squeal of protest as Trina watched her mother go. But the toddler was apparently secure in the knowledge that her mother would be back. She smiled up at Sarah and handed her a purple plastic doughnut, one of half a dozen in graduated sizes and different colors that she was stacking on a plastic spindle.

"Thank you," Sarah said, taking it from her. Trina stood and put her hands on Sarah's knees and reclaimed the doughnut. Then she clutched Sarah's skirt for balance and leaned down to grab an orange doughnut from the stack on the spindle. She gave it to Sarah and waited expectantly.

Concluding that she was expected to somehow entertain with it, Sarah put it on her index finger and twirled it. Trina was thrilled. Encouraged, Sarah spun it again, then put the tip of that finger against Trina's arm so that the spinning doughnut tickled her until it stopped. Trina shrieked her pleasure, then handed Sarah the purple doughnut again.

Sarah held a doughnut in front of each eye and leaned toward Trina, whispering, "I see you, Trina. I see you!"

Trina climbed into Sarah's lap and took possession of the doughnuts, holding them to Sarah's eyes herself.

"You two are serious show pests," Jack said, taking the chair beside them. "You being tested for glasses?"

Surprised by his sudden appearance, unsettled by his sexy good looks in his jacket and jeans, Sarah stammered, oddly breathless. "We…I…"

Trina, meanwhile, took one look at Jack and stretched out her arms toward him. Without hesitation, he circled her little torso with his hands and pulled her into his lap. To Sarah's knowledge, this was the first time Trina had ever seen Jack. He laughed and said, "You gotta love a girl who knows what she wants— even if she's only two."

Trina looked interestedly into his face and then pushed her tiny index finger against his nose. To her delight, Jack made the sound of a horn. She pressed his nose again with the same result. Then, tiring of the game, she played with the Saint Christopher medal around his neck.

Jack met Sarah's eyes. "I thought you didn't want one of these," he said, brushing the child's hair out of her face.

"Her mother went to the restroom and asked me to watch her. She's a cutie, isn't she?"

"She is. To hear Mario talk about her, she'll be going to Oxford next year."

Sarah watched him nibble on Trina's fingers as she grabbed his bottom lip. He finally had to disengage her fingers to avoid having his mouth reshaped. He winced as Trina grabbed his ears. "Easy there, Trina. I need those things."

Mercifully, Mario arrived before Trina could relocate Jack's ears. Trina went to him excitedly just as Margie returned.

"We're going to Betty's Burgers," Mario

said, tucking the baby onto his hip. "You guys want to join us? Rico and Ben are coming."

Sarah opened her mouth to decline, but Jack caught her elbow and pulled her up with him as he got to his feet. "Sure. It'll be fun. There's nothing like onion rings at nine thirty at night to keep you up and working until morning."

They followed Margie and Mario out, a raucous Rico, Ben and a few other police officers who'd come to harass Ben following behind.

"I have to be up in the morning," Sarah said quietly.

"Then we'll order you tapioca. I swear, you're spending too much time with older people, Sarah. You need some night life."

She laughed as she went to the borrowed RAV4. "And you're in sad shape if you consider a family restaurant at nine thirty in the evening night life."

He grinned and headed toward the truck he and Ben had come in. "Touché."

Coming up behind him, Ben caught him by the collar and redirected him toward Sarah. "You have to bum a ride. Sam and Rico are coming with me." Sam Wagner worked with Ben and was helping with the lighting for the show. He was in his forties, balding and handsome in an Ed Harris sort of way.

Jack turned to Ben suspiciously, but he was already climbing into the truck.

Sarah unlocked the doors, staring after Ben as Jack joined her. "I heard that. Was that Ben, trying to push us together?"

"Maybe. He probably thinks the more time you spend with me, the more inclined you'll be to pick him."

"Pick him for what?"

"For a husband. When and if you decide to have children."

She blew out air inelegantly between her lips. "I think we should start a commune for dysfunctional people to just live together in platonic friendship for the rest of their lives."

He shook his head at her mild indignation and let himself into the car. "Bad plan. You have to come up with something else."

BETTY'S BURGERS WAS SPACIOUS, with booths along one side and tables and chairs in the middle and along a glass wall that looked out on the ocean. The hostess helped them push several tables together to accommodate their small crowd.

Jack's friends all took turns entertaining Trina. She seemed to be most comfortable with Ben, who'd spent a lot of time with her parents. She settled into his arms when their food came. He put aside a french fry to cool for her while he gave her a sip of his cola.

Margie tried to take her, telling Ben, "You don't have to entertain her. You should enjoy your—"

"We're fine," Ben said. "Eat up while you have the chance."

Watching Ben with the little girl, Sarah knew without a doubt that he had to be a father one day. Jack, too, had been happy with the toddler on his lap. She, Sarah, was holding both men back from what they wanted out of life.

Looking around at the warm, lighthearted group of friends, she felt suddenly like an outsider. Or, possibly, like a child herself in a world of adults, as though, with all her fears, she wasn't ready for the real world.

She sat a little straighter and nibbled on an onion ring. The fact that a woman didn't want to be a mother was no longer a blight on her character, she told herself defensively. This was the twenty-first century. If someone didn't want children for whatever reason, society had nothing to say about it. Parenthood should be a choice made after considerable thought.

Jack, sitting beside her, leaned close and said in her ear, "What is it? You're frowning."

"I'm just listening and watching. I'm fine."

"Who are you watching?" he asked with teasing seriousness. "'Cause you know Mario and Rico are both taken. Ah." He followed the direction of her gaze to Ben. He'd given another of his fries to Trina. She handed it back, pointing to the ketchup on his plate.

"Of course, ketchup," Ben said, dipping the fry lightly in the red stuff and handing it carefully back to her. He looked up and noticed Sarah and Jack watching him. He arched an eyebrow in question.

"Nothing," Sarah replied with a smile. "Just noticing how good a child looks on you."

Mario jumped in. "Sarah had Trina earlier," he said. "A child looks pretty good on her, too. If she can decide which Palmer brother she wants."

Margie gasped and elbowed him hard. "I swear to God, Mario. You have all the social smarts of a raccoon."

"Oh, come on," he said with no visible awareness of the discomfort he'd caused. "She was going with Ben, now she's sitting with Jack. I didn't mean anything. It was just...I don't know, social commentary."

Rico shook his head and said something under his breath in Italian. Ben covered Trina's ears. "Hey, she probably understands."

"You all know the Palmers hired me to cook for Ben and Jack while they're in Arizona," Sarah said into the embarrassing silence. She tried to smile as though nothing at all was wrong, while the truth was that Mario's simple statement had said it all. "Then my apartment burned down. You know...the Bay Apartments' fire?" Everyone nodded. "Ben invited me to stay with them since I have no family here and, at that moment, had nowhere else to go."

"Why do you have to cook for them?" Sam asked. "Can't they just eat ribs and Doritos for breakfast like the rest of us?"

The men cheered and the women made sounds of disgust, though they laughed.

"She's also a nurse," Margie said. "With Jack just back from Afghanistan and suffering from—" She stopped abruptly. She doubtless realized it wasn't her job to share personal information about Jack.

"I came back physically healthy," Jack finished for her, smiling into her worried expression. "But I was a little screwed up emotionally." He looked around the table. "I'm among friends, I presume."

"Not sure." Mario stood and said, "We really should take a count. Raise your hands if—"

Margie yanked him back into his chair.

Everyone laughed, Jack included. "All right. Seriously. You all know what kind of childhood I had. Well, life at war has brought a lot of that back and I have trouble sleeping. Nightmares. My mom thinks good nutrition solves everything."

Another ripple of laughter from his friends. Then there were a few seconds of heavy silence. Sam stood and lifted his glass of soda, toasting Jack with it. "Thanks for your service, man," he said.

Glasses of water and soda and cups of coffee rose all around the table, and everyone toasted Jack.

The discussion turned to critiques of the Wild Men's performance. Sarah let the conversation flow around her. Then she spotted Vinny Caruso and Margaret Brogan in a dark corner of the restaurant. She had to lean forward to be sure she was seeing correctly. Neither looked particularly happy, but they weren't shouting at each other, either.

Sarah gave a tiny gasp and put a hand to her heart at the possibility they might be working out their problem.

Jack leaned toward her. "What?" he asked. "Something wrong?"

She turned to him, looking right into his eyes. "No. Something's *right*. That's Vinny and Margaret." Realizing he wouldn't know what she was talking about, she began to explain, "See, Vinny's..."

"Yeah, I know all about it," he said, smiling. "Vinny and Margaret don't like each other. She wouldn't date him sixty years ago or something." He scanned the room. "Ah. That must be them. Little guy and Mrs. Brogan. I'll be... They've stopped fighting?"

"How do you know about Vinny and Margaret and their long-standing dislike?" she asked in surprise.

"Ben told me," Jack replied.

"How did that ever come up?"

"Ah..." He thought back. "As I recall, he was grumbling that you shared with him that you were worried about them." He grinned and added, rather eagerly, she thought, "And you talked about it a lot."

She frowned across the table at Ben, who looked at her in innocent bemusement. Unwilling to shout at him over the noise of their loud companions, she turned back to Jack. "I thought he was interested."

"I'm sure he was," Jack conceded, stroking her arm gently. "He just missed my being there for you to talk to."

"Hmm." She wasn't entirely appeased, but when Ben looked at her worriedly over Trina's head and mouthed, "What?" she smiled and waved dismissively to wipe away any suggestion of a problem.

The bill paid, everyone scraped chairs back and stood. The women hugged, the men shook hands, and with promises to meet for next week's rehearsal, the families left first. Trina was reclaimed by her father, who thanked Ben for watching her.

Ben slapped Mario's shoulder. "My pleasure. Take care." He turned to Sarah and said, "I'm taking Sam and Rico back to the church where they left their cars. I'm sorry, but you've got Jack again."

"Some friend you are," Sarah returned.

"Hey!" Jack complained.

SARAH DROVE HOME in silence, clearly preoccupied. At home, Jack thanked her for the ride, said good-night and headed up the walk to the carriage house. There was a definite bite in the air. It was spitting rain and he thought wryly that it was time to prepare for the wet late fall and early winter. Every Oregon resident complained about it, but after the heat of Afghanistan, he'd never complain again.

Tonight had been a good evening all in all, he thought as he pulled off his jacket. His moment of soul baring had been only a little uncomfortable, but he hadn't wanted Margie to feel badly about having brought up the subject. He was sure their friends wondered what on earth was going on at the Palmers' with him and Ben and Sarah sharing space.

He wandered through the small rooms, wondering what project he should attack tomorrow. The bathroom was almost complete, except for some paint touch-up and ordering the mirror—provided his mother wanted it. He was a little surprised she hadn't gotten back to him. Maybe he should try hanging the bedroom curtains himself. He started in that direction when a knock on his door made him turn. He flipped on the outside light and opened the door to find Sarah standing there, a phone in her hand.

"It's your mom," she said quietly, handing him the phone. "One of the things you should do is add an extension phone back here. Or keep your cell phone charged. Good night."

"Hey, Mom." Jack watched Sarah walk away, wishing he was going with her, then turned back into the carriage house and focused on his mother's voice. "Did you like the mirror?"

"I did, but I called to tell you I've found a mirror," she said, her voice lively despite the hour. "And we're bringing it home with us. We found this wonderful place in Sedona with antique fixtures and hardware. The mirror is from an old theater dressing room. It's large and square and just what a writer needs to look at himself and determine where the heck the story's going."

"Great. So, second week in December?"

"No, we're on our way home right now."

He wondered whether or not to be worried. They loved their Arizona winters. "Anything wrong? You both feeling okay?"

"We're fine," she assured him. "It's just that the weather's been awful, a lot of our old friends didn't make it this year for one reason or another and we're feeling out of it. So we're coming home early. We're taking our time, though, so if you've been messy, don't panic. It'll be four or five days before we arrive. How's Sarah doing?"

"Ah…good. She's working on a fund-raiser for the seniors' community."

"She told me a little bit about it when she was walking the phone out to you." His mother's cheerful voice became concerned. "Why are you working out there so late? It isn't healthy to overdo. Especially if you're having trouble sleeping." There was a momentary pause. "Are you still having nightmares?"

"No," he lied. Well, he hadn't had one since he'd been staying in the carriage house. If he told her that, though, she'd want to know why, and he was sure the romantic triangle going on in her home would upset her. "I'm feeling great. Carriage house is almost done and I'm going to be helping the seniors with the new building—providing the seniors get it."

"It's not a sure thing?"

"There's a lawyer who wants it, too. Ken somebody."

"Oh." Her voice expressed disapproval. "Forman. I know of him. He's a divorce lawyer. Left Elaine Parsons with nothing to show for thirty-five years of marriage but an old car."

"Hopefully, the fund-raiser will give the seniors the edge. You and Dad want to do a duet?" he teased. His father was notorious for a singing voice that sounded like a wounded walrus.

"Ha, ha. But you could get us tickets. Sarah said the Wild Men are performing. How did she get you to volunteer?"

"She yelled at me."

"Hmm. That never worked for me. Well, good night, Jack. Tell Ben we said hi. See you next week. Love you."

"Love you, too."

Great. He could explain his living in the carriage house to his parents by telling them he'd worked long hours and it was just simpler to be here.

And by the time they got home, the carriage house would be finished—except for the bathroom mirror—so he'd have no reason to live in it. Except that when his parents were home, they'd have to move Sarah out of their room and into his, so he'd *have* to stay in the carriage house.

Okay, that worked. But how was he going to explain to them that he now loved Sarah?

CHAPTER TEN

JACK DREAMED THAT his adoptive parents were on the turret instead of Curry, and they seemed to be free of injury. Helen held up a mirror to Jack's face. His reflection looked hollow under all his combat gear, and over his right shoulder, he saw his natural mother coming down the road.

He was afraid to turn and look, but he knew he had to. She was coming and they had to duke it out. It seemed required.

There she was in the white garment that billowed in the breeze. Again, he held his weapon, wanting to fire but unable to move even his trigger finger. He watched her climb up, reach for him and try to take his weapon. She held tightly to it as he shoved her away, screaming his name in a way that tore at his heart. She went flying into the air. But this time she flew and flew until she disappeared.

He woke up into darkness, gasping for breath, shouting for her. The word "Mom!" reverberated around him, the sound tortured and filled with the deep loneliness of his childhood.

He sat there until his breath evened out and his heartbeat steadied. Then he got up, went to the refrigerator for orange juice and sank onto the stool.

So, obviously, his adoptive parents coming home wasn't going to be good for his nightmares. So much for the carriage house protecting him from them. Or the absence of Sarah freeing his subconscious. Not that he'd ever really believed that.

He finished the juice and went to bed. No person or place was going to protect him from the knots in his past he had to untangle.

SARAH SORTED THROUGH the few pieces of mail addressed to her that were in the mailbox last night. Looking through them this morning as she walked down the stairs, she noticed an envelope from her insurance company.

She stopped halfway down to open it and gasped delightedly at the check that was enclosed. Though she hadn't had all that many possessions, or much of serious value, her insurance had paid for everything, including a new set of tires for the Jeep, which Ben had

had towed to Mario's auto repair shop the day of the fire. This meant she could find a new place to live. Though the sound of Jack's and Ben's voices coming from the kitchen made her realize that leaving here would be hard. In fact, she hated the thought. And she still had an agreement with Helen to prepare meals for the brothers.

Tucking the check into her shoulder bag, she continued down the stairs, greeting her housemates as though nothing in their lives was different.

"You're going to have to move back into the house," Ben said to Jack as he filled a thermal mug with coffee. Whenever Ben was upset he became super cop, assuming control of the world. "If Mom and Dad think we're not getting along...well, you know how Mom gets."

Jack did. She'd take it all personally, blame herself for allowing Jack to feel excluded. Or Ben to feel overlooked. She'd make herself crazy trying to restore balance.

"You're right," Jack said, "but unless you want to get bunk beds for your room, that isn't going to happen. Only three bedrooms, remember? Mom and Dad, you, Sarah."

Sarah opened her mouth, presumably to

offer to find somewhere else to live, but he and Ben shouted her down simultaneously. "No!"

"It's logical that I'd be in the carriage house. I work twelve, sometimes sixteen hours a day. Sleeping there makes sense." He gave Ben a level look. "Just try to get along with everyone and they won't suspect there's any problem."

"But it doesn't make sense you're staying there," Ben challenged. "The heat's not working in there yet. And it's mid-October."

"It hasn't bothered me."

"So you're cold-blooded?" Ben turned to Sarah, his tall, covered mug held loosely in his fingers. "Is that what you want in a husband?"

Sarah, having packed fruit and muffins into her food carrier, zipped it closed and shook her head at him. "Come on, Ben. Don't do that."

Ben bounced a dark glance off Jack and walked out the door with his coffee.

Sarah carried her bag to the door. "How's the search for your sisters coming?" she asked Jack, indicating the computer on the table in front of him.

"At a standstill for the moment," he replied. "I just can't seem to pick up a lead on Corie *or* Cassidy. I found an obituary for a Miguel

Ochoa—but Corie's name wasn't among the family mentioned."

"Maybe they were estranged for some reason."

"Yeah. Ben told me to check the Tomb-Stones.com website where anyone who loved or cared about the deceased can mount a sort of memorial, leave a message. He says the police use it sometimes because it shows where the message originated."

"And?" She smoothed the nubby red sweater she'd borrowed from his mother's closet.

"Nothing. The only message was from someone named Isabel, who *was* mentioned in the obituary. He probably remarried and had more children."

Sarah straightened, stopped fussing abruptly and met his eyes with a smile.

"What?" he asked.

"You said Corie—or Corazon—is her middle name."

"Yeah."

"What's her first name again?"

"Elizabeth."

Her smile broadened.

"What?" he demanded again.

"Isabel is the Spanish version of Elizabeth," she explained. "When my sister was looking for baby names, I helped her go through hundreds. I remember Isabel because of Bella from the *Twilight* series. That name was so popular that there must be two million little girls with it these days."

He looked stunned. "So…I've *found* her?"

"Maybe you have." She pointed to his computer. "Go to work on it. I have to leave. Good luck, Jack." She paused in the doorway to say, "I hope it's her."

SARAH THOUGHT THE whole world's prevailing mood was grumpy. At least it was in Beggar's Bay. Vinny was exceptionally quiet while she made his breakfast, Margaret said the fruit was delicious but the muffins a little dry, and Jasper was simply feeling blue.

"It's okay," he said when she tried to cheer him up with the current status of the fundraiser and failed. "It just happens sometimes, then I get over it."

She sat on the footstool of the chair he occupied and touched his hand. "I'm sorry. You make it look so easy, but blindness is an awful reality day after day, isn't it? I mean, particularly since you were sighted once and know what you're missing."

"It is," he admitted, "but everyone has their

burdens. I know I'm luckier than most. I just have to indulge myself in self-pity once in a while and get it out of my way." He squeezed her hand. "Thanks for breakfast. I'll be fine. Go on to your meeting."

Sarah left him sipping coffee and listening to Whitman's poem.

She should try to talk to Ben sometime today to make it clear to him that their romantic relationship was over. She loved his brother, not that anything could come of it with their thoughts of having children poles apart.

How had she ever gotten into such a tangle?

HER STRESS LEVEL went up even higher when she arrived a little late to the meeting and found it chaotic. "The lawyer's talking to a furnace repairman and picking out lighting." Carol Winston worked for Senior Services and was the seniors' fiercest advocate. "My daughter works at Beggar's Bay Lumber and overheard him with Pete Daley, the owner."

"Maybe the lawyer's just thinking positive," someone from around the table said. "The mayor insists the city council is still undecided."

"Pete Daley," Carol added, "is one of the

councilmen holding out for the other side. I'm sure he stands to make a considerable amount if Forman wins and buys his remodeling supplies from him. I hear he plans to go big."

"I hope we make enough in this fund-raiser to compete with the lawyer."

Someone else snickered. "How would we ever make enough to outbid a lawyer?"

"We won't," Carol replied. "The money from the fund-raiser will help us show that the community cares about us, but we're going to have to count on a vote in favor of us from the city council."

"What if we fail?"

"Then we find another building and start again."

"But this one's perfect. It's right downtown. It has an elevator, a working kitchen and a view of the ocean from the second floor."

Carol nodded. "So let's think about success rather than failure. So far, the council's evenly divided. We just have to move one member to our side. Everybody think hard. Meanwhile, let's have committee reports."

A considerable number of tickets had been sold already, several donations had been made, Clancy's Catering was offering refreshments free of charge and the high school was providing ushers, decorating the auditorium for the event, as well as staging a dramatic scene as part of the competition.

"We owe the kids big," Carol said. "How is sign-up going for participation, Sarah?"

Sarah reported eighteen acts registered, many of them already in rehearsal and looking good. "Do you think that's enough?" she asked. "Should they go on before or after Cooper's performance?"

Pros and cons were discussed and it was finally decided that Cooper should be introduced and allowed to speak, that the talent show should follow—and eighteen performers was a good number to prevent the evening from going on forever.

Marcie Thurgood, whose family had been friends with the Coopers and still kept in touch, knew Bobby Jay Cooper and had convinced him to help the show. She preened a little in the spotlight. "He's going to sing a song to welcome everyone," she said, her manner suggesting they'd had an intimate conversation about it, "then do the judging." She smiled and added, "Then he'll do four or five numbers afterward. We have to be sure to advertise that. And that everyone in the audience gets his latest CD."

There was applause from her fellow committee members. The uncertain mood lifted. Sarah caught a little of their excitement as they all packed up to leave.

She crossed the street to the Cooper Building and found the downstairs open as the maintenance crew worked. She went in quietly, needing the sturdy, welcoming aspect of the building to reignite her excitement over the project. At the moment, her own issues—the Palmer brothers, her lack of possessions, her unhappy clients and her own seemingly ineffectual handling of all of them was dampening her enthusiasm for everything. She had her insurance check, but it meant only that she had no excuse to stay at the Palmer home once Helen and Gary returned. That was depressing, too.

She stood in the middle of the room and admired the beautiful details. Then she went to the room in the back, remembering that Jack had reacted to it and the memories it had inspired. She was happy to know he had some good memories of his childhood.

She was surprised to find a well-dressed man with thinning hair and rimless glasses, probably in his forties, standing in the middle of the room. A Coleman lantern on the floor illuminated the retractable tape measure in his hand.

He turned to her with recognition in his eyes. "Miss Reed," he said, putting the tape measure in his left hand and offering her his right.

She had a horrible feeling she knew who he was, too.

She put aside what Helen had told her about him and remembered the rules of courtesy her parents had taught her. People's reputations always depended on your perspective. He was in the way of what her seniors wanted and needed, but that didn't mean he was a bad person.

"Yes," she said, shaking his hand. "Mr. Forman. How did you know who I was?"

"One should always know as much as possible about an adversary."

"But I'm only one of a large committee."

"You care a lot and are vocal. Everyone knows you're involved." He pointed the tape measure to the area behind him, his expression annoyingly happy. "My desk would be perfect right there. No windows to distract me. What do you think?"

He was taunting her. Maybe not a nice man, after all. "I think it's good to be prepared for any eventuality," she said. "That's why I'm here, too. Thinking about where to put the pool table."

"Can those old-timers bend over to shoot pool?"

She'd been willing to be civil, but now she was angry. "As well as you can sit in a room with no light."

"You mean no window."

"No. I mean no light. The wiring was fried in this room when this place was a restaurant. It hasn't been replaced since. You'll have to have wiring done if you want to put your office here." She paused significantly. "If the city chooses you."

"I pay taxes," he said, as though that somehow made him holy.

"My seniors have already paid taxes. Years and years of taxes."

He nodded. "I know. But the city could use the funds I'll generate. Your seniors will cost the city more than they contribute." At her sudden bristling, he added quickly, "I mean in a monetary way."

She made herself calm down. "Well, money isn't everything, even to a city."

He gave her a condescending look. "It's important to this city, Miss Reed. Revenue is down the length of the Oregon coast. This isn't the time to do anything for the common good. But there's little point in arguing. I'll get out of your way so that you can look around freely. Once I occupy this space, you won't be able to do that." He grinned. "Unless, of course, you need a divorce lawyer. Pardon me."

She stepped aside so he could leave the room, her body trembling with anger. It would have been so satisfying to trip him as he passed, but she let him go unscathed.

All right. It was good that she'd met him, she told herself, taking a deep, restorative breath. She was energized anew, reinvigorated, rededicated to doing everything possible to make the fund-raiser a success so that her seniors and not Ken Forman bought this building.

She marched out to the RAV4, righteous indignation fueling her steps. Ken Forman had a thing or two to learn about whom and what was important. Her cell phone rang while she dug in her purse for her keys. She pulled it out of an inside pocket. "Hello?"

"Sarah!" Jack's voice was quiet but urgent. "Where are you?"

"I'm just leaving the Cooper Building. Why? What's wrong?"

"Wait there," he said, "and I'll come and get you."

That was odd. "I've got your mom's car. What's the matter?"

He hesitated a moment.

"Jack!" she demanded.

She heard him sigh. "Ben's been shot," he said finally, adding immediately, "he's going to be okay, but…"

It felt as though someone had punched her in the face. She'd almost met him for lunch today, but she'd been too busy.

She had to clear her throat to ask, "Is he at Bay Memorial?"

"Yes," Jack replied. "I can pick you up in five minutes."

"No, I'm fine. I'll meet you there."

CHAPTER ELEVEN

"HE WAS DOING a simple traffic stop," Sam Wagner, Ben's friend on the force, had told Jack by phone. "When he called in the plate, the guy shot him in the arm. Turns out he was on the run from a bank heist in San Francisco. Ben's going to be okay, but the bullet hit a muscle. He's in surgery right now."

Jack's entire being on high alert, his first thought had been to call Sarah. He wished she'd let him come for her. She'd sounded shaken and he worried about her making it across town in the early afternoon traffic.

When someone honked at him because he failed to stop at a stop sign, he refocused on his own driving.

After all his jabs about the level of danger in policing Beggar's Bay, his brother had been shot. Relax, he told himself. This isn't Afghanistan. There won't be snipers on the road. You just have to drive to the hospital. He's going to be fine. Sam said he's going to be fine. He's in surgery, but he's going to be fine. Jack couldn't stop trying to convince himself.

Sarah stared at him when they met in the parking lot, her eyes huge and anxious. "Where was he shot?" she asked as they ran inside.

He repeated what Sam had told him.

Ben was in the recovery room when they arrived. A small crowd of blue uniforms was in the waiting area, along with Mario in his coveralls, on the phone with Rico.

It did a lot for Jack to see them laughing. They must know that Ben was well, but he still wanted to hear it from an authority.

A very large, very all-business nurse behind the desk in the surgical area told him the surgery went well and that Ben would be wheeled back within an hour. Her badge read Jeannette. She pointed to the loud group in the waiting room. "Could you see if you can keep them a little quieter?" She pointed a pen at the monitors all around her. "Blood pressure's up all over the unit," she said with a wry glance before turning back to her paperwork.

"…And not only did Ben get the guy," Grady was telling Mario, now off the phone, "but the dude was running away, so he got him in the a—" Laughter drowned out the end of the story.

Jack walked into the room and made a lower-the-volume motion with his hands. "Nurse asked us to keep it down," he said. He grinned at Sam. "Good story, though. I'm sure Ben will be telling it a lot."

As conversation continued at a lower decibel, Jack crossed to Sarah, who stood in the middle of the room with Sam. "Surgery went well," he told her. Sam had put an arm around her. Jack presumed he meant it only in comfort, but it still annoyed him. Sam was older but had the moves and a certain style women responded to.

"Thank God." Sarah sagged visibly. Jack took her arm and led her toward a very basic sofa.

"Want something to eat?" Jack asked. "Some coffee?"

She leaned back. "I don't think I could eat anything, but coffee sounds good."

"I'll get it," Sam volunteered. "You, too, Jack?"

"Please."

And so they drank coffee, and someone produced a bag of cookies, which was passed around while they waited.

Finally the all-business nurse stuck her head into the room and spotted Jack. "Your brother's back in his room," she said. "You and the girl-friend can go in, but the rest of you—" she delivered the last four words in a louder tone as everyone moved to follow "—have to wait here. He's groggy and probably won't make sense for an hour or more, so you might want to come back, just two or three at a time."

Sam spoke for Ben's friends on the force. "Give him our best, will you? I'll wait in the hall for you to come out and tell me how he is. The guys who couldn't come are going to want to know when I get back."

The parade of Ben's friends headed down the hall toward the exit, except for Sam, who stood near the door as Jack went inside. It was unsettling to see Ben hooked up to tubes and monitors with a stillness about him that was completely unfamiliar.

Sarah leaned over the side of the bed and said his name quietly. "Hi, Ben. It's Sarah and Jack."

"Hey," Ben replied, his voice barely a whisper. "Hi, Sarah."

"How do you feel?"

"Like...I've been shot."

Sarah winced and put her hand over his,

being careful of the tubing connecting his hand to a drip. "I know," she said. "But you're going to be fine." She looked at the monitors with a critical eye. Satisfied with what they indicated, she returned her attention to Ben. "You're going to be here overnight," she said. "Maybe tomorrow, too. Is there anything we can get you?"

"I want…Jack."

Jack moved closer. "Yeah," he said quietly. "I'm right here."

Ben swallowed slowly and spoke with obvious difficulty. "So much…for animal control and…fairgrounds parking."

All right. The real Ben was in there, Jack knew. "True. I understand you were very heroic and brought down the perp with a shot in the butt. But good job not doing anything to upset Mom and Dad."

"Yeah, sorry."

"Hopefully you'll be home by the time *they* get home. But you'd better be on your way to perfect health or there will be hell to pay."

Ben smiled and coughed.

"Sam's waiting before going back to the station. He wants to tell everybody how you are."

"I hurt and…I'm tired. But fine."

Jack went out into the hall to report to Sam. "Call us if he needs anything," Sam said.

Just as Sam walked off, Sarah appeared beside Jack. "He's drifting off. We should get some lunch, go home and come back tonight. I'm going to call my boss and get a few days off, then we should lay in some groceries."

"Ah…why?"

She spread both arms in a confused gesture. Something new for her. "I'm not sure. I always go grocery shopping when I'm upset. It makes me feel like whatever else happens, I can eat. And your parents are on their way. We should be prepared. Does that make sense?" She looked at him hopefully.

He didn't want to say that it didn't. "Getting ready for my parents does, but I don't know about your need to grocery shop. Although I do like knowing that whatever else happens, we can eat. I'm sure Ben would concur." He rubbed her shoulder gently. "You okay?"

"Yeah," she said, her voice thin. "I'd just like to smash the guy who hurt Ben."

"I'd help you. But Ben kind of did a job on him, and the law's got him now. They don't need us. Come on."

THEY SAT QUIETLY over lunch at Betty's. Sarah played with a fruit salad while Jack ate half a burger and a few fries.

"You can leave Mom's car here," he said, "and we can stop back for it later."

She nodded. He caught a glimpse of her face as they separated to get into opposite sides of the SUV, and realized she wasn't as calm and together as she pretended.

He put the key in the ignition, but didn't turn it, stopping instead to look her way. Her gestures were quick and catlike as she pulled her seat belt across her body and snapped it into place, carefully avoiding his eyes. "What's troubling you," he asked, "besides Ben?"

"Nothing. Just Ben."

"Sarah…"

Apparently the sound of her name tripped her safety valve. "Well, that's a stupid question, isn't it?" she demanded with sudden, surprising vehemence. Then realizing she'd made an out-of-proportion response, she sat back with a sigh. "Well, it is," she insisted more quietly.

"You're right. Apart from my brother having been shot, your apartment burning down with all your stuff in it, and now having to take a few days off to help us when you're trying to put together a fund-raiser, what's troubling you?"

"I'm happy to help you," she said in a tone that belied the words. Then her face crumpled and she burst into tears. The cab of his truck filled with her sobs.

He wished himself anywhere but there. He never knew what to say when women wept— or when anyone wept, really. During his deployments, other soldiers often wept openly. He knew it was therapeutic. He guessed he didn't have that gift. He remembered clearly when they'd dragged him and his sisters away from their mother, and then when they had taken his sisters away from the Palmers to send them to their fathers, inside, he'd wanted to die, but he'd never wanted to cry.

This was different, of course. No one had died, or committed murder, or been torn away from loved ones. Sarah was probably just on overload. Or maybe she still had feelings for Ben she'd been unaware of until she'd seen him in the hospital bed.

"You can tell me," he prodded gently.

She struggled to get control, but every time she was quiet for a minute, a sob erupted again and she was unable to communicate.

"Would you rather go home?" he asked. He wanted to take her hand or put an arm around her, but she seemed unreachable in her meltdown.

She shook her head and gestured forward while she continued to cry. "Groceries," she choked out.

"Okay." He drove to the market while she took in deep breaths, cried a little more, dabbed at her eyes, sniffed. He pulled into a parking spot near a cart return and turned off the engine.

"Wait here," he said, going to the back of his truck and the toolbox, in which he kept everything necessary for truck maintenance and the occasional odd job. That included a flask of brandy and paper cups. He climbed back into the cab and poured a small amount of brandy into a cup.

"Here." He handed it to her. "Have a couple of sips."

Taking it from him, she sighed while giving him a self-deprecating look. "I hate this. This is what the hero always offers the hysterical heroine." She sniffed suspiciously. "What is it?"

"Brandy. Not particularly expensive, but good and sturdy. Take a sip, then tell me what's wrong."

She opened her mouth to reply and when

her mouth began to tremble, she took a quick sip instead. Then another one. She put a hand to her chest and patted, as though that would help the brandy go down.

"Sturdy is right," she said, her voice raspy. "I don't understand why people like that stuff."

Taking the empty cup from her, he put it in a plastic trash bag he kept behind his seat. "You will in a minute, when the fire in your throat becomes just a nice warmth in your stomach."

She picked her purse up off the floor, put it in her lap and began rummaging through it. She turned to him, her expression grim. "I started a shopping list," she said, zipping her purse closed and resting both forearms on it. "But it's still on the kitchen table."

"Not a problem. Whatever we forget, I can come back for."

Her hand went to her stomach. She sniffed and sighed and seemed to relax. He guessed the brandy was doing its work.

A COMFORTABLE WARMTH spread through her chest and stomach. Still scarily close to tears, she closed her eyes and tried to focus on the warmth, let it restore some sense of control over the situation. She wasn't sure what had come over her, so she had no idea how to answer his question about what was wrong. Unless it was that she had never in her life felt this overwhelmed. She'd known grief, but that was different. This was—oh, God. Love? Not infatuation, not just sexual attraction, but serious, always-and-forever love?

And why now? Why in the middle of a crisis within a crisis?

Because—and she remembered the moment exactly—her heart had recognized his heart. It had slammed against her ribs as though reaching for Jack's. When she'd seen Ben in the hospital bed and touched his hand, she knew he'd always be a light in her life, a great friend, but not the man to share the rest of it with. He was practical, in charge, heading in a well-thought-out direction, and she was none of those things.

Then Jack had bent over him and spoken quietly, adjusted his blanket, laughed at his teasing about catching strays and directing parking, and she'd felt her heart swell in her chest.

Where did Jack find that kind of love to give when he'd been without it for the first eight years of his life? How could he love, when his mother hadn't loved him and, worse, was a murderer?

Another feeling that contributed to her sense of being overwhelmed was terror. Because loving someone meant having to at least try to meet their needs. And he wanted and needed children and she didn't.

She looked up into his face to see that he'd been watching her, trying to divine her thoughts. She saw turbulence in his eyes— and something just a little sad.

"Did you look at Ben in that hospital bed," he asked quietly, "and realize that you almost lost him? That you still love him?"

Interesting, she thought absently, *how completely we misinterpret each other.*

"No," she said simply.

He blinked. "Then what?"

She linked her fingers together and reached forward to stretch her arms. That failed to reduce the tension in her neck, but she was beginning to feel steadier.

"I saw you adjust Ben's blankets in his hospital room and suddenly realized how much I love you."

It was obvious that wasn't the answer he'd expected.

"Me," he repeated.

Her mood lightened. "Yes. I love Ben to pieces, too, but in a very different way. He was a sweet, sexy introduction to Beggar's Bay. He's warm and fun and it was so easy to like him." Her mood dipped again. Her forehead wrinkled and her bottom lip trembled. "But I still won't have children. Jack, what are we going to do?"

A smile played at his lips. "We'll figure it out. One thing at a time."

"That's simplistic, head-in-the-sand thinking."

"No, it's sane, logical, take-things-as-they-come thinking. We don't have to decide today how we're going to live without each other. We have to get groceries, get Ben well, get ready to catch my parents when they see Ben and freak out, then we can think about what to do about us."

"We do have to figure out what to tell your parents about you and me. And I have to tell Ben. When he's home."

"Right. Stuff for tomorrow and the next day. Right now, let's get groceries." He leaned toward her and brought his mouth to hers with a confidence she found both thrilling and comforting.

MAYBE HE WAS RIGHT, Sarah thought, her brain mildly fuzzy under the influence of his lips. The kiss melted her resistance and erased her insecurities. He pulled back slightly, banked passion alight in his eyes.

"It's going to be all right," he said. "We'll all be all right. Ben knows you love me."

"But your parents will hate us for hurting Ben."

"They won't hate us," he said. "Mom might get upset, but she always does when one of us has problems. We'll explain and she'll understand."

Sarah considered all the inexplicable, seemingly unsolvable feelings and situations surrounding her and remembered the peaceful life she'd led in her quiet apartment with her clients and a nice, undemanding man in her life. Then Jack had returned from Afghanistan, she'd had a proposal of marriage, a fire, an emotional Tilt-A-Whirl, and here she was, in hot water again.

Jack jumped out of the truck and came around to offer her a hand.

"Geez!" she complained, having to leap before her toe could touch ground. "This thing should come with rope and harness."

He caught her at the waist midjump, held

her suspended for one long, delicious moment while she held his shoulders, then lowered her to her feet. The slow, easy slide down his body accelerated all the processes in hers. "It comes with me instead," he said, and kissed her again.

He caught her hand and pulled her with him toward the grocery-store entrance. She didn't know how she kept up with him with no air in her lungs and her heart thundering in her chest.

Somehow she managed to remember most of the list she'd started and now finished with Jack's help. He did the running when she forgot a product in an area they'd already passed, reached for things too high for her.

"Ben's into comfort food," Jack said when she asked him what he thought Ben would like. "When we were kids, Mom used to make the best meat loaf, lasagna, chili and giant salads with all kinds of greens in them. Pot roast with vegetables. Roasted chicken. Yum."

She stopped the cart in front of the meat counter, looking over the possibilities. "I could lighten the recipes, I think, so they'd be healthier and so Ben, who'll probably be sedentary for a couple of days, won't feel stuffed."

"Okay." Jack sounded doubtful. She looked

up into his worried grimace. "But no tofu, okay?"

She laughed. The tough soldier was reduced to pleading by soybean curd. "I promise." She bought chicken, lean hamburger, tilapia and shrimp. She looked up from organizing the contents of the cart to find Jack holding several bags of candy. "Halloween day after tomorrow," he said. "We don't usually get too many kids, but we should be prepared. What? Don't give me that look. Do you want to have to face the consequences of tricks if we don't have treats?"

She took note of the bags he placed in the cart. "I suspect they're all the kind of candy you prefer."

"That only makes sense, doesn't it? It's the application of experience to the iffy matter of sound purchasing."

"You make yourself sound so noble."

He grinned. "Hey, I'm a war hero. Didn't I tell you?"

On the way to the checkout, they passed a rack of flowers supplied by a nearby farm. "Oh." Sarah was taken by a clutch of mums, half yellow, half burgundy. Jack pulled them out of the metal cone that displayed them.

"My gift to you," he said, placing them

carefully in the cart. He put an arm around her and kissed her temple. "For being…"

"What?" she asked, touched by the gesture.

"Everything," he said.

AN HOUR LATER they'd picked up the RAV4 and were home, unloading groceries. Sarah played back phone messages while carrying milk to the refrigerator. Helen's voice told them she and Gary were in San Francisco and they'd be home the day after tomorrow.

Jack set down an armload of canned goods and called his mother back.

Sarah heard one-sided pleasantries as she climbed onto the step stool to move things around in the cupboard to make room for the new groceries.

"I'm great," he said, leaning back against the counter. "Making headway in the carriage house. In fact, I've been sleeping there to be able to work early and late without disturbing anybody."

Sarah turned to him to smile approvingly at his artfully phrased scenario. He playfully took a bow.

"Yeah. Ben's good. He's…working today. They'd been down a couple of guys, so he's been working extra shifts. No, he can do back-to-backs standing on his head."

There was more conversation and then Jack said, "Sure, she's right here. Sarah? Mom wants to say hi." He handed her the phone.

Sarah greeted Helen warmly, asked after Gary, then suddenly experienced a pinch of guilt that took her completely by surprise. She was going to have to lie, and it didn't sit well with her, even though she understood the importance of not upsetting Jack's parents when they still had such a long drive ahead of them. And so there was a gap in the conversation while, unable to think of a thing to say, she waited for Helen to speak.

Jack, putting apples and bananas in the fruit bowl, looked at her, eyebrows knitted in concern.

Helen asked if Jack was telling her the truth about everything going well.

"Yes, everything's fine," she fibbed. "I…I'm putting groceries away while we're talking and…I hesitated because I almost lost my balance. I'm on the step stool."

"Be careful, Sarah. Jack can reach that top shelf without needing the stool."

"Yes, but he's doing other things."

"He has a reach like Godzilla."

Sarah couldn't help the giggle that erupted. "I know. And sometimes the personality to match if I make oatmeal for breakfast."

Helen laughed loudly. Jack's concerned expression relaxed.

"If you put it in a cookie," Helen said, "those boys will eat anything. Well, I have to go. Give our love to Ben when he gets home, and thank you for taking good care of him and Jack."

"It's been my pleasure." She ignored Jack as he mouthed, "Ha, ha." Curiously, it *had* been a good time, despite their personal conflicts. That was all going to change now, of course. The parents were coming home, and Ben had been shot. The rarified atmosphere of the house she'd shared with two of the world's dearest men was over. Life was now serious. She had to figure out what she was doing. And even more critically, where she was going.

She put the phone back on the dock and turned to find Jack right behind her.

"Don't look so worried." He put his arms around her and pulled her close. Her arms looped around his waist as though they did that all the time. It was so easy to lean into his warm, solid chest and simply absorb his comfort. "Everything's going to be fine. We'll find a way to explain about us."

She loosened her grip on him to be able to look up into his face. "Can you explain it to *me*?"

"Sure." He pulled her close again and cleared his throat. "I'm attracted to you because you're generally so sane, and though the Palmers have helped me acquire some sanity, my life had been without it until I was eight. And then there were all those years of war." He sucked in a breath. "I have no idea why you're attracted to me, unless it's that I can give you a lot of what you want—love, home. Of course, you'll have to figure out that you can't have all that without children. I'm not sure where we go from there, but we're two smart people. We'll figure it out."

"Really." She should move, take this conversation seriously, but it was wonderful to be in his arms as though for the moment, at least, everything would work out. "Then you have to stop trying to kill me in your sleep."

"Hey, every time I've shoved you away there was a mattress for you to fall on."

"Don't tell that to your parents, okay?"

"Okay."

CHAPTER TWELVE

BEN WAS WATCHING one of television's dumber reality shows when Jack walked into his hospital room after dinner. Carrying a carton of Ben & Jerry's Cherry Garcia ice cream, Jack had to stop and stare at the screen to make sure he was seeing correctly.

"Did you have a lobotomy when they fixed your arm?" Jack asked as he sat on the chair beside the bed and pulled the carton and a spoon from home out of the bag.

"Funny." Ben winced as he tried to boost himself against the pillows with one hand. Jack put the ice cream down and put his hands under Ben's arms, careful with the wounded one, and pulled him up. He fluffed the pillows, then sat again and tore the top off the carton.

"Thank you." Ben looked exhausted, entirely lacking his customary invincibility. But at least his eyes lit up at the sight of the ice cream. "You even brought a spoon from home. Those plastic things never survive the desperation to get that first bite." He propped the carton on his thigh, steadied it there with the hand on the injured arm, and spooned with his right. He took a bite and closed his eyes, making a deep sound of approval.

He pointed the spoon at the television. "I've been too lazy to change it."

"You look a little worse for wear tonight. Lot of pain?"

Ben indicated the tube of medication running into his arm and the very easy reach to the button so that he could dose himself. "No. This works pretty well. I've just been...thinking."

Jack leaned forward, elbows on his knees. It wasn't like Ben to analyze. It wasn't that he was superficial; it was that he was sure of what he knew. Sometimes even what he *didn't* know.

"About what?" Jack asked.

Ben took another bite of ice cream and gave him a look that told him he didn't want to talk about it. "Just...stuff."

Okay. He was going to have to pull it out of him. "Sarah?" he asked. No point in dodging the issue. They were going to have to talk about it sooner or later. Ben's being in bed unable to use one arm seemed like a good time.

Ben met his gaze, clearly surprised and displeased that he'd brought her up. "No," he finally said. "Me."

Ben lost control of the spoon and dropped it on the bedclothes. Jack picked it up, took it to the small sink, washed it off and brought it back.

"And what is it about *you*, who made a good collar today despite the bad arm, that makes you look so gloomy?"

"I… Jack, can we just let it go?"

"Sure." Jack sat back, pretty sure agitation wasn't a good thing for someone in Ben's condition, but worried about him and feeling guilty at the same time. "Mom and Dad should be back day after tomorrow."

Ben gave him a dark glance as he continued to eat. Then he sighed, stabbed the spoon into the carton of ice cream and handed it back. "I know what you feel for her is important."

Jack put the lid back on and placed the carton and the spoon back in the bag, just to give himself something to do. This was going to be a hard conversation. He considered the fact that Ben had opened it up a good thing. "It *is* important," he said.

"She's a good person."

"Yeah, I know that."

Ben smiled to himself. "She's not very big,

talks quietly, gives an impression of softness. But then I remember her marching around the kitchen, checking on what we're eating, ordering us around if we get messy. She's like some crusty old sergeant."

Laughing, Jack nodded. "She is. So much for an impression of softness." Then he remembered holding her in his arms, recalled her easy slide down his body when he'd lifted her out of the truck, and for an instant he was the one distracted. When he came back to the moment, Ben was watching him.

"So you're thinking about living without children because you love her that much?"

"Maybe. She's not going to budge."

"You can give up what you want to give her what she wants?"

That took it down to its basic truth. "Again. Maybe."

Ben leaned back against the pillows and closed his eyes.

"Getting too tired to talk?" Jack almost wanted him to say yes so that they wouldn't have to.

Ben's eyes remained closed. Jack was about to gather his jacket and the ice cream and leave when Ben said without preamble, "I thought I was going to die when the perp shot me and I was scared."

Jack sat again. At last. Something he knew a little about. A lot, actually. "Who wouldn't be scared?" he asked.

"For an instant," Ben went on, "the pain was huge, like a fire all over me, and I couldn't isolate it. It took a few seconds to realize it was just my arm. Then I saw him running away and remembered that I still had another arm and a weapon. I took him out first try."

"Good man. Where was Grady?"

"We were so short of guys, we were operating solo." Ben rolled his head on the pillow to look at him. "How did you manage to live every day of your deployments, feeling like that?"

Jack had tried so hard to put that behind him that it took a minute to remember how it felt. "Well, you're not terrified all the time. There are some quiet periods where you're surrounded by your friends and you know how capable they are, so you feel safe. Then the crap hits the fan. Things are exploding, joes are going down, and it's like the lowest level of hell. But you try to keep your head and fight back, or you die. Or somebody crouched next to you dies. A lot of it is instinct. Like when you remembered you had another good hand and a weapon and took your shooter down."

Ben rolled his head back to stare at the ceiling. "I hated it."

"Everybody hates it. Unless you're crazy."

"I've never felt like that before. I've wrestled a few perps to the ground and then swaggered around thinking I could handle myself. It was a serious takedown of my pride to know how different it is to take a bullet, and how scared I was."

"Fear is healthy. Keeps you sharp."

"It shook me to come face-to-face with myself like that." Ben sighed and his voice went down an octave. "And to know that somebody wanted to kill me. How did you deal with that for six years?"

Jack remembered trembling inside with that first sharp awareness that his life as a cavalry scout wasn't about the heroic guy on the poster or the BS they told each other every day to pump themselves up. It was about blood and bone that didn't react well to flying shrapnel and high-caliber bullets. It was about hating everything going on and trying to find that still-beating heart inside that would fight to do the right thing. To fight without hating, and to find that nugget of fearlessness that had kept him alive as a child and let him wear it like a shield as a soldier.

"Well, childhood was a lot like combat for me, so I was experienced." It wasn't funny, but he laughed. "My mother didn't mean to neglect us or to let us wander into danger, but her need for drugs was too strong. Moments of sobriety were rare. Sometimes you have to forget how ugly it all is and remember that you're going to somehow be better, do better. And you have to stay alive to do that. As a cop, you're making a better environment for this community, and if you don't stand up to the bad guy, if you don't fear and face that fear and keep going, you won't be here to do it."

Ben was silent, stretching a leg out and messing with the bed cover. Then he sighed again. "For a couple of hours this afternoon, I considered taking the post-office employment exam." He smiled grimly.

"Yeah, well, you'd still have to wear Kevlar. Try telling some woman her QVC order is late, or some old guy that his social security check is lost. And you won't even get to carry a gun."

"I think you get pepper spray."

Jack snorted a laugh.

There was another brief silence, then Ben said, "In those few seconds when I was feeling like I was on fire and too scared to move, everything came back to me. Our lives as kids, our fights with the Duffy brothers, all the things we feared and somehow survived." He shifted his body laboriously to lean on his good elbow.

"Careful." Jack reached out to unkink the tubing in Ben's arm and give it some slack.

"I got to thinking that it's no wonder your childhood is all tangled up in your nightmares about war. That's kind of what happened to me. So, even though you're a hero, you've got an unresolved fear somewhere. There's something you haven't dealt with." He paused to just gaze at Jack, then said, "What is it?"

It occurred to Jack that Ben was thinking pretty clearly for a man who was pumping pain medication straight into his bloodstream. "I've thought about it, too, but I don't know what it is. I mean, I have all the fears everyone else has, but I've pretty much learned to kill them to keep going."

Ben asked with surprising gentleness, "Even the old one about your mom?"

He had an easy answer for that. "That's not fear, that's fury. She was beautiful, and when she noticed us in rare moments of clarity, we felt blessed, but those moments were just a fraction of one percent of our lives. It's her fault that the tight little unit my sisters and I were was torn apart by her selfishness and inability to cope with anything without being high. I can't forgive her for that."

Ben fell back against the pillow. "Just a thought. But you'll have to stop hating if you're going to get married, even if you don't have children." He was beginning to sound tired.

Jack wasn't sure about that. Love and hate had lived side by side in him his entire life. He loved his sisters and hated his mother. He loved the Palmers and hated his mother. After his adoption, he loved his new life and hated the old one. On one level, hate fueled him.

"I'm going so you can get some sleep." Jack pulled up Ben's blankets and made sure the tubing was clear of entanglement. He held up the water glass with the flexible straw. "Want a sip of this before I go?"

"No, thanks."

The nurse pushed open the door and walked to the foot of the bed, consulting an electronic tablet. "You're going home in the morning, Mr. Palmer," she said to Ben. "Everything's looking good. We're going to set up physical therapy for you, but not for a little while. So, you get some sleep and I'll get everything in order so that you can leave."

"I thought you liked me, Jeannette," Ben said with a grin.

She grinned back at him. "You're mistaken, Mr. Palmer. Good night."

Ben shook his head at Jack as the nurse left the room. "I'm losing my touch with women."

Jack picked up his jacket and the bag with the ice cream and spoon. "That's because you look like Homer Simpson."

"No! I thought I looked like Nathan Fillion."

"In your dreams. Call me in the morning when you're discharged and I'll pick you up."

"All right. Thanks for the ice cream."

"Sure."

"And, Jack?"

He turned back at the door. "Yeah?"

Ben propped himself up on his good elbow, looking exhausted but somehow more relaxed than he'd been in some time. "Give Sarah a hug for me. And then, you know…whatever you want to do for yourself. I'm good with it."

"Okay." Jack waved, a whole layer of tension dissolving. "Thanks, Ben."

SARAH HAD MADE turkey sandwiches and salad—an easy dinner for a night when she was tired and still had a lot to do. She put the food on the table when she heard Jack's SUV in the driveway.

"How is he?" she asked.

Jack came directly toward her and wrapped her in his arms. "He said to give you a hug," he reported, "then told me to do whatever else I wanted for myself."

She looped an arm around his neck. "And what would that be? Bearing in mind that I have ninja skills."

He wove the fingers of one hand into her hair and tugged her head back so that he could look into her face. His eyes flashed with wanting her, softening her spine.

"I thought, a little of this," he said softly as he lowered his mouth to hers. He kissed her slowly, soundly, then lifted his head. "And a little of this." He nipped at her earlobe and then placed kisses down the side of her neck. Sensation raced everywhere he touched. "And, maybe…" His lips dipped to the opening of her blouse, but she laughed and pushed at his shoulder with her free hand. She had to put distance between them so she could think.

"You get back to finding your sisters," she

said, "and I'll change the sheets on Ben's bed and try to straighten up his room. Then I'll come down and make coffee."

"I don't know," Jack said wearily. "My mind's full of Ben and all he—"

Sarah cut him off. "You can go back to finding your other family, Jack. Don't be afraid. I'm sure no one will hold it against you."

He was about to deny that he was afraid, then wondered if it was true. It had been so long since he'd seen his sisters. So much could have happened. What if they didn't remember him? What if he wasn't as important to their lives as they'd been to his? What if they had new lives in which the brother who reminded them of those awful days didn't fit anymore? What if Helen and Gary didn't understand?

Well, what if none of those things was true? He wouldn't know unless he found them.

He settled at the kitchen table with his laptop.

Working on the premise that the Isabel who'd left a message on the TombStones website was the Elizabeth Corazon who'd been his wild little sister, Jack first located Querida, Texas, the place from which Isabel's post originated, on his road atlas. It was a town of 2,000 near McAllen, which was five miles from the Mexican border.

Jack put her name into the telephone directory search engine for McAllen and vicinity and was exhilarated when a list of three Isabel Ochoas appeared. One was twenty-two, one sixty-eight and one, C. Isabel Ochoa, had an address on Rio Road. She was twenty-seven.

Jack's heart lurched. It was her. *C* for Corazon. *Isabel* for Elizabeth. Ochoa. Twenty-seven, the right age.

He'd found her. Well, almost. He had an address on a road on the river that separated the United States from Mexico in the State of Texas.

He printed out the address, a tremor of excitement at work in a chest that was usually rock solid. He knew where Corie was!

He got out his bank card and paid for the extra search, then stared at the screen when an arrest warrant popped up. It was for assault charges filed by Robert Pimental, 47, deputy mayor of the city of Querida.

He imagined a young woman so hurt and angry because of her childhood that she became abusive. Remembering the bright, scrappy little girl she'd been, he hated his mother even more. Well, one bad decision didn't have to ruin a life.

He clicked on the second page and felt a catch in his throat at a photo of Isabel Ochoa. Her blunt-cut hair was blond and poorly dyed, her large eyes dark and angry, her nose and mouth beautifully sculpted above a chin angled with attitude. The collar of a tattered jacket was visible. At the time of the arrest, she was twenty-six. So. Not that long ago.

He stared at the photo, completely relating to the image there, loving her as he'd loved the little girl she'd been. He hated to think about what had led that little girl to become a woman with an arrest on her record.

It was well after ten o'clock when Sarah finished with Ben's room and came downstairs.

"There was a tennis shoe in with his CDs," she reported to Jack, stopping to look over his shoulder. "And you weren't kidding about being able to hide an elephant in his room. I'm off to bed. You want a cup of decaf or anything before I go?"

He pointed to the screen and what he'd found. She leaned closer, concentrating on the document, then gasped when he paged and she saw the photo.

"Jack!" she breathed. "You've found her! I can't believe it. That is her, isn't it?"

"I'm sure it is."

"She looks so…tough. Strong."

"She was a feisty little kid." He felt a pain in his gut at the knowledge that his life had been so good after their mother went to jail, and hers probably had not. He swore he could still see that little girl in those angry eyes looking back at him. "Apparently she hasn't lost much of that."

"You've got an address." There was wonder in Sarah's voice.

"Yes. I'm giving Ben a few days to recover, and I want to explain what I'm doing to my parents, then I'm going to Texas."

She put her arms around his neck, her cheek to his. "I'm sorry you have to wait."

He patted the arm around him. "It's all right. It's been so long, another few days won't matter."

But he went to bed with Corie's pretty, angry face on his mind, and prayed that she wouldn't do anything to get herself arrested again before he could reach her.

IT WAS RAINING hard the next morning. Sarah ran outside with an umbrella when she looked out the window and saw Jack's SUV pull into the driveway. Ben was in the passenger seat. She ran to open Ben's door and hold the umbrella over him as he climbed out, his bandaged arm in a sling. She offered him her free hand to help him balance as he stepped out.

He put his good arm around her shoulders. "Hi," he said. His voice sounded friendly, affectionate. She looked into his eyes to find a warm, easy expression. He kissed her temple.

"Good to be home. I'm sure Jeannette will miss me, though she denies it." They walked together toward the door.

"Jeannette?"

"My nurse. She was in love with me."

Sarah pulled the door open for him, holding the umbrella over him until the last minute. "We all are, Ben. Sit at the table. I made a cranberry-orange coffee cake."

"You two go ahead," Jack shouted with an exaggerated note of petulance. He carried Ben's things in a large white plastic bag with the hospital logo on it. Rain fell on him as he rounded the hood of the truck, his hair already plastered to his head. "Don't worry about me. I was Scotchgarded as a child and I can breathe through my gills!"

Laughing, Sarah hurried back to hold the

umbrella over him. "Oh, pipe down. You're a heroic tough guy, remember? This is just rain."

He hunched down to fit under the protection as they headed for the house. "Well, it's a *lot* of rain."

At the door, Ben took the bag from him and hauled him inside with his good hand. "Oh, shut up. What a lot of fuss. You're just jealous because I had all Sarah's attention. I've been shot, for God's sake."

"Big whoop. I was blown up more times than I care to count. And you don't see anybody following *me* around to meet my every need."

Sarah watched the two of them in amazement. They'd obviously cleared the air. Must have been when Jack visited Ben last night. They were harassing each other as though she was no longer an issue between them.

Jack helped Ben off with the jacket he wore on one arm, the other side just draped over his shoulder.

"Stop fighting," she scolded. "We have to be on our best behavior so your parents believe that everything's okay."

Ben smiled at her. "Everything *is* okay."

She absorbed the magic of that and then

added as she went for coffee, "Right. Except that you've been shot."

He sat. "Yeah. And you've thrown me over for my brother. Otherwise, everything's fine."

Sarah kissed his cheek. "You're a prince, Ben."

Jack head-slapped him as he made his way to the kitchen sink to wash his hands.

"Well, as he reminded us," Sarah said to Ben, pouring coffee, "he's been blown up many times and you've only been shot once, so as heroes go, he's got it all over you."

"How many times do I have to be shot before I have more appeal than he does?"

"You'd be dead first, Ben," Jack said, sitting opposite him. "Pass the coffee cake."

SARAH LEFT JACK and Ben together early the following morning to attend an emergency meeting of the fund-raising committee.

"We have a lot on our plate, people," Carol Winston said gravely. "One councilman on the tax-rolls side wants to cross over to us, but Pete Daley is still holding out and convincing him to stay put. I'm not saying he's thinking selfishly of his own profits, but, you know, it has to cross his mind."

"I don't think we have to worry," Brenda

Brown, the representative from Hospice Care said. "He's married to Lucy Daley, and she's chairman of Historic Preservation in our county. Forman's present location is a contemporary monstrosity he had built."

Carol tossed her head impatiently. "If we didn't have to worry, we'd already have the vote. And to update the situation, the Daleys are getting divorced. And guess who's Lucy Daley's attorney?"

There was a communal "No!" of disbelief. Fate couldn't be that cruel.

"Yes. Forman. Public opinion is all we've got right now. I know you're all talking it up, so keep doing it. And pray that this is the most well-attended talent show in the history of Beggar's Bay."

CHAPTER THIRTEEN

BEN SQUARED HIS shoulders and smiled in an attempt, Sarah guessed, to look healthy. "I don't look like I've been shot, do I?" he asked as he struck a pose, feet firmly planted.

"Except for the mile and a half of gauze on your arm," Jack answered, "and your fingers swollen to twice their size sticking out of the bandage, you look good. I'm going out to move Ben's and my car so Mom and Dad can pull in and unpack." They were due any moment. Sarah had parked the RAV4 near the carriage house.

"If it makes you feel better," Ben said to Sarah, "I'll tell them I dumped you for another girl I pulled over for speeding. That's how I met you, after all."

She swatted his good arm with a pot holder. "Thanks. Two more weeks to the talent show. You have to be recovered by then."

"I'm practically recovered now," he replied.

"We have a rehearsal on Friday. The Friday

after that is the dress rehearsal, and Saturday is the show." She pulled a light dip she'd made with Neufchâtel cheese out of the refrigerator. "Can you reach the crackers on that top shelf, please?" She pointed.

"Sure. I will be at rehearsal." Ben handed her the crackers. She opened the box, handed it back to him and placed an empty bowl in front of him.

"In there, please," she said.

"Did you finally convince Vinny and Margaret to work together?" He poured fairly well and nibbled on the overflow.

"They're a little cool but talking. Some progress."

He carried the bowl to the other end of the counter where she worked. "I relate to Vinny a little bit. I think I'm off women for a while."

She looked up at him guiltily. "Don't say that."

He helped himself to another cracker, then snagged a bite of dip. "Oh, it's not self-pity or abandonment of the man-woman principle. I knew you'd fall in love with Jack and it's okay, really." He hugged her with his good arm. "It's just that I don't know myself as well as I thought I did. I have more to learn before I try to be everything someone else needs."

She turned to him in pleased amazement. "That's the most enlightened thing I've ever heard any man say. I'm going to circle this day on the calendar. Wow, Ben."

The powerful sound of Gary Palmer's truck and trailer came from the side of the house and Sarah pushed Ben toward the hallway. "Hide! Let them come in and have the satisfaction of being home a few minutes before they have to face the fact that their son has been shot."

He disappeared and she went to meet Jack and his parents in the driveway. His mother came into her arms and held her tightly. "It's good to be home. We had a wonderful, leisurely trip, but I'm pooped."

"Go inside," Sarah said, "and I'll help Jack with the bags. Gary, put that down."

He tried to pull a garment bag out of the back of the truck and Jack stopped him. "I'll get that, Dad. Go inside."

Sarah opened her arms to Gary now and he walked into them, smiling. "Sarah, you're a vision. My life has been full of backseat-driver wife, selfish tourists and slow motor homes."

She hugged him fiercely and walked him into the house. "You're driving a motor home,

Gary," she pointed out. "And someone was probably behind you. I've moved out of your room into Jack's while he's in the carriage house, so you can go right in and lie down if you want to."

She hurried back out to help Jack with the bags. "I can manage," he said with a wry grin. "At least it isn't raining today."

She took Helen's tote from him.

"Kiss me right now," he said softly, leaning toward her as they entered the kitchen.

She pushed him back. "We have to be careful until we've explained—"

"If you'd kiss me instead of taking time to argue…" Just as the words came out of his mouth, his mother wandered through the kitchen, went to the Keurig and poured herself a coffee.

Sarah smiled. "Later," Sarah murmured to Jack. "Hold the thought."

"Where's Ben?" Helen asked, standing in the middle of the kitchen with her coffee. She closed her eyes and simply stood there. "It's so nice to be home. I must be getting old that I was in that beautiful spot and all I could think about was being home again." Her admission was followed by her gasp of alarm as Ben walked in.

Sarah gave him full credit for a bright smile and the sincere effort to appear whole. Helen put her cup down on the table and went to him. He put his good arm around her and tried to give her a hug, but she pushed against his chest. "What happened?" she demanded, staring at his bandaged arm, the shirtsleeve hanging slack.

"I'm fine," Ben insisted, trying to direct her toward a chair. Gary came into the kitchen, frowning over the mild commotion.

"That doesn't answer my question." Helen examined the thick gauze wrap on his arm and the purple, puffy fingers protruding.

Everyone converged at the table. Jack pulled out a chair for his father and Ben pushed on Helen's shoulder until she, too, sat. Sarah got plates and napkins while Ben explained about being shot. Helen put a hand to her heart, her eyes intent while she listened.

"I really am fine now," Ben said, putting a hand over his mother's at the table. "It was a pretty minor thing all in all. Drink your coffee, Mom."

Helen ignored the cup he pushed toward her and said finally, looking from Ben to Jack, "I wish the two of you would do me a favor and pitch in together to buy a hardware store that you can run."

Ben and Jack looked at each other in confusion.

"Then I can stop worrying about the two of you being killed!" she shouted and stormed off to the bedroom. Sarah followed with Helen's coffee.

JACK'S FATHER HELD his cup toward him. "Do we still have brandy in that cupboard?"

Jack retrieved the bottle and added a shot to his mug and his father's. When Ben protested being passed over, Jack reminded him, "You're on pain medication. You can't drink."

Ben groaned, then shook his head. "I tried to put a shirt on, but the padding's too thick. I hate that Mom's upset."

His father relaxed in his chair and smiled faintly. "She's always thought her job was to keep all of us in perfect health. She forgets the world is a dangerous place. I guess that's just a wife and mother's job." He took a sip of the laced coffee, seemed to savor it, then smiled and put the cup down. He looked from Ben to Jack. "I, on the other hand, knew the first time I saw the two of you jumping off the garage roof together, holding opposite ends of a bedsheet for a parachute, that prayer and health insurance was going to do me more good than worrying."

Jack and Ben both laughed. Jack remembered that clearly. The awful events that changed his life hadn't happened yet, and he'd still been Ben's friend, not his brother. He guessed they'd been about six and filled with the adventures of Batman, Spider-Man and Captain America. They'd felt fairly sure that if they caught a good breeze and jumped high enough, they'd fly.

Reality had broken Ben's ankle and sprained Jack's arm.

"So how's your arm, really?" his father asked Ben, his gaze direct. "Is it going to heal completely? Are you really fine?"

"Yes and yes," Ben assured him quickly. "It's a little painful. I was trying to do without the pain medication because I can't go back to work on it, but Sarah insists I need it, and if I forget to take it, she literally puts it in my mouth, then pours water on me until it goes down."

His father laughed. "Good." He turned to Jack. "And how are you doing? Still having nightmares?"

Jack wanted to relieve his dad's mind and

deny that he continued to be plagued by them, but those eyes saw everything. "Yes, but I think I'm starting to figure them out. I imagine once that happens, they'll stop."

"Really."

"Yeah." He grinned. "At least, that's what Ben says. And we know what a great shrink he is."

"Oh, yeah," Gary agreed. "The kind that gets shot."

Jack took a big swallow of coffee. "I've been looking for my sisters since I've been home," he said. "Before I tell Mom, are you okay with that?"

Clearly surprised by the question, his dad said, "Of course! We don't own you and we have no exclusive right to your loyalties. What have you found out?"

He told him about thinking he'd found Corie and everything he'd discovered, even the arrest warrant.

Ben, who'd been in the hospital when it happened, leaned forward with concern. "The Mexican border? I think that's dangerous territory, Jack. You're going out there?"

"It's *near* the border. I want to make sure you're recovered before I set out."

Ben groaned impatiently.

"But," Gary told Jack gravely, "family comes before everything."

Jack gently punched his shoulder. "Right. That's why I'm staying with Ben. And you and Mom just got home. You might need me around." When Gary would have protested, he waved that away with a swipe of his hand. "I know. But I'm one of those rare people lucky enough to have two families who mean everything to me. This can wait a few days."

His father nodded on a noisy swallow. "No, it can't. You go find your little sister."

"I'M SORRY TO be so emotional," Helen said, sitting on the window seat in the master bedroom. There was early November sun just beyond the window, sparkling on the mountain-ash leaves and the grass Jack had just mowed.

"It's been such a good life, you know. Ben's been a wonderful son, and then we got Jack..." She took in a breath, trying to maintain her composure. "It's scary to think that one single moment could change all that."

Sarah, sitting beside her, put an arm around her. "Helen, Ben was shot, but luckily only in his arm, and he's so strong and cussed, he's already on his way to full recovery. Jack's happy to be home. He still has the occasional nightmare, but he's dealing with it. Your boys are going to be fine."

"I hope so. I want to see grandchildren— and soon."

Uh-oh. Not only did this seem like the wrong time to tell her about Jack and her, but the wrong time to explain that she'd have to wait until Ben got married for grandchildren.

"While I was getting groceries," Sarah said, "I also got you some bubble bath. Thought you might enjoy it after the long trip home. Want me to fill the tub? Or would you rather nap first?"

Helen looked fondly at Sarah. "How did we get so lucky to have you in our lives?" Before Sarah could reply, Helen answered her own question. "I guess we can attribute our good fortune to Ben's good taste in women and your lead foot on the accelerator… I think I *will* take a bath."

Sarah laughed and got to her feet. "All right. I made some snacks in case you guys were hungry. You can have them after your bath."

Downstairs, Gary, in his recliner, and Jack and Ben on the sofa, were watching a reality show that seemed to be about a family who bought and sold antique weapons. They laughed about a cannon set up on someone's lawn as a garden sculpture.

"I'm not sure that sends the right message to visitors," Ben observed.

"Yeah," Gary contributed. "Wipe your feet or you're cannon fodder."

Sarah was happy to hear the laughter. She still had things to tell Gary and Helen, but that could wait. Laughter was good for the soul.

BEGGAR'S BAY'S HIGH-SCHOOL drama class was busy decorating the stage to be used for the talent show. Students and a few mothers and teachers hung mirrors alternating with strings of beads at twelve-inch intervals around the stage. Sarah admired the way they caught and reflected light as she and her seniors walked into the space, everyone distracted by the beautiful environment.

Jack, Ben, Mario and Rico were in the middle of their number, dressed in their nineties' boy-band look for full effect. Some families who'd come to watch and lend support sat in the front rows. Gary and Helen were there. Helen held Trina De Angelis on her lap. Gary talked with Margie.

The boys were applauded loudly, a little feverish screaming coming from the moms in attendance. The students looked at each other with nervous smiles, clearly a little embarrassed by the women's behavior.

A group of firemen performed "Stouthearted Men," a 1920s song with heroic lyrics written for a male chorus, to great enthusiasm from the audience. Someone from parks and rec juggled plates, and Sarah ran to Mario's father's aid when one of the plates went rogue and landed on his head. He insisted he was fine, and a few simple hand tests suggested he was.

Vinny and his friends did a surprisingly sweet rendition of several Sinatra numbers. Then Margaret stood in the middle of the stage without instrumental support and, with every ounce of her dignified-lady persona in place, sang "Among My Souvenirs" in her crystal-clear alto with a surprising rock quality. The song was about searching through old memories and finding a broken heart. Everyone stopped to listen, the young people working on the stage included.

Margaret was nervous at first, but Sarah saw the moment she lost fear and became a part of the lyrics. She was wonderful.

When the last note dissolved on the air, there was complete silence for several seconds, then the applause was deafening. Margaret smiled shyly and put a hand to her heart and began to laugh. Vinny, Sarah noted, looked stunned.

Margaret walked off the stage and the decorating group assembled into a tableau and began the balcony scene from *Romeo and Juliet*.

Jack slipped into the seat beside Sarah. "You may have to hire an agent and take this whole show on the road," he whispered. "The talent is amazing. And I'm not even talking about Ben, Mario, Rico and me."

"I know," she whispered. "The reporter from the *Bugle* is here. The publicity is going to help us make a killing. I can't wait to—"

She stopped abruptly when she heard a sound that yanked her out of the moment and back into another time and place. It was completely wrong here, her brain was telling her even as she scanned the stage for the source.

It had been a gurgle, the sound of a body at war with its air supply, and it made her heart thump. No, she thought anxiously. Please, no.

Then she heard it again and a boy of about sixteen standing stage left with a string of beads in his hand dropped where he stood.

CHAPTER FOURTEEN

THERE WAS SILENCE, then gasps, then shouts. Sarah ran for the stage, hearing a cry from a woman somewhere behind her. She'd thought she'd never have to do this again. It wasn't fair. She hated the memories of her old life, the terrible tension, the grim realities and the heartbreaking vulnerability of sick children.

She dropped to her knees by the boy, his eyes now rolled back into his head. The gurgling noise continued and the *No!* in her head screamed. The boy was in full cardiac arrest.

From somewhere in that black and hated past came old knowledge and, under the panic, the steps to follow. She tried not to think about how they sometimes didn't work.

"Jack!" she shouted as she checked that the boy's airway was free and began chest compressions.

"Right here," he said.

And he was, right at her elbow. "Find the defibrillator! There has to be one."

"I'll show you." One of the students kneeling nearby sprang to her feet and Jack ran after her.

"Someone call 9-1-1!" she shouted again.

Ben's voice shouted back, "I'm on it!"

Now Sarah leaned down to begin breathing into the boy's mouth.

A woman knelt beside her, putting a hand to the boy's arm. "Breathe, Justin," she said through her tears. Sarah remembered the scream she'd heard behind her. This had to be the boy's mother. "Please breathe."

Sarah resumed the chest compressions as the mother said, "He has arrhythmogenic right ventricular dysplasia." She uttered the scientific term as though she'd had to deal with it for a while. Sarah hadn't heard the term in several years, and even then, the condition had been a relatively rare thing that caused the heart muscle to slowly change into fatty tissue and scar. It was a dangerous threat to normal life. She wanted to tell the mother that implantable defibrillators were available, but now wasn't the time.

Sarah had just begun the breathing again when the distraught mother said, almost as if she'd read her mind, "He's scheduled to be implanted with a personal defibrillator next month. Please, *please* keep him alive for that."

Jack knelt beside her with the automated external defibrillator. "Turn on the power," Sarah said quickly between breaths. "It'll give you voice instructions."

"Got it," Jack said. "I've used one of these before." After he applied the pads with the electrodes to the boy's chest, he added, "I'm going to hit Analyze, right?" He paused, then caught Sarah's quick glance in his direction. "It says to shock."

"Okay," she continued the breathing as Jack told everyone to move back. Sarah herself sat back as he hit the shock button. Justin's body jumped, but the monitor showed no heart rhythm.

She felt the air pressure change in the room when everyone gasped. Jack followed the procedure again and this time the line jumped on the monitor, frail at first, then steady, regular.

Justin's mother wept as Justin's leg moved and then a hand stirred.

Somewhere outside, a siren whined and grew louder. Sarah kept breathing into Justin's mouth until an EMT knelt beside her. "You've got a rhythm," he said, studying the line. "Good job. What's his name?"

Sarah stopped doing CPR. "Justin. This is his mother." Then she stood and stepped out of the way as the EMT took over. He told Justin that he was going to be fine, to just hang in there.

Justin's mother threw her arms around Sarah, sobbing, "Thank you, thank you, thank you!"

"I'm so grateful that it worked," Sarah said, feeling as though she might just collapse herself.

Justin was lifted onto a gurney and, with a final hug for Sarah, his mother joined the procession down the stage steps and out of the auditorium.

Sarah watched them go, unaware of her surroundings, as she thanked heaven this event had had a good ending, one of joy rather than horror.

When she came back to awareness, she realized everyone was staring at her and smiling. And as she stood just where Margaret had stood to sing, it occurred to her that it was as though she'd performed for the house.

Showed off her talent.

Her talent.

A shudder went through her that she felt in every extremity, then seemed to settle like a weight in the very core of her being. The truth was that it didn't matter that she'd decided she didn't want to take care of sick children, that fifteen to eighteen percent of them were still out there with chronic disease. She had the knowledge to help, and whenever they crossed her path she had to try, or be a horrible human being. She felt her spirits dip under the weight.

Jack put an arm at her back and peered into her face. "You're not going to faint, are you?" he asked gently. "You're pale and trembling."

She turned and looped her arms around his neck. "I won't faint, but can I lean on you for a minute?"

He pulled her closer. "Absolutely."

She relaxed and simply relished in the security the strong arms around her provided. In a perfect world she'd be able to extend this moment forever—no painful past, no scary future—just this blissful embrace.

Then she became aware of the sound of applause.

"I believe that's for you," Jack said, dropping his arms to cup her elbows. "That was remarkable, Sarah. I think you're going to have to take a bow." He turned her toward the people collected around them. A part of her wanted to deny the praise, but another part knew they meant their appreciation in the kindest way.

"Sometimes awful things have a good outcome," she said when the clapping finally stopped. "The defibrillator brought him back. All I did was keep him going until it did."

Everyone continued to look at her as though she'd performed a miracle. The family of a patient often thought medical people had heavenly powers because they understood the workings of the body. But understanding how it worked and making it work well were entirely different things.

Jerica's parents had had that look on their faces, but when Jerica died it had turned from adoration to bitter disappointment.

"How did you know what to do?" Margie asked.

Sarah hunched a shoulder. "I used to be a pediatric nurse, and we were drilled on CPR." When everyone looked at her in surprise, she added, "It's a long story, but for right now, I think we should all go home. Our acts look really good, so let's just keep practicing until our dress rehearsal next Friday night. Whoever learns news about Justin has to promise to share, okay?"

They agreed and began moving toward the

exits. Helen, Gary and Ben came to join her and Jack onstage.

"Good work, Sarah," Ben said, giving her a quick hug. He clapped Jack on the shoulder as his parents moved in to embrace Sarah. "You, too. You use those in the military? We're just starting to get them in our units."

"Yeah. I helped use one on a Medevac helicopter."

"You taking Sarah home? I'm going with Mario and Rico to the hospital. Justin's their cousin. Mom and Dad are having dinner at the neighbors' tonight, so the two of you can relax."

"Okay."

"And I don't think you have to worry about explaining anything to them about you and Sarah." Ben gave him a rueful grin. "When she shouted to *you* for help, then turned into *your* arms when it was over, they figured it out. They even looked happy about it."

Jack felt relieved and confused. "They did?"

"Yeah." Ben hooked his good arm around Jack's neck. "Dad said I need a woman more 'out there' than Sarah."

"'Out there'?"

"His words exactly. I don't get it, either. I mean, I'm so...what's the word?"

"Difficult? Insane? Argumentative?"

Ben tightened his grip. "I was going for sensitive."

"Like the sensitivity you're showing right now," Jack said.

Ben lowered his arm. "I don't know. I don't know what I want in a woman. They're too complicated for my simple mind."

Helen and Sarah joined them. "She should go home," Helen said, placing Sarah beside Jack, "and have a hot bath and a drink." Helen's look into Jack's face told him she wasn't happy about being kept in the dark about his relationship with Sarah, but that they would talk about it later.

"I have to take Vinny, Margaret and Jasper home first," Sarah said.

"I can do that," Ben volunteered. "I can easily drive with one arm."

She thanked him with a smile. "That's nice of you, Ben, but I'm fine. I always walk Jasper into his apartment, and I also have to make sure Vinny takes cold medicine for his cough. I'm fine. Really."

JACK KNEW IT was pointless for Ben to argue. "All right, Sarah. I'll see you at the house." He herded his parents toward the stairs. "Why don't you come home with me since you have a dinner date next door tonight? Then Ben can go straight to the hospital."

When his mother asked him about Sarah in the car, Jack wished he had thought through his offer to take his parents home. "It's not my business," she said, "but I'd like to know anyway. Ben seems okay with it, but is he really? The two of you have been so close for so long, I hate to think that anything would come between you."

"We've talked it out, Mom," Jack said, alternately watching the road and his rearview mirror to try to judge his parents' expressions. "We're okay with each other."

"He isn't heartbroken?"

"She was never right for him," Gary said unexpectedly.

His mother's eyes widened. "That's the second time you've said that. Why not?" she demanded.

"Because she runs deep and he would just go for what he wanted to do without stopping to tell her. That's okay if you're willing to deal with the consequences, which he seems to be. But it isn't a healthy way to run a marriage."

His mother seemed taken aback by his father's

profound observation. Then she asked Jack, "Why did she stop being a pediatric nurse?"

He told her about her patient's death and the resultant rift with her love of caring for children.

"That's so sad." Helen sighed. Jack pulled up to a red light and watched her lean her head back against the seat. "She was so perfect today, just what you want to see in a crisis—someone capable and calm."

He had to agree.

Jack escorted his parents to the neighbors' front door, then crossed the walk and let himself into the quiet house. He exhaled a sigh of relief. He'd done nothing today except sing with the Wild Men, support Sarah in her effort to save Justin and deal with his parents' questions, but he felt as though he'd done it while carrying a Humvee on his back. He'd learned something profound this afternoon that he had to tell Sarah.

Not sure how long she would be, Jack made a cup of coffee and sat to read the newspaper.

"The Wild Men are very good," Sarah said as she walked into the kitchen an hour later. She made no greeting of any kind, simply that statement, and Jack noticed in confusion that

the tone of it was critical, rather than compli-
mentary.

He looked up from the editorial page and
knew instantly that she was in a dangerous
mood. She'd tied her hair back, her mouth
was set in a tight line and she had that crusty-
sergeant air about her.

"You have to keep rehearsing this week,"
she went on, "so you don't lose that. You're
working together in harmony now and that'll
be a showstopper. The ladies love you." The
way she shot out the words, like bullets out
of a clip, that compliment, too, sounded like
a bad thing.

"Thank you." He watched her drop her
purse on the step stool and make a production of rinsing a single plate and cup left in the
plastic basin and put them in the dishwasher.

He wasn't sure how to read this behavior.
She'd been shaken this afternoon after the episode with Justin. And though she'd seemed
all right when she'd turned to him for comfort, she'd had time to think about what had
happened while taking her seniors home. The
afternoon had probably brought back a past
filled with painful memories. Memories she'd
been so determined not to relive.

"Want to talk about this afternoon?" he asked, folding the paper.

"Nope." She breezed past him to the laundry room and returned with a stack of dish towels.

"Mom thought you should have a bath and a drink," he reminded her. "You know, to help relax you."

She looked up darkly from putting the towels in a drawer. "Which one of us is the nurse, Jack? I don't need a bath, and I don't want coffee."

Her mood was darkening. He had to attack this head-on before he lost her altogether. "*You* are obviously the nurse," he said. "You certainly proved that today."

She continued to fiddle with the towels. "The defibrillator proved what modern medicine can do. That's what happened today." She shoved the drawer closed.

He put his cup down, got up and closed the small distance between them. "I know that must have been hard for you," he said quietly, turning her to face him, "but can't you focus on the happy outcome? You saved a kid's life, Sarah. You can't tell me you find no satisfaction in that."

"I did. I do," she said, putting her hands on

his arms and trying to push him away. He held on. "But it's hard to explain to someone else the terrifying responsibility of having the live-or-die outcome in my hands. A lot of medical professionals thrive on that. It makes me ill."

"Yeah. You don't have to explain it to me. I've been there, and without the expert medical knowledge you have. In the field, we're all medics."

She wrenched her arms away from him. "Yeah, well, I've had it with that. I don't want to do it anymore."

He turned to lean on the counter beside her. There were only a few feet of air between them, but there may as well have been a stone wall. "I think you just have to resign yourself to the fact that, even if you're not working in a hospital, whenever there's a health issue anywhere you happen to be, you'll be the one everyone turns to."

"I'll keep my nursing skills to myself from now on."

"It's painted all over you, Sarah. And your inherent love for the patient, whoever he or she is, makes you act. You didn't think twice today. Nobody called you to help Justin. You just ran for the stage and put your skills to work."

Her eyes were seeing the scene again. The fear that hadn't been present then, or at least not something that would rear up and stop her, was upon her now. She knotted her hands together. "I didn't want to be there."

She looked small and vulnerable, but she'd faced her fear today.

"I think," he said gently, "that you may as well step up and accept that, scared or not, you're a nurse." He hesitated a moment, then asked with a smile into her grim face, "Will you marry me?"

Her eyes widened in shock, closed, then opened again, as though she feared she had dreamed the moment. "What? Jack, I'm not—"

"Having children. I know." He smiled gently at her and put an arm around her shoulders. "I'll agree to live without them. I understand what that cost you today, and I wouldn't ask you to do it for me. I love you, Sarah."

He was thrown off balance when her eyes filled with tears. They didn't look like happy ones, either. "Sarah..."

"I'm sorry." She tossed her head and sniffed. "I never cry, but loving you has made me do it twice in a couple of days!" She punched him, hard rather than playfully. There was something behind it she wasn't telling him.

He took her hand and pulled her outside, the lights at the back of the house illuminating the lawn. He led the way to the fanciful gate his father had installed all those years ago, just because it looked nice from the kitchen window.

"I'm happy to hear that you love me," he said, stopping her at the gate. The air smelled of salt and grass and all the perfumes from the South Pacific that traveled on the wind. It was cold. He ripped off his sweatshirt and pulled it over her head. "What I don't understand is why you're upset. I thought finding a husband who'd live without children was what you wanted." Then a thought occurred to him. "Unless it isn't me you want."

"Of course, it's you." She wrapped her arms around his waist and held on. "But now that you'd do that for me—" she hesitated, a groan vibrating against his chest "—I can't let you. You're good with children. You should have them. I love that you're willing to do that for me, but…no. I don't want to marry you. I mean, I do, but I won't."

"Sarah Reed, you're going to make me insane." He caught a fistful of her hair and gently pulled her head back. Her sad eyes caught the moonlight. It broke his heart to see her so unhappy. "I'm offering you what you want."

"But it isn't what *you* want. And that's as important to me as my happiness is to you."

"I love you. The only children I'd want in this world are those that are half you, anyway."

She frowned at him. He saw it clearly, even in the dim light. "Children are children, Jack. Anybody's, any size, any color, eventually they worm their way inside you and make you care. You become so vulnerable, it's like having *ectopia cordis*."

He blinked. "And that is?"

"A condition where babies are born with part of the heart growing outside the body." She shook her head, her lips working unsteadily. "It's almost always fatal."

He crushed her to him, putting his lips to her cheek. "Love gives life, Sarah, it doesn't kill it. I know loving costs you. The girls and I loved our mother and she disappointed us every time. But I'm still here. And I still want to love. Even if I don't get the chance to love my child, I'll love you with everything I have, I promise."

Sᴀʀᴀʜ ᴄʜᴏᴋᴇᴅ ᴏɴ a sob, emotion making every attempt to blind her to good sense. But for tonight, at least, she couldn't push him away. The day would come when that would be her only option, but it didn't have to be now. Now she would hold him, let him hold her and let her exo-heart beat wherever it wanted to be.

CHAPTER FIFTEEN

JACK HEARD HIS parents' laughter as they said good-night to the Bergs shortly after ten. He left the carriage house and followed them into the kitchen.

"Have a good time?" he asked.

His father nodded, pulling out a chair at the table. "Yeah. Patty's not such a great cook, but she and Gordie are good company."

"Gary!" His mother sat opposite his father and scolded him with a look, then laughed. "She just likes to try unique things. Rutabaga, leek and sausage casserole just isn't something you'd rush toward on your own."

Jack took one end of the table. "I don't know. It's always been my conviction that sausage can save any dish."

His father shook his head mournfully. "Not in this case." Then he studied Jack with a frown of concern. "So, how's it going?"

Jack knew he meant how was it going with

Sarah. But he wanted to talk about something else. "It's going fine."

"Then how come you're here and she isn't?"

"Justin having that issue today just brought it all back. She thinks she doesn't want to have children."

His father crossed his arms on the table. "And you do, so you don't want to be serious about her, but you can't help yourself?"

"Not exactly, I asked her to marry me. She's warm and wonderful and would be a spectacular mother. I'd give up having children if it meant I could have her."

His mother looked pained. "Jack. Are you sure about that? I don't think it would be wise to marry her, hoping that one day down the road she'll change her mind."

"I know. You're absolutely right. She didn't make that decision because she doesn't like kids or doesn't want to be bothered with them. She made it because it hurts her to see *them* hurt." He blew air inelegantly and then ran a hand over his hair, further disheveling his nineties look. "She knows all the statistics about kids living with chronic diseases because, obviously, all she dealt with was sick kids. I'd love it if she could accept that disease could happen, but probably won't, but if it did, we could deal with it. But she can't. So maybe I'll have to be happy being an uncle, provided Ben—"

His father winced. "That's not good, Jack."

His mother shushed his father. "You can't tell him what's good for him. I hope you're doing the right thing."

"Well, right now," Jack said, "nothing's good. She doesn't want to marry me because she loves me and knows I'd love to have children. She doesn't want to hurt me." He ran both hands down his face. "Did you ever hear such a mess?"

"Life is messy," Gary said. "We all deal with our awful things in our own ways. She respects her fears. You fly in the face of yours, so you have nightmares."

"But I'm trying to figure them out."

"She's probably trying to figure herself out. The fact that she doesn't come to the conclusion you want doesn't mean she isn't working at it."

That was true. A difficult thing to accept, but true. He looked from one parent to the other. "You adopted me to torture me, didn't you?"

"Of course." His father pretended exasperation. "Ben complained so much when I did it to him, we needed another kid to pick on."

"Sounds like I got here just in time to defend myself." Ben came to the table and pulled out the last chair, resting his arm in the sling on the tablecloth. "I always know what to do. That's why I hate being told."

His mother said flatly, "Sometimes you're wrong."

Eyes filled with laughter; Ben maintained a straight face. "I maintain that life is often wrong and when I'm doing the right thing, that makes it *seem* wrong."

Helen turned to Gary. "That's the part of him that takes after your side of the family."

"Incidentally," Ben added, "Justin is doing great and they're stepping up the implantation of that thing—it'll be done tomorrow."

They all agreed that was good news.

Jack cleared his throat and looked from one parent to the other. "You know how much I love both of you." Then he met Ben's eyes and added, "Not you."

"Right."

"Yes," his mother said warily.

"You understand about my wanting to find Corie and Cassie?"

"Of course."

"I was telling Dad earlier, Mom, that I think I've located Corie."

His mother leaned toward him, clearly pleased and excited. He answered all her questions. His sister was in Texas, he had an address, and that was about all he knew. But he wanted to go in person to meet her.

"You go find that girl right now," she said.

"Corie's last address is on the Texas-Mexico border."

Helen said, turning to Ben, "That's not always a safe and friendly place, is it?"

"No, it isn't," Ben replied. "But he's going to have a cop along."

"You're going, too?" his mother asked. "But your arm—"

"Yes." Ben put his good hand up to stop whatever protest Jack intended to make. "I'm fine, Mom. And I'm better with one arm than he is with two."

"Yeah." Jack made a scornful sound. "Someday we'll put that to the test. I'll be fine on my own, Ben."

"You'll be better with me."

His mother groaned. "I'm going to buy that hardware store for the two of you myself."

"I speak a smattering of Spanish." Sarah's voice came from the living-room doorway.

She stood there, face free of makeup, hair tied tightly back, wearing Jack's sleep pants and sweatshirt. "I'd like to come. Everything for the fund-raiser is under control for a few days."

Ben frowned at Jack, who frowned at Sarah. He'd been planning on a quiet meeting with a young woman who might be his sister. What if she didn't want to meet him? What if she didn't care? He'd been hoping to experience that possibility in private.

"Just agree, Jack," his father advised. "If you don't let them go with you, Mom and I are going. Do you really want Backseat-Driving Beulah on your trip?"

Helen gasped. "Backseat-Driving Beulah?"

"Can you be ready tomorrow?" Jack asked Ben.

Ben nodded. "I travel light."

Jack turned to Sarah.

"I don't have many clothes to pack, anyway. How long do you think we'll be gone?"

"Couple of days. If it isn't her, it won't take long. If it is, maybe I can talk her into coming back with me to meet the rest of the family."

"Wouldn't *that* be a Thanksgiving?" Helen put her hands together in anticipation. "Both your families together in the same place at the same time."

"It would." He'd dreamed about that for years, but it might be more than anyone had a right to ask for. Still… There was nothing to lose by asking, anyway.

JACK DROVE THE dusty road to Querida in the silver Navigator he'd rented at the airport, Ben in the passenger seat, reading the map, Sarah in the back, unusually quiet. He caught a glimpse of her in the rearview mirror. She'd pushed up the sleeves of the sweatshirt she wore because the air was hot and heavy and the air conditioning wasn't working well. Neither was the GPS. Her hair was caught back in a high ponytail and she wore the Cavalry cap he'd given her.

He was a little worried about her. He'd given her everything he could give—especially the willingness to live a childless life—but she didn't want him to do it. So they still hadn't resolved anything. He'd talked to her about that this morning when they were getting in the car and Ben had stopped to dig a map out of his bag.

"Please don't worry about *us* on this trip," she'd said. "I just came along to provide moral support. Some things are too hard to do alone. I'm sure that's why Ben's here. He is a cop, but you're every bit as tough as he is. He just doesn't want you to do this by yourself. Just think about Corie, and we'll deal with you and me when we get home. Okay?" She'd kissed his cheek and climbed into the back.

Now he dealt with equal parts terror and excitement. It wasn't as easy to put the matter of Sarah and him aside as she seemed to think. He wanted to resolve his past, but that wouldn't help him if he couldn't have Sarah in his future. He turned his focus to keeping the car on the bumpy road.

The excitement had that element of fear that kept cropping up the closer he got to finding Corie. What if she just wanted to forget her childhood and he just fostered a bad memory?

"Knock it off," Ben said without looking up.

Jack glanced at him, saw him run his finger along a line on the map. "Knock what off?"

"The worry. I can hear your brain clicking on options. She's going to be glad you found her. She's going to want to be family again. She's probably been looking for *you*."

"Why didn't she find me?"

"You've been all over the globe, you nitwit. And in some very inhospitable places. Your name is different. She was four, Jack. Will you keep your eyes on the road? About two and a half miles. On the map, it looks like the only turn to the right. It'll take us into Querida. Then I presume we'll find Rio Road by following the Rio Grande."

Jack nodded. "Brilliant detective work."

"Don't get smart with me. You stole my girl."

"No, he didn't," Sarah chimed in from behind them. "You're very sweet, Ben—well, not this morning, but usually—but I fell in love with Jack."

"Why, in God's name?"

"Because he gave me his hat and changed my lightbulb."

That remark hung among them for a moment and then Ben sighed and said, "Maybe you two are a case of a couple of loonies deserving each other. I, on the other hand, feel free. Loving a woman demands a lot of attention to details that I'd really rather not worry about for a while. A whole world is opening up for me. I'm thinking about quitting the force and starting a detective agency."

A dual "What?" came from his companions.

"No, don't brake," Ben said to Jack. "We're

almost there. Yeah. I've learned a lot I could apply to that. It'd probably be a lot of spouse-tracking at first, but I have quite a few connections. I'll bet I could make it work. Maybe I could even find your sister Cassidy, if Corie doesn't know where she is." He strained to see ahead, consulted the map again and then pointed to a break in the dry brush on the right side of the road. "There. There it is. We follow this for a quarter of a mile, then we'll run into Rio Road." He sat back again. "Of course, I'll be pricey. Based on how much you want to find her, I can charge you double what I charge anyone else. And there's the world of hurt I've suffered from most of a lifetime of having to put up with you. You owe me big, pal."

"Okay. I'll get right on that." Jack turned onto the narrow road, bumped along for a quarter mile, checking the rearview mirror to see how Sarah was doing. She simply bounced along with the movement of the car, watching the high grass go by.

Ben pointed to the Rio Road sign. The road was unpaved with high weeds on both sides. "Aren't you glad I came along?" he asked.

"No bandits to save me from yet. But, yes,

I am. Your incessant yammering has helped me forget that I'm nervous."

"Relax. She's going to be thrilled to see you."

"Yeah."

Querida was a very small town, its downtown only two blocks long. One side of one block seemed to be devoted to public buildings; city hall, post office, library, all built in the hacienda style. Across the street was a small but verdant park with old playground equipment.

The second block held a small café, a beauty shop and a clothing store. Jack pointed it out to Sarah. "We could buy you something lighter weight than what you've brought along."

"Yeah. I didn't realize temperatures would be in the seventies in November. But all their fall stuff is in the windows. Looks more classic than trendy. Probably has a small fashion-minded customer base."

"Down-on-its-luck little town," Ben observed as they passed a little bodega, a bakery, a hardware store, a pharmacy and a run-down bed-and-breakfast.

The commercial buildings, Jack noticed, weren't getting much attention from the municipal government. The city hall block was well maintained with a green lawn and a walkway lined with fall flowers.

He doubted that anything on the commercial block had been painted in years. The bakery had a scraggly pot of flowers hanging from a lamppost, and a row of hardy geraniums flowered in a window box in front of the pharmacy. Otherwise, there were few amenities that suggested prosperity. He remembered the details on Corie's arrest warrant. It was strange that a town this small and in such obvious financial straits would have a deputy mayor.

"It looks like tough times here," Sarah said.

"Yeah. Ah…" Ben consulted his MapQuest printout. "According to this, we follow this road out of town, take a right on Hidalgo and it's a two-minute drive to her address."

"All right." Jack followed Ben's instructions, noting the natural, somewhat barren beauty of their surroundings while being aware of the ramshackle little dwellings along the way.

He made the turn onto Hidalgo, then drove for about a mile and came to a stop in front of a chain-link fence that surrounded a large dusty yard where young children played with a basketball and a soccer ball, and chased each other while screaming and laughing. The condition of the yard was less than optimum, and the large home beyond, also built in hacienda style, looked like something from an old Western movie. The children playing in the yard seemed happy with nothing but a couple of balls and each other to chase. He found himself smiling. Children who were cared for could have fun anywhere.

"Do you think she runs a day care?" Ben asked, peering out his window. "This is the right address."

Jack wasn't sure what to make of all the children.

"Could be. Although, with an arrest on her record, I'm not sure she could do that."

"Yeah, maybe not. But I count eleven children here. They can't all be hers, unless she's had one a year since she was fifteen. And the fence suggests something…you know, institutional, like a school or day-care center."

Jack turned in his seat to look at Sarah. She watched a little boy walking a low stone wall around the house as though it were a tightrope. She looked nervous, thinking probably that if he fell, she'd have to do something about it.

Jack reached behind and touched her knee. Her eyes smiled at him under the brim of his hat. "You want to come?"

"Do you want me to?"

"Sure."

Jack pushed open his door, stepped out and opened hers. Ben remained in the car. Jack leaned in. "You're not telling me you're going to stay behind and risk missing me have the door slammed in my face by someone who isn't my sister, or rejected by someone who is, are you?"

"I thought you'd want to do this by yourself. Or just with Sarah."

"No, I want you to come. If the woman in there gets hostile, we're ducking behind you."

Ben and Sarah followed him through a gate and up a concrete walkway to the big old house, the pale pinkish stone burnished with age. Jack noticed that the porch was swept and pots of Christmas cactus stood on either side of the doorway. He stepped up to the large wooden door, a metallic taste in his mouth.

He heard Ben, standing behind him, shift his weight. Sarah put an encouraging hand to his back.

Jack took a breath and knocked; heard footsteps on the other side. His heart raced as the footsteps grew louder. The door opened, he braced himself, and a woman with a toddler on her hip looked at him in surprise and smiled, the gesture moving to Sarah. The smile changed subtly when her gaze landed on Ben. Jack understood two things at once. The woman somehow knew Ben was a cop. And she wasn't Corie.

She refocused her attention on Jack and the smile returned. "Good afternoon," she said. "What can I do for you?"

Jack offered his hand. "Hello. I'm Jack Palmer. This is my fiancée, Sarah Reed." He felt Sarah react with a start to the title but went on. "And my brother, Ben." Ben and Sarah shook the woman's hand. She smiled politely at them.

"I'm Teresa McGinnis." She indicated the baby. "This is Roberto." The boy, about eighteen months old, reached out to Ben. Ben laughed and took him from her.

"I'm trying to find my sister," Jack said. "We were separated as children when she was four. We called her Corie. I found an Isabel Corazon Ochoa online at this address."

He caught an almost indiscernible flicker in her eyes, a reaction to his explanation that she tried to hide. "I know Corie, but she doesn't live here," she said. "Her mail comes here, but the last I heard she was somewhere near Acapulco."

He absorbed that information with an almost debilitating disappointment. He felt Sarah's touch to his back again. Then he realized he was grateful to know he was on the right trail. He also now knew a third thing about this woman Teresa. She had not been born in Texas. There was nothing slow or Southern in her voice or her manner. She was from somewhere in New England. Massachusetts, he guessed. And she was probably in her forties. "Do you know how I can get in touch with her?"

She shook her head regretfully. "I'm sorry. I wait to hear from her. She's somewhat of a vagabond, and she doesn't believe in cell phones and GPS devices." She laughed lightly. "You'd think she was eighty rather than twenty-seven."

He smiled at that. Eccentric or evading the law? he wondered.

"What does she do?" Ben asked.

The women met his gaze, hers carefully even. "Do?"

"For work? How is she able to travel for such long periods that you wait to hear from her? That her mail has to be taken care of?"

Ben's tone was pleasant but still demanding. The woman clearly didn't like it. Before she could express that dislike, a young woman came into the house through a rear entrance, shouting Teresa's name.

"Tee! Teresa! I have Berto's—" She stopped abruptly at the sight of visitors. Framed in a shaft of light from the window, she was small, wore skinny jeans and a short leather jacket, and possessed a haughty manner as she looked Jack over, then Ben. Her eyes ran over Sarah in a completely different way and showed less suspicion than interest.

She was Corie's age, with an inky sheet of hair that fell past her shoulders, and large dark eyes caught in some kind of storm.

She looked away from the three of them in a gesture of dismissal and delved into a brightly colored woven purse. She pulled out a white paper bag that she handed to Teresa. "Berto's medication." She also pulled a book out of the bag. "And Lita's math book." She smiled at Teresa, said a few words in Spanish, then turned to leave.

"*Momento*, Magdalena," Teresa said, catching the young woman's hand. "This is Jack Palmer and his brother, Ben. They're looking for their sister."

"Actually, by birth she's just *my* sister," Jack

corrected. "When Corie's and my family was separated, I was adopted into Ben's family."

Teresa made a sympathetic sound. "I'm sorry. He thinks Corie might be his sister," she said to Magdalena. "Have you heard from her since we got that card in June?"

Magdalena shook her head. "No, I'm sorry. She was in Acapulco. That's all I know."

"How do you know her?" Ben asked.

Magdalena met his eyes, cool distance in hers. "We worked here together, helping Teresa when we were teenagers," she replied. "I still help once in a while, when she needs a run to the pharmacy or somebody forgets their homework." She backed away again, waving. "Nice to meet you. I hope you find your sister. Bye, Tee. Bye, Berto." And she was gone.

Jack handed Teresa a business card. "Will you give this to Corie when she comes back?"

She pulled Berto from Ben's arms. "I promise I will," Teresa said. "The moment I hear from her, I'll tell her you're looking for her."

Jack shook her hand again. "You've been very kind. Thank you."

Berto waved at Ben, who waved back as Teresa closed the door. Sarah ran down the steps after Jack. Ben put a consoling hand on Jack's shoulder, walking beside him toward the car.

"I'm sorry you couldn't find her today, but at least you know we're on the right track."

Jack kept moving. "You're not going to make much of a detective, Ben. That *was* her. Magdalena *is* Corie."

"What?"

"That was Corie. I don't know why she doesn't want to admit it, but that's her. I was afraid I wouldn't recognize her, but she has that same royal-personage attitude, and the smiling dark eyes hiding fear way down in the depths."

"She didn't *know* you, Jack," Ben said gently.

"Yes, she did. I saw her recognize me."

"I think she did," Sarah corroborated. "I saw that in her eyes, too. And when she spoke to Teresa in Spanish, she said, 'Don't tell him anything.'"

Jack put an arm around her. "I knew it. There's something going on. Teresa made you as a cop right away, Ben, and didn't like it. I don't know if she knows Magdalena is Corie or not. But Corie was a tactical genius, even at four. Come on. We're going to find out what's going on with her. If I can figure out how to find her again."

"Easy," Ben said. "When we said goodbye to Teresa, I saw Magdalena through the window to the back. She drove off in a black Ford pickup. That shouldn't be too hard to find parked somewhere in this little town."

Jack slapped his shoulder as they separated to get into opposite sides of the car. "You're a genius," he praised.

"That's what I keep telling you."

"Oh, please," Sarah groaned, climbing into the back.

CHAPTER SIXTEEN

THEY FOUND CORIE'S truck parked in the driveway of a decrepit little house on a side street downtown. Jack bought a sandwich, Ben a tamale and Sarah a chocolate bar at the bodega; then they made a production of leaving town with the windows open and the radio blaring before circling back and parking behind a low bush a block away from the little house.

They took turns watching and sleeping. Ben elbowed Jack awake in the middle of the afternoon. "Look," he said quietly, pointing through the windshield.

Corie, dressed in a white blouse, a black skirt and low heels, was climbing into the truck. She pulled away with more speed than necessary, spewing dust as she headed for the main street. Ben followed her at a distance, then stopped abruptly when she parked in front of the café. Ben pulled into the drugstore parking lot across the street and parked beside a tractor.

"She could have walked those three blocks," Ben observed, "without using four dollars' worth of gas. You think she works there? That did look like a waitressing uniform."

Jack pulled out the binoculars he'd bought at the airport. "Sounds reasonable," he said absently as he tried to find her through the restaurant window. It took just a moment before he spotted her wearing a ruffle-trimmed apron and carrying a coffeepot to a table in the window. "I guess you'll make a good detective, after all."

Sarah snickered. "That wasn't much of a test. White blouse, black skirt, walking shoes. Nun or waitress. And she's obviously not a nun."

Ben made a face at her. "I thought you came along for moral support."

"I did. For Jack." She snapped off a square of chocolate. "Want one?"

He snatched it from her. "Some clues are more obvious than others," Ben said, defending his investigative powers. "Not everything is shrouded in mystery. But what if she's doing something illegal? If she did recognize you, Jack, that would be about the only reason she wouldn't want to admit she's your sister." He coughed and sipped at his soda. "Except for the obvious reason."

Jack turned to him. "And that is?"

"Well, it's you. Who'd want to admit being related to you? I mean, *I* can always say you were adopted, but if that is Corie, she shares blood with you. Poor thing." He shook his head in a helpless gesture. "I don't know what Sarah's problem is."

She patted Ben's shoulder. "Probably that I dated you first."

Jack sighed and handed him the binoculars. "There's still an hour and twenty minutes left on your watch. Wake me up again if anything happens. And you were pretty glad I had your back when the Duffy brothers caught you in that alley behind Safeway when we were kids. Just because Susan Federer made eyes at you in the cafeteria when she was supposed to be Eddy Duffy's girlfriend."

Ben thought back and winced. "We lost that fight."

"I know. But I still waded in to help. You can't get that kind of support from just anybody. Especially when you're outnumbered."

"Go to sleep. And I've always been a stud. I can't control it."

"Saints preserve me!" Sarah said. "I feel

like I'm stuck in a bad episode of *The Bachelor*! Please do me a favor, and both of you go to sleep and I'll watch."

BEN DOZED IN the back and Jack in the passenger seat when Sarah, behind the wheel, saw Corie come out of the café well after 10:00 p.m. "Jack!" She elbowed him. "Wake up! There she is."

Jack sat up, blinking against the darkness, peering through the windshield. They still sat in the parking lot and the tractor had long since moved on. "We'll just sit here until she takes off, then follow slowly. Can you do that?"

Sarah tried not to be offended by the question. "Of course I can do that."

Ben woke in the back. "I'll drive, Sarah."

"You've been shot in the arm. I'll drive. And there she goes. We don't have time to change seats. She's changed her clothes, though."

Corie had climbed into the truck in the black jeans and jacket they'd seen her in at Teresa's. But her hair had been shoved into a watch cap—also black. "Aha," Ben said. "She's probably military and this is some kind of black ops thing."

"She's probably just going home to take a bath and feed the cat," Jack said.

"Go!" Ben said. "There she goes. Keep your distance, but don't lose her!"

"Relax," Sarah said. "I've had defensive-driving training."

"Then let's see some of it!" Ben said. "She's turning the corner!"

Sarah followed her up a narrow country road. "Where is she going?" she wondered aloud, relaxing a little as they reached the state highway headed east. Darkness still seemed to absorb the frail light from the side of the road and the highway lights posted at distant intervals.

"Not a clue," Jack replied. "Maybe she's got a boyfriend."

Ben made a scornful sound. "I'll bet he's up to his eyeballs in frayed nerves."

That was probably true, Jack thought, but all he could remember was the screaming little girl who'd been ripped away from him all those years ago. "She was such a cute little kid," he said.

"She's a beautiful young woman," Ben conceded, "but she looks like trouble, Jack. And she's obviously up to something if she didn't want you to know who she is."

"We all have things to hide."

"No, we don't. Just promise me you're not going to do anything stupid."

"Like what?"

"I don't know. Hard to say when we don't know what's going on. But I know you. Hero through and through. I've got a bad feeling."

"That's the tamale you bought at the bodega. Look, her blinker's on. Looks like we're going north on 77, Sarah."

"I know, Jack," she said patiently. "It's not like I'm driving with my eyes closed. What's up there? Check the map."

Jack held the map under a dash light. "Ah... Raymondville, Kingsville and, just off this road, Corpus Christi. But that's a couple of hours away."

"What time is it?"

"Almost eleven."

Sarah allowed a BMW to get between them and Corie's truck. She relaxed and prepared herself for a long drive.

A couple of hours later, when Corie turned off onto Interstate 37, Jack had a feeling they were headed for Corpus Christi.

Sarah followed Corie silently, staying back, making sure they didn't lose sight of her.

"You getting tired?" Jack asked. "I can take over."

"Thanks, but I'm fine."

Corie made several turns, then followed a sign that promised only two miles to Corpus Christi.

"I wonder what's here for her," Sarah said.

"We'll see soon enough."

And they did. Corie went through the brightly lit downtown to Ocean Drive and an area of elegant, upscale homes.

"Okay, Jack," Ben said, an edgy tone to his voice as he leaned forward. "What's she doing *here*?"

"I don't know. Stay with her, Sarah."

"Sit back and let me drive," Sarah said.

"When did you get so bossy? You were never like that with me. Jack's been a bad influence on you." He punched Jack in the shoulder, still leaning forward.

Toward the end of Ocean Drive, Corie slowed, turned off her headlights and drove at a crawl up a narrow, tree-lined lane that led to a plantation-style home. There were lights on in the veranda and the shrubbery that surrounded it.

Sarah turned off their headlights. She waited until Corie had reached the house be-

fore following, and then went only halfway
up. "If I get any closer," she said quietly to
Jack, "she'll see us."

"Right." He opened his door. "You two stay
in the car."

"Jack—"

JACK DIDN'T STAY to listen to whatever caution
Ben or Sarah had to offer. This was his little
sister.

Binoculars in his pocket, he ran at a crouch
through the trees on the side of the lane until
he could see her truck. She'd gotten out of it
and, a small bag slung over her shoulder, did
what he was doing—stayed in the shelter of
the trees until she got to the garage.

Afraid to let his brain reach the obvious
conclusion, he simply watched her creep along
the garage wall, then around the corner. The
moment she was out of sight, he followed,
moving as silently as possible.

At the edge of the garage, he peered around
it and saw her on the back porch working on
the entry door with a tool, a small flashlight
in her mouth pointed at her work. She did it
with remarkable ease, as though this wasn't
the first time.

Now the conclusion reached *him*. She was a thief. Oh, good. His sister was a crook.

He had just made the decision to take her by surprise and stop her from entering the house when she let herself in. Though he hurried to the door, he was momentarily distracted by wires dangling in his face. Apparently the little girl who'd once eviscerated one of his GoBots could disarm a security system. With a silent groan, he pushed the door open the rest of the way, but she was nowhere in sight.

He was in a very large kitchen. It was hard to tell in the shadows, but it appeared to be all white and stainless steel with no place at all to have cake and coffee.

He heard a floorboard creak above his head and noticed what had once probably been the servants' stairway at the back of the kitchen. He moved toward it, listening. He was guessing no one was home, but the garage doors had been closed, so it was impossible to know for sure.

Some minutes later the floorboard creaked again and then he heard the scrape of a chair being pushed back and heavier footsteps. A deep male voice said, "Who's there?"

His heart in his throat, sure he was going to have to save Corie from being shot, Jack put one foot on the steps, about to run up them, when he heard a whoosh of movement at the top, and from the moonlight through a side window saw Corie come flying down—straight into his arms.

This time, fear in her eyes, her mouth open in an O of astonishment, she threw her arms around his neck and held. "Jack!" she whispered against him. She was shaking.

Heavy footsteps started down the stairs accompanied by a loud string of invectives. Jack turned quickly, yanking Corie after him. He shoved her ahead of him onto the back porch, whispering "Run!" and stopping just long enough to turn the lock and pull the door closed after him. He heard her racing away and chased her into the night.

As floodlights went on all over the property and the owner stepped out onto the porch, angry curses spilling from his mouth, Jack ran for the trees. He was almost there when he was tackled from the side and went down on his stomach beside a knee-high bush, the air knocked out of him.

Thinking the angry owner had friends, he elbowed backward, prepared to struggle. Then he heard Ben's grunt and a whispered plea.

"It's me, genius! Stay down! You, too, you little crook!"

A soft hand touched his face. "You okay, Jack?" Sarah whispered.

"You were supposed to wait in the car!"

"Yeah. That's what you thought."

Jack heard a struggle going on right behind him. It sounded like slaps and punches and grunts. Then Ben gasped in pain. "Hey! I've been shot in that arm. Stay down or I'll hand you over to this guy!"

"How'd you like me to punch that arm again? Who made you king, anyway?"

"Corie!" Jack looked over his shoulder. "Stay down and shut up!"

Sarah said, "It's okay, Corie. Ben just wants to help. Nobody's going to let this guy have you."

The owner walked down the steps, still swearing, a shotgun at the ready as he scanned the yard.

"We've got to get out of here," Ben said under his voice. "He's coming this way."

"Take Sarah and Corie to Corie's truck," Jack ordered Ben. "I'm going to distract the guy. Drive the truck to the road and wait by our car. I'll meet you there."

"Jack…" Ben began to caution, but Jack

didn't listen. He ran silently through the trees, aware of the big guy scanning a grid pattern through the garden, looking behind the tall, ornamental pots. Jack made it to the alarm Corie had disabled. He reconnected it and was immediately deafened by the blare of noise.

Flattened against the side of the house, he saw the guy turn and race back in his direction. He threw a pot of geraniums at the garage wall, then ducked behind the house as the guy turned back in his direction. Jack ran around the house to the other side and stayed in the trees until he reached the road.

He saw the rented Navigator about ten yards away, Corie's truck idling beside it, and he rushed toward them. He opened the passenger door of the truck and pulled Corie out. "Can you follow me in the truck?" he asked Ben. "Is your arm up to it?"

"Yeah," Ben snapped. "No thanks to your sister." Sarah, however, had already jumped out of the middle and into the driver's seat, giving Ben a shove.

"Move over. I'm driving."

"No, I—"

"This is no time to argue!"

"All right, let's go."

"Jack, I can't go with you!" Corie said. Her voice was high, breathless. "I—"

"We'll talk about it when we can stop. Get in the car."

He pushed her toward the Navigator. When she resisted, he said, "You'd rather get caught?"

With a despondent shake of her head, she got in the car. He climbed into the other side and drove off doing seventy, Sarah and Ben in the truck right behind him.

They were on 77 heading south before Jack felt safe enough, calm enough, to speak. As far as he could tell, they weren't being followed, except by Ben. He shot a glance at his sister, the excitement that had lived in him throughout the trip not even fractionally diminished by the knowledge that she was a criminal. He'd just seen her disable an alarm and break into an elegant home in an upscale neighborhood. He hated that, but he still loved that he'd found her.

"Do you want to tell me what you were doing in that house?" he asked. He pointed to the glove box. "There's a bag of peanuts in there if you're hungry."

He felt her turn to him and took his eyes off a clear patch of road for just an instant to glance her way. It was dark inside the car, but he saw the anger in her eyes. Under it, though, was shock and worry. And something else he couldn't identify. She was beautiful and looked a lot like their mother, except that she had dark hair and eyes. She'd ripped her hat off a few miles back, combed through her hair with her fingers, then knotted it up like he'd seen Sarah do with hers—with a carelessness that looked messy, yet somehow attractive.

She turned away. "No, on the telling you what I was doing in the house, and no thank you on the peanuts." She had a surprisingly raspy voice. "You want to tell me where we're going? How on God's earth you found me? And why?"

"No, on the telling you where we're going, and no on the how I found you," he replied. "If I get nothing, you get nothing. Except the why. It's because I've wanted to find you and Cassie since the day they took you away. I've imagined it, dreamed of it, almost gave up, hoping you'd be looking for me. But you weren't, so I had to keep trying. Because you're my little sister and though you made me crazy when we were kids, I loved you. I love you now. And it seems you're still going to make me crazy."

Without warning, she burst into tears. The

car filled with the sound and Jack said her name evenly, hoping to calm her. But the sobbing only increased, seeming to come from deep inside. He put a hand out to her and she caught it, grinding her fingernails into his palm. "Jack!" she wept. "Jack. I can't believe you're here."

He spotted a rest area sign and turned on his right turn signal. He checked his rearview mirror to make sure Sarah saw him. She, too, signaled a right turn and followed Jack off the road into a small park surrounded by trees. Streetlights brightened the darkness but left a picnic table in the middle in shadow.

Jack led Corie to the table and sat her on the bench, then straddled it and wrapped his arms around her. She held him as the sobs continued to rip out of her.

Out of the corner of his eye, he saw Sarah and Ben approaching, then stopping, obviously reluctant to intrude on this intense moment between Corie and him.

At last Corie stopped crying enough to say, "For years I hoped you'd find me—" her eyes still swam with tears "—but then I gave up. I mean, *really* gave up." She looked down at the bench, fresh tears flowing. "My father died. Life was awful. I'd lost touch with Cassie—"

"You've heard from Cassie?"

"A long time ago. I was twelve when I got the last letter. She went away, I think. Europe or somewhere." She pressed herself closer to Jack. "I can't believe you're here."

So she *did* care. She hadn't forgotten.

She straightened abruptly and dragged the sleeve of her jacket across her eyes. "But I can't go with you. Whatever you're thinking about us...you know, being family again, I can't do it. I've got my own life now. I...I have plans. Things I have to do."

Jack gestured Sarah closer. She came to sit beside Corie. "This is Sarah. We're getting married. I'd really like you to get to know her."

Corie looked Sarah over, suspicion in her tearful gaze. After a moment she said, "Hi, Sarah. I'd like to get to know you, too, but I have a lot to do right now."

Ben appeared beside them and offered Corie a thermos cup filled with water. "Like break into another house?" he asked.

"Ben," Sarah scolded.

"Okay," he said. "I got the thermos from your truck, Corie. Thought you needed some water."

Corie took the cup and drank from it, then

handed it back to Ben. "I have my own life now," she said.

This was the very thing Jack had feared. She had her own life and he would be a reminder of her unhappy past. But there was more at work here. He'd witnessed her big-brother adoration. Was she somehow protecting *him* rather than herself?

"Are you married?" he asked.

"No."

"Do you have children?"

"No."

"Then it's a life that could use a little livening up. I'm taking you home to Oregon with us. My mother, my adopted mother, wants you to have Thanksgiving with us. Maybe together we can find Cassie."

He saw longing in her eyes for the scenario he'd painted. Then she shook her head. "I can't right now."

"Why not?"

She looked up at him stubbornly. "I just can't." Then she added in a high, frail voice, "But I love that you came for me."

Ben leaned over her. He pointed to a small fabric bag strung across her chest. "Can I have a look at that?" he asked.

She stiffened and wiped at her eyes again. "Can't you see it from there?"

He acknowledged her deliberately obtuse response with a phony smile. "I'd like to see *inside* it."

She turned away. "Well, you can't."

"What is it you don't want us to see?" Ben persisted.

She studied him for a minute and Jack remembered the little girl who'd told him she hadn't eaten his Twinkies when she had cream all over her lips.

"The mysteries of my makeup routine," she replied, returning his phony smile. She gestured toward her face, mascara and lipstick smeared. "Can't have everyone copying this CoverGirl look."

Without warning, Ben caught the strap in his fingers and tore it off her.

"Hey!" she complained at the same moment that Jack and Sarah shouted simultaneously, "Ben!"

She grabbed for the purse. Ben held her away with his good arm and handed the contents to Jack with his swollen fingers. Overturning the bag onto the table, Jack swore. He hoped his eyes were deceived by the shadows where they sat, but the jewels that spilled out gleamed like the real thing. There were several necklaces that appeared to be diamonds in various sizes, a large pendant that was probably gold, and a cluster of brilliant green stones. Emeralds.

"Omigod," Sarah whispered.

When Jack looked up, he could see that Ben was beyond exasperated. "If we go to jail for this, Jack, you're going to be sorry," Ben said. He looked at Corie, his expression turning severe. "You tell us right now what's going on. Your brother just spent half his adult life in Iraq and Afghanistan and came home wanting nothing more than to find you and your sister. If he ends up doing time in the State of Texas because his little sister is a common thief, I will make you miserable, young lady."

"You're already doing that!" she shouted at him. Then she turned to Jack and demanded, "Who *is* he?"

Jack had to smile. "Don't you remember Ben Palmer?"

She frowned as she turned reluctantly to study Ben.

"He was my friend." Jack tried to encourage the memory. "You and Cassie and I used to play ball with him and Marty Brogan at the park. We spent a couple of days with him and his parents before the state sent you and Cassie back to your dads."

He saw the pain move in her eyes; the same thing that always happened to him when he thought about that time.

Ben offered her the cup of water again. "You used to love to walk on that old brick path in front of Mrs. Brogan's house, and I used to hold your hand to keep you steady while Jack carried Cassidy."

Her eyes lit up for an instant and she looked into his face. Then something dark seemed to crowd out the memory.

"He's my brother," Jack said, trying to pull her out of whatever bad thoughts she was having. "My dad was dead, so I had no one to go to. Ben's parents adopted me."

She nodded grimly. "Wow. Lucky."

"I was," he said. "I am. I'd like you to meet them and to share them with you."

Her smile saddened. "I had a fairy-tale life, too, in the beginning. My father died when I was twelve. His wife never really liked me. She had two daughters, just like Cinderella's stepmother." Corie laughed, the sound hollow. "She sort of sold me to a friend who turned me into a housekeeper-slave and usually forgot to feed me. One day I met Teresa. She was at the bodega, buying fruit, and she caught me stealing a banana from her bag. She took me home with her."

"You mean, Teresa from the day care?"

"It's not a day care. It's a sort of unofficial foster home. In a border town like Querida filled with people coming and going, some legal, some not, no one pays much attention as long as no one gets in trouble. I've been helping her support it with my job as a waitress and—" she shrugged "—a few freelance jobs."

Ben held up one of the diamond necklaces. "Freelance?"

She snatched it from him and put everything back in the bag. "That rat is throwing Teresa out," she said, sadness gone, anger back, "and I won't let that happen. So I can't go anywhere."

"What rat?"

"Cyrus Tyree. The man whose house I broke into. His father owned the house and property Teresa rents, and he never cared if she was occasionally a little late with the rent. But he died two years ago and that guy you saw tonight is always trying to throw her out. She's behind only two months, but he's added penalties and says he's going to make her pay for damage to the kitchen, which wasn't her fault anyway, because a water pipe broke, and that was because he never fixes anything. I have to find her thirty-five hundred dollars by the day after tomorrow or Teresa is out."

"Why did she pretend that you were Magdalena, and not Corie?"

She looked away, shaking her head, then back at him. "Because the deputy mayor likes to hassle me and the chief of police is his friend. At the moment, I'm not in their good books. Teresa didn't know who you were. Magdalena was the name I thought I wanted when I was twelve and dreaming of rescue."

"But I told her I'm your brother. That I was trying to find you."

"We don't trust just anybody. It's safer."

"Why are they hassling you? That assault charge?"

When she looked surprised that he knew about that, he explained about finding it in his search for her.

"That charge was filed by the creepy deputy mayor, who was trying to get *payment* from me—" the emphasis indicated that the payment wasn't necessarily in money "—in exchange for his cooperation in helping Teresa fight Tyree. I didn't give him his payment.

In fact, I had to hit him with my purse so he
didn't *take* it. Needless to say, after a year of
scrounging for every dime, Tyree is about to
throw Teresa out."

"You did enough damage with a purse to
warrant your arrest?"

She grinned. "It had my tips from the restaurant in it. In a coffee can." Then she sighed.
"So Teresa struggles every month with her ba-
sically crooked landlord, and no one will help
because the mayor's office is corrupt. Anyway, I'm going to sell Tyree's wife's jewelry."

Ben arched an eyebrow. "To who?"

It was clear she didn't want to answer, but
she was beginning to know Ben, so she replied, "There's a guy in the courthouse who
can find a buyer."

"Corie, I'm a cop," Ben said. "You can't
keep or sell this stuff."

Suddenly, Corie was up and running, with
her bag, and would have beaten them to her
truck and driven off if she hadn't tripped and
fallen. Jack helped her to her feet and hung on
to her, while Ben took the cloth bag and lec-
tured her on the ramifications of what she'd
done. "You're going to get us all thrown in
the slammer."

"Listen to them, Corie," Sarah said. She'd followed Jack and Ben. "They're right."

Corie struggled against Jack's hold, but he held fast.

"You have to return those jewels," Ben said. "There are other ways to handle someone like Tyree."

"Yeah?" She scowled. "You mean call a *cop*?" The word writhed with scorn. "The guy who can get me a buyer is a cop. The local pimp is a cop. Every store owner in town pays twenty-five percent of his take every month to a cop! There's no justice in Querida, brother Ben, so that's not an option here. I suppose if I gave you this to return it, it'd find its way into *your* pocket."

"He's not that kind of cop," Jack said. "And he's right. The jewelry has to go back. We'll find another way to help Teresa."

"How? If she's tossed out of the house, Berto's going to get sick again and Lita and all the other kids who have no one but her..."

"Did you say thirty-five hundred dollars?" Jack asked.

She stopped ranting and stood quietly. "Yes."

"I can get two thousand out of the bank," Jack said, then turned to Ben. "Sorry. My savings is in Certificates of Deposit. What about you?"

Ben stared back at him disbelievingly, then sighed. "I've got a thousand on me," he said. "And I can get the rest out of an ATM. But you're going to owe me so much interest—"

"I've got a couple hundred," Sarah said. She patted Corie's shoulder. "See? We can fix this."

"I've got three hundred in tips," Corie put in.

Ben stared at her. "You don't have to contribute hard-earned tips. We can give the full amount."

"I was going to sell this stuff, remember? If you hadn't appeared, I'd have *had* to come up with *all* of it. Teresa gave me a home. You can't know what that means to a kid."

"Easy," Ben said. "You're like a cannon with too much powder."

"Yeah, well, I'm aimed at you, dude, so watch it." Then she looked from one to the other and shifted her weight. "But thank you," she said more quietly.

"You get the money," Jack bargained, suddenly realizing he had the upper hand, "if you agree to come home with us to Beggar's Bay."

Corie spread her arms helplessly. "Jack, I'm not going to fit in with the Palmers. Like I told you before, I love that you found me, but I can't go with you. My life—"

"If you don't come with us—" Ben backed him up "—he won't give you the money for Teresa. I'll see to that."

She glared at Ben. "Yeah. You seem like a real sweetheart."

Jack said nothing, simply opened the passenger-side door of the rental car for her. She got in without another word.

"You owe me so big," Ben said to Jack, then gave him a wide grin. "I can see this is going to be so much fun."

Jack smacked his good arm. "Yeah, I do owe you big. Thanks, Ben."

CHAPTER SEVENTEEN

TERESA STUDIED THE fat envelope of money suspiciously. It was just before noon the next day. After spending the remainder of the night in Corie's little house, Jack, Ben and Sarah had driven to the café for breakfast. Jack had gone to an ATM and withdrawn two thousand dollars and then all four had headed to Teresa's.

Teresa opened the envelope and looked at Corie with wide eyes. "What did you do this time, Corazon? Your vision of right and wrong is very imaginative but not acceptable to the law."

Corie indicated Jack and Ben. "My brother gave it to me. And his brother. And his fiancée."

"Three hundred of it is her tip money," Jack corrected. "That should keep you going until the end of the month. Then maybe we can figure out what to do so this doesn't keep happening to you."

Teresa stared at him in apparent confusion. "Why do you care?"

"Because Corie cares. Because you gave her a home and I know what a big thing that is. It makes me care about you."

Teresa hugged him, then Ben, then Sarah.

"I'm taking Corie with me to meet my family," Jack said. "You'll have to do without her for a couple of weeks."

Teresa put a hand to Corie's cheek, love in her eyes. She held her tightly for a long moment, then let her go. "It will be hard for me. She's a light in my life. And the children adore her. But I'm so happy you've found her. She needs to connect with you and her sister. Do you know where she is?"

"No. But we're going to keep looking until we find her."

Teresa hugged Corie one more time before Corie ran around the room hugging children. Jack, Ben and Sarah followed her out into the yard and watched her with a group of little boys playing baseball. They didn't want to stop playing, but something she said brought them all to her for a group hug.

Sarah had to turn away and wander toward the car as her eyes filled with tears. She felt the giant hole that had lived inside her the past two years fill with the love that vibrated in the air. Teresa's love for Corie, Corie's love for the children and theirs for her, Jack's love for his sister and the sadness he felt at her pain. For the first time since Jerica died, hope sprouted in Sarah.

When everyone returned to the car, tears were rolling down Corie's cheeks.

"It's going to be okay," Jack told her, tossing her bag into the back and holding the door open for her.

"Yeah," she said wryly. "That's what you told me when the woman from DHS came to take me away." She moved to climb in after her bag, but he caught her arm and stopped her.

"I'm not eight years old this time," he said. "I'm better able to keep my promises."

"I'm sorry." Her mouth was unsteady. "I know it wasn't your fault. It was *hers*. Mom's."

"Do you remember her?" he asked.

She nodded, old pain tightening the line of her mouth. "She was so beautiful. She should have been a good person. But she wasn't."

"Yeah." He hugged her, then urged her into the car. "Get in. We're going home."

HELEN AND GARY came out of the house to meet them when they arrived in Beggar's Bay around eight that evening. The light over the back door lit the driveway and the cold night smelled of rain.

Helen hugged both brothers, then Sarah, and offered her hands to Corie. Jack introduced Gary, who told her how happy he and Helen were that she had come.

Corie's eyes brightened. "I do remember you. And a really big kitchen."

Helen led her into it. There was commotion as everyone came in and gathered chairs around the kitchen table, snagging a straight-back from the living room, while Sarah made coffee and pulled out the turtle brownies Helen had made earlier.

"I think it's bedtime for some of us," Helen declared after she'd encouraged Corie to eat a couple of brownies. She turned to Corie now, put an arm around her shoulders and said, "We've put an extra bed in Sarah's room. There's a nice big tub up there and everything you need to have a long, relaxing bath. But if you'd rather just go right to bed, you're welcome to do that, too. Where are her bags, Jack?"

Jack stood and gestured at a worn canvas backpack he'd set in a corner. It was all Corie had brought, except for the little fabric purse he held in his other hand and a big, colorful straw bag she'd carried on her shoulder.

Corie reached toward Jack for the cloth bag. He held it away, giving her a fractional smile. "I'll carry it for you."

Her eyes met his and then went to the little bag. She sighed, apparently realizing she wasn't going to see its contents again. "Thank you," Corie said, turning to follow Helen toward the stairs.

Jack handed the small purse to Ben, who took off with it out the back door. Jack started up the stairs with the canvas backpack.

SARAH UNDERSTOOD CORIE's desperation to help Teresa, but hoped what she'd done wouldn't result in problems for Jack and Ben. Jack loved her so much.

Sarah watched him follow his sister and experienced a sense of rightness, of well-being she hadn't known in a long time. She remained still for a moment as the past two years of her life seemed to reorganize themselves in her mind into something she finally understood.

Losing Jerica had been a life-altering moment. She'd been on overload with nursing sick and dying children for some time, and watching Jerica get the best care, fight valiantly and die anyway had been more than she could deal with. The impact of the loss had spread across her plans for her future, leading her to make the decision to be childless.

But she'd been alone then. She hadn't known Jack. She'd known Ben, of course, who was warm and wonderful and the kind of man any woman would welcome into her life, but Jack's childhood had been an awful ordeal that he'd come out of hopeful and strong— and wanting to share it.

Life with Jack, she realized now, would be worth any risk. Whatever she might have to suffer, she could suffer if they were together.

She had to tell him. She waited at the bottom of the steps for him to return, but the landline rang. With no one around downstairs to answer it, and with Helen busy with Corie upstairs and Gary upstairs, too, she went to the wall phone in the kitchen.

Sarah didn't recognize the voice on the phone. "Sarah Reed?" a cheerful-sounding man asked.

"Yes," she replied.

"Sarah, this is Dr. James Weston of the new River Rose Retirement Village. Do you have a minute?"

"Uh, sure." She leaned against the wall. "How can I help you, Dr. Weston?"

"I'm sorry to call so late, but this is the first chance I've had to sit at my desk for a few minutes."

"It's all right. What can I do for you?"

"I'd like you to consider becoming the administrator for Rose River," he said. "I'm sure you've noticed we're under construction across from the grade school."

She straightened, certain she couldn't have heard that correctly.

"Sarah?" he asked after a minute.

"I'm here." She pulled over a kitchen chair and sat. "What did you say, Doctor?"

He repeated the offer. She hadn't misunderstood.

"Dr. Weston, I've never administered anything," she said, flattered but disbelieving. "You must have me confused with another nurse."

"John Baldrich sent me your résumé," he said. She heard the rustling of paper. "You seem to have a full complement of talents. You were a pediatric nurse and yet when you came to Beggar's Bay, you went to work for Coast Care as a home-care worker, though you've maintained your license. John says your clients love you. Also—" there was a pause "—Justin, whose life you saved the other day, is the son of a woman who works for me.

"She said you were wonderful. Calm. Competent. True grace under pressure. And while dealing with a group of seniors in varying stages of health is different than caring for kids, I think you'd be very good at it. I was hoping you'd come by next week and visit with the board, see what our facility will look like, talk about salary, perks, whatever else you'd like to talk about."

Her mouth stood open.

"Sarah?" he asked again.

"Uh, I'm not licensed for administration, Doctor."

"I know, but I think you could handle that easily with your credentials and experience. Maybe you'll have to take a management class. The facility doesn't open for another six months, but you're our first choice. We'd love it if you'd work toward getting licensed."

"Okay," she said finally. "It's a busy time for me. You probably know I'm helping with the seniors' talent show. And, frankly, I was imagining my life going in a completely different direction. But it wouldn't hurt to talk."

"It's always good to talk."

He suggested a date. She checked her client calendar. She'd be back to work next week and she had Vinny and Margaret that morning. "I have clients early. Can we do it over lunch or in the afternoon?"

"Lunch it is," he said before ending the call.

Sarah couldn't quite believe what had just happened. She loved her seniors, and the opportunity to help keep them healthy and a viable part of a lively community was an exciting thought. Her grief over Jerica and all she couldn't do to save sick children was now put away, love for Jack and his family blossoming over it. And hope over everything.

JACK HAD LEFT his mother fussing over Corie and gone back downstairs. He had to talk to Sarah. She'd been a stalwart companion on their trip to Texas, and her feminine approach to discord had helped a lot in dealing with Corie.

But he wanted more than a friend in her. He wanted a wife. He wanted a mother for his children, too, but that wasn't going to happen, so he'd find other ways to deal with his need to parent. He could coach soccer, help with a Boy Scout troop and, when Ben got married one day, he'd be the best uncle any kid ever had.

Downstairs, he saw Sarah in earnest conversation on the phone and detoured to the carriage house in search of Ben.

Jack found him sitting on the sofa, leaning over the coffee table and sealing a priority-mail box with packaging tape. He guessed by Corie's fabric bag, lying flat on the sofa beside him, that the box contained the jewelry.

"We're mailing it back?" he asked.

"Safer than trying to return it in person." Jack held up the package and shook it. It didn't rattle. "I packed it in bubble wrap. No one will suspect it contains a small fortune in jewelry. I made a label without a return address and got the postage online."

"It'll be postmarked from here."

"Not if I send it with Grady to Seattle to mail it. He's going there to visit his girlfriend tomorrow."

Jack sat beside him. "Thank you. I know it's hard for you to do something so…"

"Illegal? Semi-criminal?"

"I was going to say, 'helpfully discreet.'"

"Yeah, well, call it what you want. It doesn't change what it is. But we don't want your little sister to go to jail, or we might go along. At this point, the three of us are accomplices."

Jack sighed. "Thanks, Ben."

"Sure."

"You know," Jack began cautiously, awkwardly, "that you're as much my brother as she is my sister?"

Ben messed with the package for another few moments, then finally turned to him, his eyes serious. "Yes," he said. Then he pushed his hands against his knees and stood. "That must be why you stole my girl and took me on that delightful trip to sunny, southern Texas, where I drove half the night, was almost shot and got a terminal intestinal disturbance from a bad tamale."

Jack stood, too. "*You* insisted on coming. And *you* bought the tamale. I can't watch you every minute. Quit complaining."

"Okay." Ben left the box on the coffee table. "Keep that safe tonight. Grady's coming for it in the morning."

As they started toward the door, Jack caught a glimpse of something pale blue out of the corner of his eye. He turned to see a large bouquet of dried hydrangea in the fireplace. Sarah. Something inside him melted.

There was a light rap on the door and Jack

moved to answer it. Corie stood there in her skinny jeans and the red sweater he recognized as the one Sarah loved from his mother's closet. She smiled. "Your mom sent me to get you, Jack. She said you shouldn't sleep here tonight, that your dad worked on the heater back here while you were gone and it's still not working. You should come to the house and sleep in the recliner. She also said you should show me what you've done in here."

He gestured her past him and down the small corridor. She stopped abruptly at the sight of Ben. "Hi," she said stiffly. "Your mother sent me."

"I heard." He handed her the empty fabric purse. Then turning to Jack, he said, "I'll leave you to show off your talents," then skinned past Corie, who flattened herself against the wall to let him by.

When the door closed behind Ben, Jack led Corie into the kitchen, telling her about his plans to put in tin ceiling tiles and stain the cupboards a golden oak.

"That's beautiful," she said. "I love that shade of green on the walls."

"My mother picked out the colors."

He walked her through the living room, showing off the new French doors, the fireplace mantel and the new light fixture, then into the bathroom, which was now pristine with improvements. When they returned to the living room, he noticed the mirror his mother had brought home still leaning in a corner.

"Sarah seems nice," Corie said, putting a fingertip to the flowers he told her she'd dried. "Your whole family is very kind. You got really lucky, Jack."

"I did. And no one realizes that more than I do. Aren't you glad I bullied you into coming?"

She thought a moment, then smiled reluctantly. "I am, sort of."

"Why sort of?"

They walked toward the doorway and she looked away. "Because…it's nice here, but it's not the kind of place where I fit in."

"You mean you're not comfortable here?"

She sighed, seeming frustrated that he didn't understand. "No. Everyone's gone above and beyond to make me welcome. I mean that I don't belong."

"Why?"

She gave him a dark look. "You know why."

She started for the door. He caught her arm

to stop her. "You mean—" he shook his head "—your criminal tendencies?"

She wasn't amused. Tears stood in her eyes. "They're not tendencies, Jack, they're skills. I've used them for a long time and they're now a part of me. I don't fit in with cops and nurses and professional people. I was a gutter rat as a kid, and though I've learned how to survive since then, I'll always be what our childhood—what our mother and my stepmother—made me."

"No!" he said vehemently, then repeated the word with deliberate calm. "No. I've lived my entire life trying to get over our childhood, too. I had all those same insecurities— never good enough or smart enough. Then I realized it wasn't that I didn't measure up, it was that I was *afraid* I wouldn't measure up. You've got everything it takes. Just don't be afraid."

She indicated his elegant surroundings. "Easy for you to say."

"No," he said. "It's not. Love erases the fear. You'll have to stick around here long enough to feel it."

She opened the door. A fragrant fall wind raced inside. "Teresa can't do without me that long. I'm one of those people love doesn't recognize, anyway. Good night, Jack."

JACK HELD THE door open to call Corie back, but saw Sarah passing her as she came toward the carriage house. She wore a bright smile that dimmed as she looked into Corie's face.

They stopped in the middle of the walk illuminated by the light from the house's kitchen window. They spoke quietly, Corie suddenly more animated than she'd been with him. She must have said something to alleviate Sarah's concern; they hugged briefly, then each kept going.

His worry about Corie slipped behind the sight of Sarah's incandescent smile. He held the door wider; she marched in past him and didn't wait for him to close the door before flying into his arms.

He couldn't imagine what had brought that on, but he simply went with it, responding in kind.

"How many children do you want?" she asked, nibbling on his ear.

His brain had disengaged. He needed a number. But he came back with an answer, anyway. "An SUV full. With room for you, of course."

"How many is that? Six? Five? Sometimes the middle seat only holds two."

She wrapped her arms around his waist and

leaned her cheek against his shoulder. For a second, their hearts beat in unison.

"We'll renegotiate after five," he laughed. "What happened? You've done a 360-degree turn."

She sighed. "I just couldn't imagine us being able to have a life together when I was refusing to have children, which you wanted so much. Then I saw you with Corie, and Corie with the kids at Teresa's, and I realized the simple truth that's escaped me all this time." She met his gaze and finished. "Life is risky. Everybody hurts sometime. And everybody goes on."

He crushed her to him. After a long moment she leaned back to look into his eyes, hers soft with dreams realized. "Will you marry me?" she whispered. "I can finally love you without depriving you of what you want out of life."

"Yes! All I want is you. Children are a bonus."

She was beginning to tremble. He pushed the door closed. He kissed her again and said on a laugh, "This really did just happen, didn't it? You proposed to me? Offered to have my children?"

"I did. And you said yes."

"I did. Dreams coming true all around."

"One more thing."

"Yes?"

"I was just invited by Dr. James Weston to meet the board of the River Rose Retirement Village about a job," she said.

That was the last thing he'd expected. "Wow. Is that good? I thought you felt burned out with nursing."

"This would be as the administrator."

"Sarah!"

"I know. It shocked me, too. They just want to meet me. I'd have to do some preparatory things to get licensed, but the place doesn't open until early in the summer. The doctor said I was their first choice."

"You've done a lot of hard things. Maybe you deserve a rest."

She looked into his eyes, her gaze softening further with love for him. "You've been to war, but you're not resting. You're restarting your dad's business. You're trying to reclaim Corie as family and looking for Cassidy. You're willing to love me and start your own family. That's very brave."

He caught her hands, overwhelmed. He had a lifetime to make his love worthy of her. "I'm going to so love being married to you. I want you to do what will make *you* happy."

"I absolutely don't want to go back to pediatric nursing, but I love working with seniors, and I think this could be my answer to work that's important but a little less hard on the soul."

He felt compelled to say, "But, you'll be losing your senior friends from time to time. That's kind of the nature of that work, isn't it?"

She nodded. "It is. I'm not dismissing them lightly, but often they're ready to go by the time they reach that place in their lives, so losing them is not quite as hard as a life unlived. My job will be to make them comfortable, keep them engaged and interested and happy as long as possible."

"All right. You're going to be pretty busy."

"The board hasn't even met me yet. They might not share the doctor's enthusiasm."

"They'll love you when they meet you."

"We'll see."

He leaned down to kiss her, unashamedly joyful in the newness of their relationship.

She reached up to wrap her arms around his neck, her lips clinging to his. She pulled back slightly to whisper, "I love you, Jack."

He put his lips to her ear. "I love you, too.

And I can't wait until there's time to show you how much."

They walked back to the house hand in hand. She kissed him good-night.

"I like Corie a lot," she said. "I promised her I'd find her a nightgown. She sleeps in socks and T-shirts at home. So I have to go." She blew him a kiss and hurried to the stairs.

JACK WENT BACK to the carriage house to put the contents of his bag away, laundry in the hamper, jacket on a hanger. Then, exhausted but still on an emotional high, he walked through the place, planning projects for tomorrow.

By the time he went back to the main house, it was quiet and dark. Ben lay on his stomach on the living-room sofa, one arm hanging off, his hand on the floor. Jack fell into the recliner across the room and tipped back, covering himself with the nubby throw always folded over the arm. Thankfully, he told himself as he began to drift off, he was too tired to dream.

His subconscious, unfortunately, was unaware of that.

CHAPTER EIGHTEEN

HE STOOD ON the turret, the wind blowing the woman's white hijab as she came toward him. This time he knew she was his mother and he was determined to keep her away. He aimed his sidearm at her.

"Stay away!" he warned. "You're not getting up here. You're not getting my weapon."

The air rang with his warning, but she climbed up the Humvee with the strength and agility that always surprised him.

Okay, but she wasn't getting on the turret.

He put a foot out to kick her off when she reached the turret, but he missed somehow. He didn't understand how he could have, but he did. She stood beside him.

Okay, but she wasn't getting his weapon.

"Jackie," she said, that soft, scratchy voice reaching inside him. "Get away from me, Jackie!"

Jack, the observer, felt fresh pain at the sound of her last words to him. Jack, the sub-

ject of the dream, morphed from the adult he
was to the child he'd been the last time he'd
seen her. They were no longer on the Humvee,
but in the living room of the house in Beggar's Bay. He saw the old flowered sofa, toys
all over the floor, a tricycle and a clear push
toy that played music while marbles bubbled
inside. He saw his mother without the hijab in
a pair of jeans and a black T-shirt, her curly
hair in disarray. A man's voice shouted angrily
in the background.

She reached for the weapon Jack held.

He was puzzled. It wasn't the M4 he'd carried in Iraq, but a fat-handled, skinny-barreled
Luger. While he dealt with that inconsistency,
she continued to try to get it from him. He
didn't want to give it to her. The angry male
voice grew closer.

Her grip was so strong.

His observer self didn't understand it. He'd
fought off big men with these hands, but he
had been a child then.

She peeled his fingers off the gun. Still, he
held on.

"Jackie," she said again. "Get away from
me."

She gave one last vicious pull.

The shouting voice grew closer.

The gun fired, startling him.

He heard himself cry out, saw his mother on the floor, bruised and bloody. He stood over her. She had that look in her eyes that paralyzed him. That look he'd always hoped to see and never had. The look that said she recognized him as her son, that she knew he loved her, that she loved him. Then her eyes closed.

"Mom!" His voice was high with desperation. "Mom!"

"Jack."

"Jack!"

He heard sobbing, high voices, shouts of alarm as arms came around him, crying his name.

He awoke to find himself on his feet, a small crowd around him in his parents' living room. He stood near the sofa Ben had been dozing on, Ben holding his arm as though to steady him. Sarah wept against him, his parents stood apart, watching worriedly, his mother crying. Corie had both hands over her mouth, her eyes huge and terrified. She looked just as she had the night his mother killed—

Wait.

The whole world seemed to jerk to a sudden stop.

He put a hand to his head. There were pictures there, fragments of the dream that had changed location from Iraq to the old house in town, like a jigsaw puzzle spread out on the table, random, misshapen pieces of memory without connection.

"Jack," Sarah said, putting a hand to his cheek. "Sit down, Jack. Ben, make him sit down."

Ben pressed lightly on his shoulder but Jack resisted. "No," he said. "This time we were at the house in town. I had a Luger instead of an M4." His voice was agitated, disbelieving. "She fought me for it and I thought she was going to shoot me, but..." He hesitated, uncertain. "The gun went off. She was on the floor, bruised and covered in blood. What is going *on* in my brain? What does that mean?" He turned to Sarah.

"I don't know, Jack," she said, tightening her grip on him. "I wish I could tell you and end all this."

Jack turned to Corie. He didn't want her to have to remember, but he needed relief from his dreams or he would go insane. "Do you remember that night, Corie?"

She nodded and lowered her hands from her mouth. "Yes," she whispered. Images flashed in his head, passing too quickly to sort or even see very well. He tried to recount the story for himself, to slow down the images.

Ben pushed him forcefully onto the sofa and beckoned Corie to sit next to him. Sarah sat on his other side.

"Mom shot Brauer," Jack said, "and when I tried to take the gun away from her, she told me to get away." He turned to Corie for corroboration.

Tears ran down her cheeks. She looked miserable. "Jack…" she said.

"That's what happened, right?"

She stared at him and he saw the denial she was trying so hard not to say out loud.

"What, then?" he asked. Had his memory been wrong all these years? That was impossible, wasn't it? "What do *you* remember?"

It was easy to see that she didn't want to say anything. He caught her hand. "Please. I know it's horrible to remember, but I have to know."

She shook her head, unwilling to speak. He heard the clock ticking, his adoptive mother crying softly, the sound of the old oil furnace roaring in the basement. Time stretched, pinning him to this painful moment.

Ben knelt beside Corie. "Tell him what you remember," he said gently. "Say the truth.

Please. It's the only way the nightmares will stop for him."

She looked from Ben to Jack and then sucked in a breath that seemed to make her shudder.

"I woke up and heard the screaming," she began. "I wanted to stay in my room but I heard you run out, Jack, so I followed you." She closed her eyes and took another breath. "When I got to the living room, Mom was on the floor and he was punching her. He was kneeling over her, and there was blood everywhere." She looked up at him and her face crumpled. "Then..."

"Tell me, Corie."

"*You* had his gun, Jackie," she blurted. "You told him to stop, and when he didn't..." She burst into sobs and blurted, "*You* shot him!"

The images stopped flying by his face and came into sudden, sharp focus. He relived them aloud.

"I remember Brauer astride Mom's waist, punching her with one fist, then the other. Oh, God." His heart was thumping. "I did have his gun. I pointed it like...like Ben and I used to practice after watching *21 Jump Street*. I screamed at him to stop hitting her or I'd shoot him!

"He didn't stop." Jack saw himself pull the trigger.

"Mom screamed when Brauer fell on top of her. It took her a minute to react. Corie was screaming but I was quiet, the gun still aimed at the spot where he'd stood. I remember being glad I'd stopped him.

"Mom pushed him off her and got up. She was bruised and bleeding, and holding her side.

"You ran to her," he said to Corie, who nodded as she wept. "But she held up a hand to keep you back. She said, 'Get away from me.'" He had to strain to pull the sound of his mother's voice from his memory. "'You can't have blood on you,' she said. 'Go back to bed and make believe you're asleep.'"

Jack saw his eight-year-old self look up at the sound of sirens. "We heard the police coming. She told me to give her the gun. She said, 'Careful, don't get blood on you.' I handed it over. She wiped it off with the hem of her bathrobe and pointed to my bedroom. 'Get away from me, Jackie. Pretend you're asleep and don't tell anyone, *ever*, what happened. Promise?' She looked like a loving mother, a look I was always trying to see in her and couldn't find."

He repeated those last words she'd said to him that had haunted him all his life. She hadn't meant them the way he'd thought. He couldn't breathe.

"I promised her I wouldn't say anything. Then she said, 'Good. Go to bed, Jack.'"

The images disappeared. He stared at blackness. Corie gripped his arm and sobbed against him.

Sarah said in a tortured whisper, "Oh, Jack."

"So…" he began. As a kid, as a soldier, he'd had to face the night, no matter what. He had to do that now. He forced himself out of the sucking darkness of his memories and made himself examine the truth. "I killed a man," he said simply, "and my mother went to prison to protect me."

"You killed a man who was beating your mother," Ben said, getting in his face. "I've covered enough domestic calls to know that if you'd waited for the police to arrive, he might have killed her. Or Corie. Or Cassidy. You did what you *had* to do. You've done that enough times as a soldier to know you bear no guilt in it. No guilt, Jack. No guilt. Do you hear me?"

It was hard to remember Brauer and feel badly about his absence in the world. But *he'd* killed him, not his mother.

"Yeah," he said. "But my mother gave away her life…" He felt the knot tighten. He swallowed and struggled to take another breath.

"Take it easy, Jack," Ben said.

"I've hated her my whole life." He needed to admit that, to get that out of him. "For what she did to our family. Sometimes hating her was all that got me through. And all that time…she'd taken the blame for *me*. And when she told me to get away from her, it wasn't because she hated me, but because she didn't want me to get blood on me. She didn't want me there when the police came. She wanted them to think I was asleep and that she killed Brauer. And all the time, *I'm* the one who did that to our family."

He put his head in his hands. "She went to prison and then died there of a drug overdose. She took the blame for me and then she died."

It was agony. And he couldn't fix it. His entire life had been about coming to terms with what he remembered, repairing his reactions to all the bad things that had happened to him, repairing himself so that he loved instead of hated. But it was too late to repair his relationship with his mother.

Helen came to sit beside him. Corie stood to give her room. "Jack," Helen said gently, "the thing to take from all this is that she was a beautiful young woman who couldn't face her life without drugs. God knows why some people can and others can't. But she loved you under it all. She did a fine, noble, *maternal* thing by taking the blame. But in the end, she still had to have drugs to get by—even after all the misery it brought into her life and her children's lives. You have no blame for what happened to Brauer or to her. All the things that happened to your family are because of the choices *she* made."

She leaned into his upper arm and held it tightly. "No one begrudges you your memories of her, Jack. And I'm so glad you know that in that awful moment, she protected you and loved you." She raised her head and forced him to look into her eyes. "Let that go, Jack. For the rest of our lives, *I'm* your mother. I know the man you are, and I'm so proud of you. This family is all together, right here, right now, and you're a critical part of it. We are your life."

SARAH WATCHED HIM as he tried to absorb his mother's words. She knew they were meant to help move him forward, but he seemed stuck in a truth so harsh he couldn't move.

"Want some coffee with brandy in it?" Helen asked.

"Thanks, Mom. I'm good." He looked at everyone gathered around him. "Why don't you all go back to bed? I'm fine. I'll be fine."

Corie said his name apologetically. He stood to put his arms around her and hold her closely for a moment. "Please don't feel badly about telling me the truth. I must have just buried it because it's so…" He shook his head. There was no word strong enough to describe what he felt.

"He would have killed her," Corie whispered tearfully.

"Yeah."

Helen took Corie by the shoulders. "Go to bed, Corie. It was all so long ago. It's been over for more than twenty years. I know it's impossible to forget, but it's time for the two of you to put it away and never take it out again." As she led Corie to the stairs, she turned to Sarah with a look that said she was leaving Jack to her. Ben and Gary wandered away.

"Jack," Sarah said gently.

He tried to meet her eyes. He did, but the man she knew didn't seem to be inside.

"Please don't do this to yourself." Frightened by her inability to connect, to find the man who was always there for her, she began to babble. "No one would blame you. No court would ever convict you. My God, you were eight years old, he was beating your mother and you had two little sisters in the house. Jack, she's gone, he's gone, and you and Corie are here together. And I'm here. Just *please* let it go."

He took her hand and held it between his two. "I can't, Sarah." He rubbed it gently, kissed her knuckles, then dropped it. There was a finality about the gesture that chilled her. "I can live with having shot Brauer because he was horrible. I can go to the police and explain. But how do I live with the knowledge that she took the blame for the shooting and went to jail? And not only that, but I hated her, *hated* her all this time, when she made such an enormous sacrifice to protect me."

"I don't think you really hated her," Sarah said, catching his hand again, refusing to let him slip into the darkness he was creating for himself. "I think deep down you loved her. Maybe you didn't even know you did, but you did. That's why it hurts so much. Jack, she did it so you could have a life. Please. Have a life with me, like we've planned."

She saw the rejection of her plea in his eyes. "I can't now, Sarah."

Desperate, she grasped his arms and shook him—or tried to. It didn't even rock him, but it did make him give her his attention.

"Listen to me," she said, her voice quavering. "The only thing wrong with you is that you've taken the blame for her behavior your entire life. Her going to jail for you was a great, loving gesture, but she did it because she knew she owed you, and even she wouldn't have been able to live with herself if you'd ended up in the system for all the selfish choices *she* made. So don't let her actions be for nothing."

He wrapped his arms around her and she thought for a moment that she'd won, that he understood. But when he pulled away, she saw in his face that she'd lost and he was simply tired of arguing. He looked bone-tired—of everything.

"I'm going out for a while," he said.

"Where?"

"Not sure. Just out."

"Can I come?"

"No." He lifted his head. "Ben!"

His brother, who'd been making himself scarce in the hallway, appeared.

"Can I use your condo?" Jack asked. "Just for a day or two?"

Ben dug into his pocket, pulled out a key ring and worked one of the keys off. Ben tossed the key and Jack snagged it out of the air.

"Thanks."

Jack went to the door, but Sarah ran around him and plastered herself against it. "I hate melodrama," she said, "but know this. I'm not going to let you just walk away from me as though what we've been through to try to understand each other was all for nothing. And I'm not picking up my life as a nurse again, sticking out my chin and my neck and my... my *heart* without you. You told me that getting people where they wanted to go was your job. Cavalry Scout. Well, I want to go forward, I want to help old people be happy and thrive. I want to have your babies and drive you crazy and make you grateful every day that we're together. So don't leave here thinking this is over, because it isn't."

He reached for the doorknob and she stepped aside.

The man had just learned awful truths about his life tonight and maybe he needed time alone to process them, she realized. She'd tried to beat him into submission with her love, but love shouldn't be used as a weapon.

He was staring at her as though he hated to leave but had no choice.

She said a crisp good-night, her tone implying strongly that it was absolutely not good-bye.

He stared at her for another few moments and then walked out the door. She turned away and found Ben standing behind her, arms open. She sobbed against him.

JACK LET HIMSELF into Ben's condo on the bay. It was a bastion of guy stuff: NordicTrack, telescope, televisions in every room, huge leather furniture and five remotes lined up on a wide coffee table. He turned off the lights and sank onto the sofa, glad to be away from his parents' house, away from the dream of Sarah, away from all the good things in his life he shouldn't have because of who he was—and what he'd done.

He closed his eyes, hoping for sleep, but secretly wondered if he'd ever be able to sleep again.

SARAH STARED AT the ceiling for hours. The glass of wine Ben had insisted she drink to help her sleep could have been caffeine-laden coffee for all the good it did.

She finally fell asleep shortly after 6:00 a.m., but awoke just two hours later with a pounding headache and an emotional clot in her chest that no amount of deep breathing or antacids would dissolve.

Seeing Corie still soundly sleeping in the extra bed, she pulled on jeans and the sweater she'd worn the day before and padded quietly out of the room and down the stairs. There was not a sound in the house. She looked out the kitchen window and saw that all the vehicles were still there. Everyone else must have slept better than she had. Must still be sleeping.

Desperate for coffee, she put a mug under the Keurig and waited impatiently for the thirty seconds it took to brew. Before it was finished, a light rap sounded on the back door.

Her only thought, going to answer it, was that Jack wouldn't have knocked. Annoyed to be separated from the aroma of Tanzanian dark roast, Sarah pulled the door open—and stared in astonishment at Marcie Thurgood, of the fund-raising committee. Her jaw dropped a little farther at the long, lean young man standing beside her. Both wore sweats, though

Marcie's were pink and black and the young man's were more traditional graphite-colored fleece.

Marcie pushed past Sarah into the kitchen. The young man shook his head at her behavior and offered his hand. "Hi, Sarah. I'm Bobby Jay Cooper. May we come in?"

The country singer, Sarah thought, in person. Still staring, she shook his hand, then stood aside and gestured him in. "Yes, please. Welcome to Beggar's Bay."

"Thank you." He had red-brown hair that fell across his forehead and a mass of subtle freckles. He also had the widest smile she'd ever seen. Sniffing the air, he said, "I smell coffee. Marcie dragged me out of the house before I could have a cup."

Sarah actually thought twice about giving him the cup that was ready and then reminded herself that this man had donated his time to help their fund-raising. She handed him the cup. "Cream or sugar?"

"No, thanks." He took it from her and seemed to need it almost as much as she did. No surprise. He was staying with Marcie Thurgood.

Sarah started another cup.

"Listen!" Marcie ordered, coming to stand

beside her. "I know it's early, but you won't believe what's happened."

"I won't? You want coffee?"

"Please. Are you paying attention?"

"Uh, yes. I just didn't sleep very well." She watched the coffee drip. "What is it?"

"Pete Daley voted to sell the Cooper Building to the seniors!" She clapped and did a little leap at her own announcement.

Oh, yeah, Sarah thought. The Cooper Building. She was happy. It was just that her heart had been smashed to powder and she didn't know how to express happiness.

"That's wonderful," she said, struggling to put enthusiasm into her voice. She handed Marcie the now full cup and started another, aching for her own caffeine. "How did it happen?"

"Well—" Marcie indicated the table "—can we sit?"

"Please. I mean, it was looking pretty good for Forman at our last meeting. Did the Daleys change their minds about the divorce?"

"No. But while Lucy Daley was in Forman's office talking about it, she noticed his plans for the Cooper Building. I guess they were over-the-top contemporary. He wanted to add balconies, an outside glass elevator, take the brick off the front…"

"What?"

Bobby Jay pulled Sarah's chair out as she came to the table with her coffee.

"Lucy fired him on the spot as her lawyer," Marcie went on, "and told Pete if he didn't vote for the seniors, she'd get a Portland lawyer and take him for everything he had."

Sarah felt a little pleasure push against her heartache. "That's wonderful, Marcie. I can't believe it. Carol must be beside herself."

"We all are. Bobby and I went out for a run this morning and I thought it would be fun to deliver the news to you in person, since you've worked so hard."

"Thank you, Marcie. That was thoughtful." Now, if she could just fix her personal life…

There was another knock on the kitchen door. Bobby Jay, who was closer, rose to pull it open. Sarah, still sitting at the table, stood in complete surprise at the trio in the doorway.

"Bobby Jay Cooper!" Vinny said, clearly surprised but in no way intimidated by the celebrity who'd answered the door. He reached out to shake hands. "I'm Vinny Caruso," he said. "One of the acts you'll be judging tomorrow." He turned to his companions. "This is

Margaret Brogan, also competing, and Jasper Fletcher."

Bobby Jay shook hands all around, gestured Margaret inside and then reached for Jasper's arm. "Can I give you a hand there?" he asked.

Sarah greeted her clients while Marcie vacated her chair for Margaret and Bobby Jay helped Jasper into his. Sarah pointed Vinny to her chair. "You all want coffee?" she asked. The quick reply of "Sure!" sent her to the K-Cup drawer in the hope that there was enough. She could always make a pot.

"How did you get here?" she asked as she pulled down mugs.

"Jasper drove," Vinny replied. Getting the laugh he'd hoped for from her other guests, he said, "We took a cab. The good news about the building is circulating like wildfire among our friends, and we had to come and thank you for helping make it happen."

Margaret held up a colorful tin. "Peanut butter cookies," she said.

Sarah remembered asking her once why she'd never been given a sample of her cookies. Margaret had replied that it was because she wasn't a "hungry little waif with a world of sadness in her eyes."

She guessed that wasn't true this morning.

Sarah carried cups to the table, put Margaret's cookies on a plate and placed it in the middle of the table. "Not a traditional breakfast, but... Thank you, Margaret."

Conversation carried on about Bobby Jay's home outside of Memphis, about the show and about the building and all the seniors would be able to do in it.

"And Jack Palmer," Sarah said, "has offered to do the repainting and sanding and restaining of the floors at cost."

It pained her to even say Jack's name, not knowing if she'd be a part of his life anymore.

"That's wonderful," Bobby Jay declared. "He's part of this family you're staying with, isn't he?"

Sarah nodded. "He is. He's been back from Afghanistan just a couple of months and wanting very much to reconnect with the community."

"Well. We'll just have to see that that young man gets lots of work around here." Marcie wagged a pink-polished fingernail. "And not at cost, either."

Sarah looked up to see Helen, Gary, Ben and Corie standing at the foot of the back stairs, clearly uncertain what to make of Sarah's early morning company. Corie looked particularly surprised. But of course she would, Sarah thought.

Sarah waved Corie and the others in and made introductions. Corie was awestruck by the presence of Bobby Jay, and Gary and Ben went in search of more chairs.

"I could make some breakfast," Helen said hesitantly as they returned.

Ben put a bench seat from the upstairs hallway behind his mother and pushed her onto it. "No, no. I'll make a McDonald's run. Is that okay with everybody?"

The affirmative was unanimous and Ben did a quick count, then left with Gary along to help him carry.

Conversation picked up, then Sarah noticed the back door opening again and couldn't imagine who else was visiting.

Jack. He took a step into the kitchen and froze at the sight of all the people around the kitchen table. He didn't look as though he'd slept any better than Sarah had. Her heart punched against her ribs. Was he coming home?

She met his eyes across the room, thought she could hear the sliding-bolt sound of their hearts connecting. "Hi, Jack," she said.

Before she could say anything more, Bobby

Jay rose from his folding chair and frowned at Jack in concentration.

"Jack...Manning?" he asked, taking a step closer. "From Cubby's?"

Jack turned to Bobby Jay in complete surprise. He took another step into the room, frowning as he studied Bobby Jay's face. "Robby Turner? No."

Bobby Jay stuck out his hand and the two men shook. Then Bobby Jay stood back and looked at Jack in amazement. "I can't believe it, either. Yes! Robby Turner. Only, my mother married Paul Cooper, who already had a boy named Robby, so I became Bobby and then Cooper when he adopted me. How are you, man?"

Sarah could see how Jack was: still shaken from the revelations of last night, stunned, exhausted, in pain. She saw him force a smile and come out of his misery to engage in the moment and this gift of fate of an old friend.

Bobby Jay shared the story with the group of how he and Jack had met. "It was a tough time for me," he said, growing serious. "My parents had separated, I missed my dad, and my mom and I were in a new town. She worked nights in the nightclub that was in the Cooper Building then." He smiled quickly at the seniors. "Jack used to always bring this cool dump truck."

Jack pointed to Margaret. "That's the lady who made the cookies that came in it. You remember, I ate all of them?"

"Oh, yeah." Bobby Jay grinned at Margaret's look of pleasure. "The cookies were long gone by the time I got to play with it, but I really liked that truck. When my mom fell in love with the man who owned the building and we moved away, Jack gave me the dump truck." He punched Jack in the arm. "I still have it. Meant a lot to me, man."

"Why'd you move away," Vinny asked, "when the building is here?"

"No Coopers had lived here for fifteen years or more. When the last renter defaulted, my father had lost a lot in the downtrend and decided to let the city have it. So when this opportunity arose," he said, "and Marcie called me, I figured I had to do something for this town and the cool kid who gave me his dump truck."

Jack looked embarrassed under the praise and the smattering of applause that followed. Sarah wished she could have him to herself for just five minutes, but it didn't look as though that was going to happen.

Ben and Gary arrived with two large boxes filled with individual bags. "They're all Mc-Muffins and potatoes," Ben said. "Hope that's okay."

The impromptu party went on for another hour. Sarah made a pot of coffee and Helen cut up fruit. Those without access to the table ate off their laps, the conversation so lively that no one noticed the inconvenience.

While Ben talked to Bobby Jay, Sarah saw Helen take Jack aside. She had no idea what they were discussing, but they looked serious. Jack nodded while his mother spoke. At one point he shook his head and that seemed to upset Helen. He put a hand to her arm and smiled, seeming to tease her. They ended their conversation with a hug.

Jack then ran upstairs and returned with the leather jacket he wore when he performed with the Wild Men. He needed it for the rehearsal that night. Her heart sank. So he hadn't come home; he'd simply forgotten something.

He went to the door, stopping to raise his hand in a goodbye gesture. "Nice to meet all of you," he said, his eyes still troubled but his smile genuine. He looked at his father. "Bye, Dad," and then pointed to Bobby Jay. "We'll get together after the show Saturday night."

Bobby Jay gestured at Ben. "Can we bring your brother along?"

Jack pretended reluctance. "If we have to. Bye, everybody."

A chorus of goodbyes followed him out the door.

Sarah felt that clot of emotion in her chest. He hadn't even looked at her when he'd said goodbye.

She explained that to Helen later when Marcie and Bobby Jay had departed and Ben had left to take the seniors home.

"He's still focused on the blindness of his memory all these years," his mother said. "I think he'll come out of it eventually, find a way to forgive himself, and when he does, you should be there."

"But when he first walked in the door, he never looked at me."

"I think he's thinking he has no right to have you."

Sarah doubted that was true, but hugged Helen anyway.

What would she do, she wondered later when she stood under a hot shower, letting it beat on the knotted muscles in her neck, if he *didn't* come out of it?

Now that she saw the road ahead, how could

she take it if he wasn't beside her? She couldn't imagine. She could go on, of course, but without the laughter and the shine he brought to her life. And without the children that she now wanted more than anything.

CHAPTER NINETEEN

THE HIGH-SCHOOL auditorium was packed for Bobby Jay's performance and the talent show. Dress rehearsal had gone reasonably well, though not brilliantly, but the drama teacher standing by to help told Sarah that was a good sign. That meant opening night would be great.

The local women's service club was handling ticket sales, and the chairwoman caught Sarah backstage to tell her they'd made a small fortune so far. And ticket sales weren't done yet. There was still standing room.

Sarah turned to share the good news and saw Margaret arm in arm with Bobby Jay. Margaret's hair, she noticed, had been softly styled, lending her a more approachable air. Sarah told her she looked wonderful.

"Marcie helped me." Margaret handed Sarah a large zip-top bag of cookies. "These are for Jack," she said. "Will you see that he gets them?"

"Uh…sure." She and Jack weren't talking much, it seemed, but she could always give them to Ben to give to Jack.

With a parting wave, Margaret left to prepare for her performance. Bobby Jay asked where Jack was. Sarah explained that he was living in Ben's condo and that she hadn't seen him since the morning they'd all been at the Palmers' for breakfast.

"Yeah. Ben told me a little bit about it. Pretty awful thing. Anyway, I'm going to see him after the show."

An image of Jack came forward in her mind as it had a hundred times since that morning. She was beginning to think his escape to Ben's condo didn't bode well for their life together. She ached to help him, but he apparently thought he had to deal with this alone. He'd experienced all kinds of things she couldn't even imagine, so maybe she wouldn't be of much comfort.

She pushed all thoughts of him away to deal with all she had to do tonight. She looked around with mild trepidation. Must be the classic opening night jitters. Mercifully, opening night was closing night, so whatever went wrong wouldn't happen again. She peeked out at the audience and saw Gary and Helen

Palmer sitting with Corie in the first row. She hoped that whatever had gone wrong in the young woman's life would right itself, too.

At eight o'clock the director of the seniors' center, a tall young man in his thirties serving as emcee, welcomed everyone and announced that the seniors were acquiring the Cooper Building, which brought a round of applause.

Then he introduced Bobby Jay Cooper, who walked onstage with his warm personality and easy charm, and sang a song about small towns, close friendships and neighbors who were friends forever. The evening was off to a wonderful start.

When he finished, he spoke briefly about the time he'd spent in Beggar's Bay, about his connection to the Cooper Building and even about Jack and their friendship forged in the stockroom of Cubby's.

He also thanked all the generous people who'd volunteered to perform and all the townspeople who'd bought tickets.

Then the lights went down, a spotlight picked out the middle of the stage and an attractive, glamorously dressed patron of the seniors' center walked on with a big placard that she placed on an easel. The placard read Beggar's Bay Fire Department Men's Chorus.

There was enthusiastic applause, then silence fell and a dozen handsome men in evening dress began to sing "Stouthearted Men."

Sarah, standing in the wings, couldn't quite believe her ears. They were magnificent, stellar and more harmonious and inspired than they'd been last night. Whatever notes weren't perfect were covered by the fervor of their delivery. Their good looks didn't hurt, either.

They received a standing ovation.

Sarah, jaw dropping, looked across the stage at Marcie, who stood in the wings stage right. Marcie gave her a thumbs-up.

The evening went on as though Michael Bennett had produced and directed it after finishing *A Chorus Line*. Act after act met enthusiastic response from the audience. The Wild Men brought the house down with "Bye, Bye, Bye." Sarah watched Jack greedily, hoping the title of their song had no significance to his future plans. His performance seemed a little less lively than usual, but she doubted that anyone else noticed. Ben and the De Angelis boys were over-the-top wild.

Margaret's performance was perfect in an absolutely silent auditorium and the high-school drama club's glimpse of *Romeo and Juliet* was stunning.

Vinny and his group, known as Caruso Plus 2, typical of Vinny's narcissism, did their romantic medley of Sinatra tunes, then shocked Sarah when Margaret joined them for their last number.

She gave "Stardust" a unique treatment with her low, moody voice, and went on to do rich justice to the Hoagy Carmichael classic. The theme, Sarah thought, was a lot like the song she'd sung earlier, bright memories of a love that was lost.

When she'd finished, there was a moment of complete silence, then a roar of approval came from the audience and everyone backstage.

Vinny walked from the piano, leaning on his cane. When the roar abated and they'd all taken a bow, he gave Margaret a hug. Sarah saw them exchange a few words and hug again. The audience continued to shout their approval.

At the end of the evening Bobby Jay announced a tie between Margaret and Caruso Plus 2 and the Beggar's Bay Firemen's Chorus. He suggested a sing-off.

Margaret and Vinny's group did "Swinging on a Star" and the firemen sang "Men of Harlech."

Bobby Jay declared the tie unbroken and both groups were awarded first prize. The Wild Men followed with second and the drama club with third.

An hour later, when the audience and most of the performers had left, Sarah sat alone in a front seat, looking at the empty stage and feeling as though she'd helped mount a Broadway production that had garnered rave reviews.

Now, if she could just do that with her life. There was comfort in the fact that Margaret and Vinny were friends again, and that the seniors would own their new center and could now afford many of the extras that would make it a great place to spend their time.

It was a bittersweet triumph.

She grabbed her jacket and purse on the seat beside her and headed backstage for one last look around to make sure no one had forgotten anything. She went to the dressing room everyone had used to primp and change and was surprised to see Jack, Ben and Bobby Jay still in it, chairs gathered in a loose circle.

"Hey, you're still here," she said, hoping no one noticed the way her breath caught at the sight of Jack.

"We're going out to party tonight at Betty's before Bobby Jay goes home," Ben said, "but

Bobby Jay said there was something he wanted to do first."

"That's right," Bobby Jay said and reached for a large FedEx box sitting on the floor. Ben pulled a chair up for Sarah between him and Jack.

"I'm not staying," she said with a smile all around, letting it linger an extra moment on Jack. "I was just making sure we hadn't left a mess."

"No, stay," Bobby Jay insisted. "In fact, you're welcome to come with us. And if you're going to marry Jack, you might like to see this, too."

She gave Jack a startled look. He looked back at her and smiled.

JACK DRANK IN the sight of Sarah. It had been most of two days since the thrill of loving her had been killed by what he'd learned about himself. He could resolve that he'd shot Brauer, but the wasted hate was hard to live with. He was trying to distill all those years into the simple truth that, in the end, his mother had loved him. He was beginning to think he could live with that.

"So." Bobby Jay handed Jack the box. It had

a FedEx label on it with Marcie Thurgood's address. "This is for you."

"What is it?" Jack asked, a little embarrassed by being given a gift.

Bobby Jay shrugged. "Open it." He handed Jack a pocketknife.

Jack slit the tape, handed back the knife, then pulled apart the flaps. He reached into a nest of shredded paper and pulled out a Tonka dump truck, not just any Tonka dump truck, but the very one he and Bobby Jay had played with twenty-four years ago. It was still bright red, though it was scratched and dinged. Jack swept a hand along a wheel and it turned as though brand-new.

He couldn't have said why tears crowded his throat. He looked up at Bobby Jay, whose blue eyes betrayed the same emotion. "We were a couple of lonely kids, man," the country singer said, "and you were kind to me. I never forgot that." He cleared his throat. "Someday you and Sarah will have a son to give it to." He made a self-deprecating gesture. "I have two little girls. Girlie girls. This should be yours now."

Before she could think twice about the gesture, Sarah put the bag of cookies Margaret had given her for him into the truck.

"Those are from Margaret," she said.

He looked down at the cookies in the dump truck and did an instant mental trip back to that moment when the world had seemed to be a dark, unfriendly place and someone had thought of him with generosity and kindness. It occurred to him now that in the years that had passed, he hadn't lost a thing. He had what had meant so much to him twenty-four years ago—and so much more.

Now that he'd had a few days to relive the night Brauer died, he had a new perspective. He knew he'd been the instrument, but everything that had brought the family to that point hadn't been his fault. He accepted that the mother he loved had been a bad mother, but she'd still loved him. He knew that the past didn't have to determine the future.

Jack looked at Bobby Jay. "Thanks, Bobby. Your friendship meant a lot to me in those days, too. And it does now."

Ben chose that moment to get to his feet. "Okay," he said, beckoning for Bobby Jay to follow him. He looked from Jack to Sarah and back again. "I imagine the two of you have things to say to each other. So we'll see you at Betty's. And, hey, don't keep us waiting too long." He and Bobby Jay left.

Sarah took the truck from Jack and looked it over. "You know," she said, smiling into his eyes, "we might have a daughter who'll just love a dump truck. Doesn't have to be a son."

He met her gaze, saw the warmth and love there. He got to his feet and pulled her up, then put his arms around her and tugged her close, or at least as close as the toy she held allowed.

"I adore you," he said, planting a kiss at her ear. "I'm so sorry I lost it and scared you."

She put the truck on a chair, then wrapped both arms around his neck and held tightly. "It's all right. I can only imagine how awful that must have been for you to remember, but those days are over. You're a remarkable man to have gone through that and come out the Jack Palmer I know and love. And want to spend the rest of my life with."

"Oh, Sarah." He kissed her and put everything he felt into the kiss, for there were no words. Then he pulled back and smiled. "Are you going to ask me to marry you again?"

"Do I have to? I believed you the first time you say yes."

SARAH WAS AMAZED that this was her life now. A couple of months ago it had been in ashes—literally—and now there was so much promise. "Come on," she said, giving him one last quick kiss. "We should go meet Bobby Jay and Ben. Are you sure you want me along? Weren't you going to talk about guy stuff?"

"No," he replied firmly. "After the past few days I don't want you to leave me ever, for any reason."

They turned to leave and then remembered the dump truck. "We'll have to find somewhere prominent to put this," he said as he retrieved it.

She felt laughter bubble up. "Until we have that son or daughter, it makes a great cookie jar."

EPILOGUE

BEN COULDN'T WAIT to get back to the RAV4 he'd borrowed from his mother to drive the honeymooners and Corie to the airport.

The Thanksgiving holiday weekend had been warm and chaotic. Everyone in the Palmer household had traveled to Sarah's parents' home in Seattle, where the Reeds, having learned of the impending marriage of their second daughter and the pregnancy of their first, had insisted on hosting Thanksgiving with tons of food and serious gratitude all around. Then Jack and Sarah had been married quietly there, in Seattle, on the Saturday of the weekend, with both sets of parents, Corie and Ben, and Kate and her husband, Drew, present.

Ben had just dropped off Jack and Sarah at the Alaska Airlines terminal, where they were boarding a flight to San Francisco. And now he was standing with Corie at the Southwest Airlines terminal, where she was taking a flight back to Texas.

Corie turned to him and smiled politely, then offered her hand. "Thank you for the ride…and for everything."

"Sure." He shook her hand. It seemed small and slender in his, though her grip was firm. "Safe travels home. Please keep in touch with Jack."

"Yes." She turned and looked in the direction of her gate. He sensed reluctance in her and experienced a moment of panic. *No, please go.* He was afraid she'd gotten a glimpse of genuine family life and didn't want to leave.

He started to back away. "Take care, Corie."

She nodded slowly, as though this was something she'd experienced before. And of course she had, he knew that. A kid nobody wanted. He felt a pinch of conscience, but it was overridden by a finely honed sense of self-preservation.

She picked up her bag and squared her shoulders. "Bye, Ben," she said and marched away.

He breathed a sigh of relief and loped to the car before she could change her mind.

THAT EVENING BEN stood at the kitchen counter in his condo, making a sandwich while watching the news.

The newscaster announced the "Funny Story" segment that ended each broadcast. It was usually some amusing event considered more noteworthy than newsworthy.

Jack put his sandwich together and went to the refrigerator for a soda when the words "Ocean Drive" and "Corpus Christi, Texas" coming from the television caught his attention.

Soda in hand, he went to stand in front of the TV and listened. A beefy, middle-aged man appeared on screen with a very blonde and buxom woman, holding up a box. The man was Tyree, Teresa's landlord. A close-up of the priority-mail box revealed the very one Grady had mailed for Ben from Seattle.

The reporter provided some background information on the recent theft of Mrs. Tyree's jewelry. Ben couldn't believe Corie's caper had made the news.

Then the reporter asked the woman to explain what had just arrived in the box. Her features in an angry pout, she said, her voice thick with a Texas drawl, "Ah thought our thief had a change of heart, but apparently he was just rubbin' it in!"

She took a fistful of the contents of the box

and held it up for the camera. Ben dropped the soda.

Strings of Mardi Gras beads gleamed garishly. Not the diamonds and gold and emeralds Ben had thought he'd sent back, but plastic junk that could be bought for a dollar a string.

* * * * *

LARGER-PRINT BOOKS!

GET 2 FREE LARGER-PRINT NOVELS PLUS 2 FREE MYSTERY GIFTS

Love Inspired®

Larger-print novels are now available...

YES! Please send me 2 FREE LARGER-PRINT Love Inspired® novels and my 2 FREE mystery gifts (gifts are worth about $10). After receiving them, if I don't wish to receive any more books, I can return the shipping statement marked "cancel." If I don't cancel, I will receive 6 brand-new novels every month and be billed just $5.24 per book in the U.S. or $5.74 per book in Canada. That's a savings of at least 23% off the cover price. It's quite a bargain! Shipping and handling is just 50¢ per book in the U.S. and 75¢ per book in Canada.* I understand that accepting the 2 free books and gifts places me under no obligation to buy anything. I can always return a shipment and cancel at any time. Even if I never buy another book, the two free books and gifts are mine to keep forever.

122/322 IDN F49Y

Name   (PLEASE PRINT)

Address   Apt. #

City   State/Prov.   Zip/Postal Code

Signature (if under 18, a parent or guardian must sign)

Mail to the **Harlequin® Reader Service:**
IN U.S.A.: P.O. Box 1867, Buffalo, NY 14240-1867
IN CANADA: P.O. Box 609, Fort Erie, Ontario L2A 5X3

Are you a current subscriber to Love Inspired books and want to receive the larger-print edition? Call 1-800-873-8635 or visit www.ReaderService.com.

* Terms and prices subject to change without notice. Prices do not include applicable taxes. Sales tax applicable in N.Y. Canadian residents will be charged applicable taxes. Offer not valid in Quebec. This offer is limited to one order per household. Not valid for current subscribers to Love Inspired Larger-Print books. All orders subject to credit approval. Credit or debit balances in a customer's account(s) may be offset by any other outstanding balance owed by or to the customer. Please allow 4 to 6 weeks for delivery. Offer available while quantities last.

Your Privacy—The Harlequin® Reader Service is committed to protecting your privacy. Our Privacy Policy is available online at www.ReaderService.com or upon request from the Harlequin Reader Service.

We make a portion of our mailing list available to reputable third parties that offer products we believe may interest you. If you prefer that we not exchange your name with third parties, or if you wish to clarify or modify your communication preferences, please visit us at www.ReaderService.com/consumerchoice or write to us at Harlequin Reader Service Preference Service, P.O. Box 9062, Buffalo, NY 14269. Include your complete name and address.

LILPDIR13R

LARGER-PRINT BOOKS!

GET 2 FREE LARGER-PRINT NOVELS PLUS 2 FREE MYSTERY GIFTS

Love Inspired®
SUSPENSE
RIVETING INSPIRATIONAL ROMANCE

Larger-print novels are now available...

ReaderService.com

Manage your account online!
- Review your order history
- Manage your payments
- Update your address

**We've designed
the Harlequin® Reader Service
website just for you.**

Enjoy all the features!
- Reader excerpts from any series
- Respond to mailings and
  special monthly offers
- Discover new series available to you
- Browse the Bonus Bucks catalog
- Share your feedback

Visit us at:
ReaderService.com

RS13